I0627184

Rain-Soaked

Also by Montana Carr

Beyond the Scent of Sugar: A Memoir by Billie River

Marti Starova Erotic Thrillers

Drowning in Broad Daylight (Book 1)
Shadow Work (Book 2)
Coming Soon!
Almost (Book 4) - January 16, 2026
The Familiar Dark (Book 5) - March 11, 2026

Rain-Soaked

A Marti Starova Erotic Thriller Book 3

Montana Carr

Northshore Noir Press

This is a work of fiction. All names, characters and incidents are the product of the author's imagination. Any resemblance to real persons, living or dead, is entirely coincidental.

RAIN-SOAKED. A Marti Starova Erotic Thriller Book 3. Copyright © 2025 by Montana Carr. All rights reserved.

Northshore Noir Press and the Northshore Noir logo are copyright and used with permission.

Northshore Noir upholds the principles of free expression and recognizes the significance of copyright protection. All rights reserved. No part of this publication may be reproduced, distributed, or transmitted in any form or by any means without the prior written permission of the Publisher, except for brief quotations incorporated into critical articles or reviews. Your adherence to and respect for the author's rights are sincerely appreciated.

Northshore Noir Press
Toronto, Canada
www.northshorenoir.com

ISBN: 978-1-998648-23-8

eBook ISBN: 978-1-998648-24-5

For more information visit: northshorenoir.com

Contents

Chapter 1

"What the fuck was I working on again?"

Marti glared at the screen like it had personally offended her. Smoke curled from the cigarette clinging to her lip, trailing up past her eyes before disappearing into the yellowed ceiling tiles. The cursor blinked. Mocking her.

Falls City PD's gold shield felt like a lifetime ago. Private investigating paid more, and nobody cared if she showed up hungover. Or still drunk. Or riding the chemical wave of Shadow that made everything sharper and softer and nothing better.

She rubbed a thumb over one temple, trying to scrape off last night: the sex, the shots, the Shadow hit she hadn't needed but took anyway. Her brain felt as if someone had filled it with wet socks.

The ashtray was clean. Which meant she'd actually done something productive this morning, probably during one of those weird bursts of guilt-fueled energy that came between hangover cramps and lighting the day's next cigarette.

"Jesus, Marti. Seriously?"

That voice. Sharp, familiar, laced with exasperation. Lori Harring walked in like she owned the place; technically, she at least paid the rent. Fifth secretary in four years, and the only one who'd lasted longer than nine months with Falls City's most disgraced ex-detective.

Heels clicking against scuffed hardwood, Lori stopped behind her chair: too close to be innocent, not close enough to give Marti what she wanted. Her hot-but-don't-touch-you'll-fuck-this-up secretary. Exceptionally competent, tragically clothed.

Marti didn't look up. She could feel Lori's body heat curling at her back, smell that maddening perfume: clean floral with a bite underneath, like lilies hiding switchblades.

"Here," Lori said.

She reached over, fingers brushing Marti's hand as she took the mouse. That single drag of skin sent a tremor down Marti's spine and straight between her legs. Fucking hell.

She pulled her hand back as if it had been burned. Thank God there was no HR here.

Lori swiped through the holographic displays with calm efficiency. "While you were out with God-knows-who doing God-knows-what, I made some progress on the West Insurance case."

Images. Charts. A timeline of someone else's bullshit organized into neat little lies. The only thing messy in the room was Marti's brain and maybe the things she wanted to do to Lori across the desk.

"You listening?" Lori asked, turning enough for Marti to catch a flash of cleavage and annoyance in equal measure.

"I'm always listening," Marti lied.

"Focus." Lori crossed her arms. "Tobias West hired us for this fraud case, remember? You were there when he cried about his precious insurance empire."

"Right," Marti muttered, trying not to sound like she'd rather be handcuffed than doing data analysis.

Lori leaned in again, her hair brushing against Marti's cheek as she pointed at overlapping charts on the screen.

"Look at these spikes in claim activity," Lori said. "There is a sudden increase right here, and then a sudden drop-off. Someone needed quick cash for something big, then backed off three weeks ago."

Marti tapped the screen. "And here: geolocation metadata is off by miles. I've been working on this all week."

Her fingers moved across the keyboard, pulling up a map that plotted reported locations against actual incident sites. "See? Miles apart. Not just once, but repeatedly."

Marti squinted at what looked like meaningless squiggles and numbers. "So?"

"So someone's tampering with it," Lori said. "I texted you about it three times."

Marti's eyes flicked to her comm unit, unread messages blinking accusingly.

"Tobias thinks it's Juanita Valenzuela," Lori added. She leaned close. "Someone wants these claims approved fast and for a shit ton of money."

Marti's heart did something unpleasant and fluttery: either from Lori's breath ghosting along her earlobe or from how tight her jeans felt.

She tried for cool detachment. She failed. Marti's eyes raked over her desk, hoping to land on something more interesting than Lori's hips. A couple of sticks of StimGum, a PulseSpec, a wireless charging pad.

Lori's hips won.

"Keep talking dirty about metadata," Marti murmured before catching herself and snapping back toward the screen. Lori pulled away with a smirk sharp enough to cut rope.

"I spent time going through the employee directory and access list," Lori continued, clicking to a profile on screen. "Valenzuela has admin access. Full server privileges. She can change records, modify data, change timestamps. Even alter the video."

"Alter how?" Marti lit another cigarette.

"Look at this dashcam footage," Lori said, pulling up a video file. "The audio cuts out mid-word, an imperfect slice of silence lasting three seconds before resuming. When I checked the timestamp against the metadata..." She paused dramatically. "Another mismatch."

A distinct meowing sound from outside caught their attention. Lori glanced toward the window.

"That black cat's back again," she said. "It hates me. Hisses every time I go near it."

Marti ignored the obvious pussy joke, and stared at the footage. But all she could think about was how Lori looked when she was angry: lip curled slightly, brow tight.

"You good?" Lori asked without looking up.

"Nope." Marti dragged on her cigarette while pretending to care about metadata anomalies instead of how she wanted her secretary bent over this desk.

The streetlights flickered on schedule. There would be full brightness in the Financial District, dim yellow in the residential blocks, and complete darkness in areas where authorities had written off the population.

Three. Two. One. Darkness outside until lightning lit up the sky.

Outside: thunder. Inside: unresolved tension and claims fraud.

"User access patterns show multiple log-ins to the same evidence files by different employees across departments," Lori said, tapping her tablet. "That's not standard protocol. It might suggest tampering. Maybe collusion."

Marti forced a nod. "Great. Cyber-fraud with teamwork." Her fingers drummed on the desk. "Someone would need serious technical skills to pull this off so cleanly."

She stared at the doctored footage, a nascent thought forming through her hangover. Whoever did this knew exactly what they were doing. The kind of precision that spoke of experience and expertise.

"Get me a list of those users and timestamps," Marti said. "Let's see who's been getting curious."

Lori hesitated just long enough for it to register. Her eyes flicked down to Marti's mouth before snapping back up. "On it."

She retreated into her office next door, hips swaying in that rhythm that made Marti's mouth dry.

Marti stared after her for a dangerous second, then turned back to the altered footage. Something about the clean edit nagged at her. Very professional. Expert.

She shouldn't be thinking about Lori like this, not while their client's servers were bleeding secrets and someone with dangerous technical skills was manipulating evidence.

She needed a distraction. From everything.

Fuck it.

She reached into the desk drawer and pulled out her Shadow inhaler like it was communion wine. Salvation in aerosol form.

One hit. Just one. It might be good. It might be a nightmare. What wasn't these days?

The drug slid into her lungs like silk dipped in lightning. Vision fractured into prisms of color: ultraviolets humming against grayscale memories. Time peeled outward until even the sound of rain seemed like an afterthought.

Gone.

Just for a minute.

Until Lori's voice crashed through the kaleidoscope.

"Marti," she called from next door. Urgent now. "I've got something."

Marti blinked hard. Reality elbowed its way back in as Shadow receded into background static.

"What?" Her voice came out thick and sticky, like honey poured over gravel.

Footsteps approached fast until Lori emerged, Holo-Tab in hand.

"Dashcam footage," she said, sliding back into Marti's space. "Someone altered it using old software: Cinemagic Editcraft."

"Sounds fake," Marti muttered, rubbing at her temples.

"It's not." Lori shoved the tablet under her nose. "The program's obsolete, fifteen years at least, but it still slips past current authentication software because no one bothers coding filters for antiques."

Marti squinted at the footage. "So what you're saying is... someone used decades old tech to cover their ass?"

"Exactly." Lori dropped into the chair opposite her. "It passed verification until I ran my tweaked version of VideoTruth through it and found this." She jabbed the screen. "Graph spike right here."

Marti stared at a colorful blip on a line graph.

"The day after the accident," Lori added.

"Of course it was." Marti dragged another long sip from her coffee, which tasted like burned regret. "And let me guess: whoever pulled this off knows their way around codebases older than I am."

Lori gave a tight nod. "Yeah. We're talking someone with vintage IT knowledge and access; probably worked inside government systems or big-money insurance mills."

"Great fucking detective work, Sherlock," Marti said with mock enthusiasm. Her gaze dropped without permission to where Lori was leaning forward now, cleavage framed by silk buttons.

Temptation pressed against restraint, hard enough to bruise.

She looked away before she embarrassed herself further.

Lori noticed anyway. Her smirk had teeth.

But instead of calling Marti out or pulling away, she stayed where she was and locked eyes with her boss.

Outside: more thunder, closer now.

"I still can't tell exactly what was altered in the footage," Lori said. "Could've been something cut, spliced in, or just morphed so clean it passes for original."

"Then keep digging." Marti stubbed her cigarette and leaned over the desk. "Start with who accessed the system that day. Full list. Names, log-ins, timestamps. I want to know who breathed near that file."

"No shit," Lori muttered, already heading back to her desk with that catwalk sway she claimed was unintentional.

Just another Wednesday at Starova Investigations. With ass, lies, and microdoses of hallucinogenic escapism.

Chapter 2

Marti stayed behind, alone with the rain drumbeat and the scent of scorched tobacco. Water chased itself down the office window in frantic rivulets, like it couldn't get out of this damn city fast enough.

She stared through the downpour, watching Lori's reflection hammer keys like she was exorcising something.

"You're staring again," Lori said without looking up.

Marti turned slowly and lied badly. "Just thinking."

"About the case," Lori said, one eyebrow arched like a dare, "or about me?"

That smile, barely there, made Marti want to commit crimes worse than surveillance tampering.

She cleared her throat. "This insurance gig stinks. Whoever doctored that dashcam footage wasn't doing it for shits and giggles. They've got a constant stream of willing clients. Someone in sales who signs them up. And a need for money."

Lori snorted but didn't argue. Instead she reached for a sheet fresh from the printer and held it out. "Cross-referenced system access logs with our tampered timestamps. Here's everyone who touched those files when they shouldn't have."

Warm paper brushed warm fingers; brief contact, but electric enough to light up Marti's spine.

She took it, eyes flicking down columns of usernames until something ugly jumped out.

"Jv491?" She tapped it hard. "That one doesn't match company naming formats. Everyone else is initials plus last name." Her gaze snapped back up. "What the fuck is this?"

Lori nudged Marti out of her chair and got to typing.

Marti watched her work: the way her bottom lip caught between her teeth when she focused, how that little wrinkle appeared above her brow.

"Oh shit," Lori breathed, sitting back fast.

Marti was moving. She stepped behind her desk and leaned in close enough her breath ghosted against Lori's cheek.

"That user," Lori said, pointing at the glowing screen, "is Juanita Valenzuela."

"The adjuster we were hired to look at?"

"The very same," Lori confirmed.

"Son of a whore." Marti straightened up and crushed what remained of her cigarette. "We've got her."

Lori hesitated. "Because she has a weird user name?"

Marti barked a laugh and started pacing. "Yeah, that's stupid." She stopped and stabbed a finger at the screen.

"I want everything on Valenzuela: her files, contacts, where she buys coffee and who she fucks after hours." Her voice dropped an octave lower.

Lori leaned back in the chair and looked up at Marti through lashes thick with implication.

"I'll start with a financial overview," Lori said, moving quickly to her own chair.

Marti yanked her leather jacket from the coat rack. "Send me screen grabs of the locations of the accidents that she touched. I'll hit the street, see if they match locations. If I can figure out angles and shit."

"Be careful," Lori called after her. "If Valenzuela's our girl and she's wired into someone higher up—"

"I'm never careful," Marti tossed back, giving a wink filthy enough to be its own liability.

Two hours later, Marti slammed back into the office drenched through: hair plastered down, boots soggy, mood fouler than a septic tank in summer. Four locations, two drinks, and one punch to a guy who got grabby. Zip. Zilch. Fuck-all.

Lori hadn't moved. Judging by the half-eaten sandwich, empty coffee cups, and the glow of obsession in her eyes, she probably hadn't even blinked.

"You need to see this." No hello, no kiss-my-ass. Just Lori's voice sharp as a syringe.

Marti peeled off her soaked jacket and let it fall in a wet heap as she stalked over.

Lori gestured to the screen with all the triumph of a cat dropping a dead bird at your feet. It was a digital altar to Juanita Valenzuela: glam shots pulled from social media feeds, slices of public record arranged like a menu of sins.

"I couldn't get her actual financials," Lori said, flipping through tabs, "but I didn't need 'em. Look at this string of posts: eighteen months of showing off like she's auditioning for Rich Bitch Weekly."

She clicked through photos. Valenzuela leaned against a luxury nuclear hybrid N-Car; draped across some oligarch's yacht; flashing labels so high-end they probably had fewer human rights violations than she did credit cards.

"Now," Lori purred, switching tabs, "this is her reported salary from West Insurance." The screen filled with numbers that barely scratched six figures.

"Claims adjuster money doesn't buy fucking yachts," Marti muttered as she leaned close enough for their shoulders to brush.

"There's more," Lori said.

She flipped to a calendar visual studded with colored points like bullet wounds across time.

"The dates on these posts? They line up with certain claims: big ones. Every flashy purchase happens within two weeks of Valenzuela signing off on something big."

"And these?" She pointed to sets of beach selfies and luxury resort check-ins. "Each vacation hits right after fat settlements landed in someone's account."

Lori tapped again, zooming in on metadata Marti hadn't noticed. "See this? The accounts getting those settlements? Some of them aren't even in the claimant's name. Shell companies. Payouts routed through firms that didn't exist six months earlier. This one is weird too: a single payment to a place called Crimson Crown. Twenty crisp three weeks ago. But the claimant's name was Samuel Barajas. A Crimson Crown employee, maybe?"

Marti narrowed her eyes. "No, I think you're onto something. She's laundering the settlements."

"More than that," Lori said, voice flattening. "She's not subtle enough to have done this. This set up takes someone who is good at staying hidden, under the radar.

These LLCs are too clean, and they're front-loaded with legal insulation. Someone else built the machine. She's just pushing the buttons."

Marti ran both hands through her short black hair until it stood up like static shock.

"Well fuck me sideways," she murmured around another cigarette already lit between her lips.

"You see where I'm going with this?"

Marti exhaled slow. "Valenzuela isn't driving this train." She tapped ash into an overflowing tray. "Someone else is laying track and paying her just enough hush money to keep posting selfies."

"Exactly." Lori zoomed into another photo: a club shot so overpriced you could hear champagne fizz through pixels. A man hovered behind Valenzuela in three different images.

Same man each time. Blurred face, generic build that screamed government-issued mannequin. Suit too neat, skin too smooth, no personality traits aside from 'camera-phobic bastard.'

"No ID yet," Lori said. "But he keeps showing up wherever she does when the money flows."

Outside, rain battered the window harder.

Marti took another drag and flicked ash onto the carpet.

"This is sophisticated. Probably even more money being taken than we can prove so far," she said finally.

Her voice was low, ragged and dangerous: the kind you only hear just before everything goes to hell. It was only a matter of time.

* * *

Hours passed, the kind that came with bloodshot eyes and sticky keys, where the clock mocked you and the coffee stopped working. Digital records piled up like bodies; messy, incomplete, hiding something rotting underneath.

Then Lori sat up. Her chair screeched across the floor.

"Marti," she breathed. "It's Stirling."

Marti leaned in, breath catching as the screen lit up with the old Thornfield murder file. Ari Stirling—second-in-command and grief-stricken—had hired her to find the killer. She found him. Stirling paid. So did Bruce Garrison, the man who pulled the trigger.

Garrison paid with his life.

Stirling paid with digital cash.

Lori's fingers tapped and spread across the monitor, pulling two windows side by side. On the left: a large settlement payment, authorized last month by Juanita Valenzuela. On the right: an archived transfer from Stirling to Marti, funds paid after the investigation.

Same bank. Same account. Same routing number: 0874920216.

Marti blinked.

"Shit," Marti muttered, eyes wide. "That's it. That's...fuck, that's the jackpot."

It wasn't metaphorical anymore: the connection was right there in glowing white text. Ari. Juanita. The money overlapping both like a bloodstain.

"What's the deal?" Lori asked under her breath. "What's his motive? This is way outside of his wheelhouse."

Marti sighed, still staring at the screen. "Diversification. But if Stirling finds out we know? We're dead before we can finish printing."

"So what do we do?" Lori murmured. "This isn't airtight. Not yet."

Marti leaned back, rubbing her temples with nicotine-stained fingers. "We got a skeleton key and half a map drawn in piss." She exhaled. "Yeah, alright. Let's figure out his angle before we tell Tobias West anything."

"Let's burn his whole rotten operation down," Lori said, mock-heroic voice engaged.

Marti snorted and waved her off. "Sure thing, babyface anarchist." She flicked ash toward yesterday's sandwich and grinned.

Chapter 3

"First thing," Marti said, voice low and flat. "We need actual evidence before Tobias starts kicking doors in. No half-assed screenshots or spooky static files. We're not sending him into a gunfight with a butter knife."

Lori didn't look up. "If he fires Juanita, or worse, gets her arrested, Stirling might get pissed that his money stops flowing and starts tying up loose ends. Dead ends."

Marti tilted her head, watching Lori work; agitated clicks of the mouse, fingers stabbing the keyboard hard enough to draw blood and solve the case at once. God, she was brilliant when she was pissed. Marti's eyes trailed lower, caught the soft scoop of cleavage visible beneath Lori's rumpled blouse, and stayed there.

Time to switch from one addiction to another.

She stood and slipped into her office, door half-closed behind her. The drawer stuck, probably from some spatula used in ways that had nothing to do with food, and she yanked it open anyway. Inside: one metal inhaler gleaming like sin under the flickering desk lamp. It looked cold even from here: sharp-edged comfort in a world gone dull.

Shadow called.

"Are you seriously doing that now?" Lori's voice rang through the room like judgment on feet.

Marti rolled her eyes and raised the inhaler to her lips. "Don't start with me. I've earned five minutes in hell."

She inhaled deep.

The hit slammed into her skull like a freight train laced with glitter. Her vision fractured: colors refracting off each other like broken glass in a kaleidoscope orgy. The ceiling melted into stars; the floor pulsed under her boots. All the dread and guilt curled up their grimy little fingers and let go for once.

Not the best trip, but not the worst.

"Goddammit, Marti," Lori muttered somewhere on the edge of reality.

Marti leaned back in her chair, pupils blown wide, heart thudding like sex and danger wrapped in velvet.

"I'm working while you fry your fucking brain," Lori added from beyond the doorframe. "Just so we're clear."

Her tone was dry as gin but laced with that soft thread of worry she never snipped away. It made something tight wriggle beneath Marti's ribs: a slithering mix of shame and want that Shadow couldn't smother.

Lori went quiet for a moment before calling out again: "Okay... got something else that caught my eye."

Marti barely registered it through the high-pitched ringing that passed for music inside her skull.

"There's a list of usernames," Lori continued. "People who accessed the footage, timestamps, everything. But after the first alteration."

Marti latched onto the words as if they were lifeboats drifting past in a sea of liquid light. She tried to speak but couldn't tell if sound escaped her throat or if she was imagining her own voice inside someone else's dream.

Then a shrill buzz sliced through everything. The phone vibrated against her desk with all the subtlety of a grenade blast.

She fumbled toward it with slow fingers and knocked over an empty bottle before catching hold of the slippery thing and dragging it to her ear.

No idea who it would be on the other end. She was too far gone to care if it was God or Stirling himself.

"What?" Marti slurred despite the single syllable, jaw barely cooperating with her tongue.

"Is that any way to greet me?" Pauline cooed, smug like she thought the sound of her voice could still get Marti wet. "Come on, be nice."

Marti blinked hard, the fog in her skull freezing into something sharp. "Fuck off, Pauline."

"Aww, don't be like that," came the pout, audible through the phone. "I just wanted to say I'm sorry."

Marti sat up straighter, spine crackling. Her thigh still ached where Pauline had sunk her teeth into it. "Sorry doesn't cut it, you psycho bitch." She rubbed at the spot out of reflex. The bruise was still there: dark purple like ripened rot. "You nearly took a chunk out of me when you were high on that Golden Shadow shit."

"Hey." Defensive now. Predictable. "We've both done crazy shit when we're high. Remember that time…?"

"I've never done anything without consent," Marti snapped back. "And never anything that required a tetanus shot."

The static on the line swelled with silence and resentment.

"I'm not saying it was okay…" Pauline began again, soft enough to pass for sincerity if Marti hadn't heard every variation of this script.

"What do you want?" Marti didn't bother keeping the edge out of her voice anymore.

A beat passed. Then two.

"I've changed," Pauline insisted. "I'll get clean. I promise."

Marti stared at the ash clinging to the tip of a dead cigarette between her fingers and let her paranoia take hold.

Pauline works for Evelyn Delacroix who was married to Marcus Thornfield who got killed by Bruce Garrison who got killed by Thornfield's right-and man…Ari Stirling.

And Stirling's name just came up in a huge auto insurance fraud case.

"You work for Evelyn," Marti said coolly, testing the waters even as they burned hot under her skin.

"That's over," Pauline whispered.

"And Stirling?" Marti asked: not because she didn't know but because she wanted to hear Pauline lie about it.

"I don't talk to him anymore."

Uh-huh.

Marti leaned back in her chair. Her eyes tracked a spider crawling across the ceiling tiles as if it had nowhere better to be.

"No."

"Please," Pauline breathed down the line, soft again, seductive again. That same purr she used when she used to leave lipstick kisses all over Marti's thighs before slipping under the sheets like sin incarnate.

Marti hesitated for half a second and hated herself for it. "No," she said. "Go fuck yourself."

She hung up mid-breath before temptation could repackage itself as forgiveness.

The silence buzzed.

Then: "Everything okay in here?"

Lori's voice broke through the tension like a dull blade hacking at rope. She poked her head into Marti's office, hesitant and wary.

Marti didn't look at her. She lit another cigarette with trembling fingers and barked out, "Get back to work, asshole."

Lori flinched. Not obviously, but enough for Marti to catch it from the corner of her eye as Lori vanished through the door without another word.

Marti blew smoke at the ceiling and imagined choking on it just enough to feel something sharp again.

"I meant, please get back to work, asshole," Marti clarified, hoping that was enough.

One beat. Two beats.

Lori reappeared in the doorway; her silhouette stark against the harsh fluorescent light. "You know what, Marti? Your 'please' is worth about as much as that cigarette ash. Next time your ex calls, don't make me your fucking punching bag." She gripped the doorframe, knuckles white. "Some of us still remember how to fight back."

Marti grunted something close to an apology or an orgasm. Lori went back to her desk, angry.

The keyboard noise was deliberate now: sharp, caffeinated stabs as if she was trying to murder every damn key. Lori's office pulsed with it. The clack-clack-clack ricocheted off the walls like gunfire in a church. Marti could hear it from her desk, where she sat staring out into the piss-colored rain and feeling just as fucked as the weather.

Her cigarette burned down to the filter without her realizing it. The smoke curled around her face as if it was taunting her for the scene she'd just caused, as if maybe even the nicotine thought she was a bitch.

She flicked the butt out the open window. It hissed when it hit the wet fire escape, snuffed out like everything else lately.

"Goddamn it," Marti muttered, dragging a palm down her face.

Apologizing wasn't her thing. She broke bones easier than she bent pride. But guilt had weight, and this one was sitting right on her chest: hot, vulgar, and shaped like Lori's clenched jaw and hurt eyes.

Fine.

Marti hauled herself upright, brushing damp ash off her jeans where rain had splattered through the open window. The air smelled like ozone. She shoved one hand in the drawer. The metal inhaler pressed sharp against her palm, but she let go.

Time to bleed out what she'd been holding in. Marti shuffled toward Lori's office like someone walking into a minefield.

The typing slammed louder as she approached, which was impressive since Lori always typed like she hated technology. When Marti stepped into view of the doorway, everything stopped. Complete silence except for rain chewing on the windows outside.

Marti leaned against the frame, hands buried deep to hide how badly they wanted to shake. "Hey."

Lori didn't look up immediately. When she did, her expression wasn't guarded: it was fucking fortified.

"What?" The word came out dry enough to dehydrate an entire lake.

Marti cleared her throat and shifted her weight, neck prickling under Lori's stare. "I just... Can we talk?"

Lori pushed back from her desk with that slow-roll posture that said she knew Marti had been dragged here by guilt and wouldn't mind watching her squirm before deciding whether to forgive her.

"Oh? Suddenly we're talking?"

Marti took another step inside but kept close to the wall, as if conversation might be contagious if she got too close. "Yeah. I mean, fuck, yes." She rubbed at her chin, tried not to look at anything too long. "About earlier."

Lori crossed one leg over the other and tilted her head. "Which part? When you called me an asshole or when you made me your emotional punching bag because your ex decided you were filet mignon?"

"Jesus," Marti hissed. "Both."

She reached up to run a hand through hair that snatched back. Her fingers drifted toward that pack of cigarettes in her pocket: the ones she'd promised not to touch unless something exploded. Well... nothing had exploded yet.

"I'm sorry," she said, each word dragged from behind her ribs, hoarse and choked but true anyway.

"For...?" Lori prompted sweetly. Too sweet.

"For being a dick," Marti snapped back. She winced and tried again with less barbed wire in it. "For lashing out at you when I couldn't handle my own shit."

There was a pause.

Then: "You gonna cry now? Or should I make popcorn first?"

Marti barked out something between a laugh and a groan of misery. "I deserve that."

"You do." Lori leaned forward now, elbows resting on thighs as she appraised Marti like something freshly peeled open and twitching on a slab.

"My drug use…" Marti began quieter. Her fingers found metal in her jacket; the Shadow inhaler cold through fabric, and dug into it like penance. "It fucks with me sometimes worse than I realize. Makes me paranoid and cruel when I don't mean to be either."

"You ever think about stopping?" Lori asked.

"Every fucking second."

That landed heavier than either expected.

Something shifted: not forgiveness exactly, but maybe curiosity holding its breath to see what she'd say next instead of slamming the door in her face.

"Anything else?" Lori asked.

Marti exhaled hard through gritted teeth, the kind of breath that tasted more like failure than relief, and gave up wrestling whatever ounce of dignity she'd carried since noon.

"I want us to be good," she admitted.

Lori blinked but didn't answer.

Outside, thunder rolled low across the skyline like bad background music for confessions no one wanted to hear aloud.

"Well," Lori said, voice cool but crackling beneath it with heat that hadn't gone anywhere even if trust had evaporated weeks ago, "if you're gonna keep calling me names during fights... at least learn some new ones."

That earned half a grin from Marti: uneven but real.

"We done?" Marti asked, voice low, like she was testing how far the moment would stretch before snapping.

"No." Lori didn't sit. Didn't flinch. She stepped close: too close. She tilted her head down, eyes peering up through lashes as if they were knives dipped in honey. "Actually, Marti, there's something I've been meaning to tell you..."

A shrill ring sliced through the tension like a boxcutter across skin.

"Fuck," Marti muttered as both women jolted.

Lori scrambled for the receiver as if it might explode if she didn't pick up fast enough. "Martina Starova Investigations," she said, trying to sound professional despite her flushed cheeks from whatever she'd nearly said.

Marti didn't wait for the end of the call. Her face folded into that careful mask she wore when someone got too close. She turned without a word, heels silent on the floor, and disappeared into her office.

Door shut. Lock clicked. Shadow inhaler pressed to lips.

Cold metal. Bitter chemical sweetness. A hit of nothingness.

Chapter 4

It dulled the edges, softened the roar in her chest, but it didn't erase shit. Not Lori's voice gone soft and brave one second before the universe slapped it out of her mouth. Not Marti's near-failure to stop herself from leaning in too far.

She'd been down this road before. Twice, if she was honest with herself (which she rarely was unless Shadow forced it out of her): heated glances across desks, flirtation bleeding into obsession. Then watching everything burn to ash while shoving another woman out of her life with a bruised ego and a severance check.

Too toxic for anyone who wasn't already sick with their own demons.

She looked toward the ceiling fan and let it spin there until a knock on the wall snapped her attention back toward reality.

"Hey, Marti!" Lori's voice, sharp and distracting, cut through the chemical lull like a buzzsaw.

Marti dragged herself upright, spine stiff from pretending not to feel anything all morning. She swung into Lori's office with her usual half-predator swagger and dropped into the cracked leather chair like it loved her.

Legs up on Lori's desk with a satisfying thud.

"I'd just gotten cozy," she drawled. "This better be about murder or money."

Lori didn't blink at the attitude. "Taylor Sezam called. Wants you to run a background check on his new girlfriend."

Marti yawned theatrically. "Another jealous finance bro?"

"He sent files," Lori added sweetly. "Bank statements, photos... and thirty thousand dollars."

That got Marti's eyebrows to twitch upward ever so slightly.

"Alright," she said slowly. "That's one hell of a girlfriend."

Lori crossed her arms but leaned a little closer anyway. "That's just the appetizer." Then, without even trying to hide the drama in her voice: "I also saw Damian Kane's name come up in the insurance scam."

Marti went still. Damian Kane was one of the smartest and most corrupt cops she'd ever worked with. He lied to suspects, took bribes. Even shot her not that long ago. Not that she'd ever give him the satisfaction of knowing that.

Every nerve inside her snapped to attention like dogs hearing footsteps behind them in an alleyway.

"You're fucking kidding me."

"I wish," Lori said carefully.

Marti stood fast enough to make the chair squeal in protest behind her. Her body coiled tight like she'd been handed live wire instead of bad news.

"What did that asshole file?" Her voice was sharp now: each syllable packed with pure venom and ghosted memories of betrayal boiled down into rage.

"Easy," Lori warned, though even she knew that particular storm was past containment now.

"He's lying about something," Marti snapped. "He always is."

Lightning flashed somewhere outside as if agreeing with her mood, followed by grumbling thunder that rattled against window panes smeared with rainwater and grime.

"I want everything he submitted," Marti said, pacing as if violence was one thought away from becoming reality again.

"It's all here." Lori turned back to her screen and tapped keys until lines of text lit up across dual monitors. "Two days ago. Insurance claim on a red ThunderBlade GT: front-end damage, broken headlight... $20K repair estimate because it's a specialty car."

Marti stopped pacing.

"ThunderBlade GT..." she repeated, voice low, eyes narrowing like a lens adjusting to a sudden light. The name lit up old circuits: LaLoLa's footage. Same make. Same flash of red at the edge of the frame, peeling off into the rain.

Marti didn't need a file to remember the case. She and Lori had chased that ghost through half the city. LaLoLa Henderson, dead in a shitty motel room with a bullet in her head. And the ThunderBlade? Leo Fehr's. Sleek, custom, built to run.

Leo had dirt under every nail and blood behind his smile. But killing LaLoLa hadn't even been his biggest mistake.

That had been underestimating Dan Devall's vengeance.

Lori glanced sideways at her boss, noting how Marti's jaw clenched tight enough to crack bone, and felt something twist hot low in her stomach that had nothing to do with fear and everything to do with admiration laced with lust laced with danger.

"And Leo…" Lori began.

"…is dead," Marti finished for her. She smiled, but not kindly, as if some piece of control had finally slipped back into place where grief had lived too long unchecked. "Which means Kane is driving his car around town."

"Could that be Kane in the LaLoLa video instead of Fehr?" Lori asked, her voice tight, as if she already knew the answer and hated it.

Marti didn't look away from the screen. "Shit, maybe. We always assumed Fehr was behind the wheel that night. But if Kane had the keys…" She trailed off, eyes narrowing. "Fehr was killed for running a drug lab in Devall's territory, but Kane was clean. He's still walking."

"You think he could have killed LaLoLa?" Lori asked.

"Let me think," Marti said as she tapped on her head. She lit a cigarette, drawing in smoke like it was brains. It almost was.

"Okay, okay. We thought Fehr killed LaLoLa because her killer is on video getting into that car. But if we can put Kane in that car at the time of her death…" Marti said.

Lori leaned forward, tapping her thumbnail against her lip as if it might help her think faster. "Fuck. If Kane was the man in the video…"

"Then maybe I can get the bastard after all," Marti muttered. She stood up so fast her chair nearly tipped over. "Pull up the footage again."

They scoured every second, frame by grainy frame, as if they could force a confession out of pixels if they glared hard enough. The resolution was garbage, black and white streaked with static, as if all those years of corruption had seeped into the footage itself.

"That could be anyone," Lori growled after the fourth rewind.

"Or no one," Marti said, slamming her palm onto the desk so sharply it echoed around the room like a retort from a gun not yet fired.

They sat in silence for a moment, frustration thick as smoke. Lori broke it first.

"What if we talk to Teli Somram? It was her name on the registration. Fehr's widow might know something about that car: who used it, who had access."

Marti didn't hesitate. "Grab your coat."

The city greeted them with rain that slapped at the windshield as if it was pissed off to see them again. Water sluiced across potholes and neon gutters while the wipers squealed their protest with every pass.

Teli's house was wedged between two gray slabs of urban decay. Someone had tried here, with flower boxes sagging under too much rain and just enough hope to sting.

Marti parked on the curb, killed the engine, and stepped out into cold wet air that bit through her leather jacket. Her boots squelched in mud as they headed to the door, a modest thing with peeling blue paint and one of those novelty knockers shaped like a lion's head.

She rapped twice, firm enough to be heard but not enough to break bone, and waited.

The door creaked open. A woman with fire-red hair stepped into view; her professional-cut bob framed cheekbones that had lost their adolescent softness. She adjusted her stylish round glasses with one hand while the other clutched the collar of an oversized sweater, the kind purchased with a career woman's first real paycheck despite being both cozy and impractical for storm season.

Her stare lingered on Marti long enough to suggest interest or suspicion, or both wrapped in lipstick and trouble.

"Can I help you?" she asked.

Marti smiled without showing teeth. "Are you Teli Somram?"

"Ouch. That's my mother. I'm Rosalyn, her daughter." The woman tilted her head like a cat sizing up whether you were food or threat before stepping aside. "Come in."

Warmth hit them like breath held: soft lighting, cinnamon-scented candles barely masking something older beneath; grief baked into floorboards and furniture cushions still shaped by bodies that no longer existed.

Photos lined every wall: Leo Fehr in uniform, out of uniform, smiling at some unseen joke only his family had been allowed to hear.

"Mom? Visitors!" she yelled. "She'll be down soon," Rosalyn said as she motioned toward a luxurious couch piled with handmade blankets. Her gaze flicked back to Marti. "You can sit... or stand if that's more your thing."

Lori sank into the cushions. Marti stayed on her feet, all angles and impatience under soaked leather.

"You want something to drink?" Rosalyn offered. Her voice wasn't flirtatious; it was bolder than that, dipped in dare and dusted with interest. "We've got coffee... tea... questionable gin..."

"We're good," Marti said, though her eyes didn't leave Rosalyn's face.

Rosalyn shrugged one shoulder and leaned against the doorway like a woman who'd never rushed for anything that wasn't worth fucking twice.

"You're detectives," she said. "Mom figured someone would come sniffing around eventually." Her glance flicked toward Leo's photo hanging above what looked like mail someone had tried to ignore. Then back at Marti with laser focus. "She didn't mention you'd send someone dressed like sin on payday."

Marti smirked but didn't rise to it. She shifted against the wall so her boot knocked into chipped floral wallpaper that might've once meant something before mildew and time did their damage.

Rosalyn closed some of the distance between them with slow steps built for better entrances than tough questioning usually deserved.

"Nice boots," she murmured warmly, eye-catching lips curling upward as she stared at Marti's Docs like they were foreplay incarnate. "Bet you get into some serious shit wearing those."

Marti glanced down at Rosalyn's stilettos: deep red leather laced tight up strong calves. She chuckled low in her throat.

"You're not exactly innocent yourself."

Rosalyn tilted her head, sly grin sharpening at the edges. "Maybe we should swap sometime," she whispered as her fingers ghosted along Marti's forearm in one careful stroke that lingered just shy of invitation, or maybe far past it depending on how long you'd been dry-mouthed.

"See what kind of trouble we stir up walking around in each other's shoes?"

"Trouble finds me just fine without wardrobe changes," Marti said. Heat curled under every syllable now.

"Well then," Rosalyn purred, stepping closer until there were only heartbeats between them, "you must have experience." She angled herself between Marti and that table piled with unopened mail and half-hidden receipts; her move casual only if you weren't looking closely.

"You strike me as someone who doesn't wait around hoping secrets reveal themselves."

"Guilty," Marti murmured without breaking eye contact.

"Then what are you really looking for today?" Rosalyn asked, not teasing anymore, but still running hot under every word she laid down as if dealing cards on velvet.

Her hand brushed Marti's arm again, bolder this time, and stayed right there waiting for permission or refusal or maybe worship depending on how long it'd been since either of them did anything reckless just because they could.

Marti stayed silent but didn't step back. For one charged moment neither woman moved except to breathe each other deeper into whatever came next.

"Looks like my kind of party," Marti muttered as Rosalyn's fingers slid over hers: too soft to be innocent, too deliberate to be accidental. That light contact sent a bolt down her spine, heat curling low.

Then the mood shattered.

Chapter 5

"Rosalyn!" The name came carved in glass and fury. Teli stormed in as if she had unfinished business with a god, eyes red-rimmed and wild. "Why are these people in my house? Don't they know my husband is dead?"

Buzzkill.

Rosalyn rolled her eyes but played sweet. "Sorry about that, Mom." She gave Marti a wink as she drifted toward the kitchen, hips swaying as if she knew Marti was watching.

Marti forced herself not to watch her leave.

"Ms. Somram," she said instead, dragging herself into stiff professionalism and regretting every syllable. "Apologies for the intrusion. I'm Marti Vega; this is Lori Reeves.

We're with SecureGuard Insurance. Standard claim check on your late husband's vehicle."

Teli blinked at them as if they were speaking Orkish. "Insurance? Why would you be interested in my husband's car?"

Marti smiled like a scalpel. "Because someone else filed a claim involving that car. We're here to verify the details, not point fingers."

"Yet." Lori offered up words with absolute innocence and nothing innocent in her eyes.

Teli snatched a tissue, flipping it with fingers that trembled more from rage than grief. "Are you accusing me of something?" Her voice cracked like dry wood.

"No one's accusing anyone," Marti said while silently cataloging every twitch Teli made: lip curl, jaw clench, throat bob. All of it screamed: I've got secrets buried under the guest bathroom tile.

"We just want to establish who was driving," said Lori. "The claimant isn't listed on the title."

Teli exhaled hard through her teeth like she'd just been slapped. "I don't know anything about any accident or any fucking insurance claim."

Her grief had sharp edges: the kind someone could bleed out on if they weren't careful.

"We understand this is a difficult time," Marti said. Even she didn't believe herself anymore. "We'll make this quick."

The room was moneyed comfort: plush chairs that were probably older than Marti but better preserved; gilded frames lining the walls with photos of champagne-smiling elites tossing cash at causes they'd forget before dessert hit their lips. One photo had Teli grinning beside Mayor Patricia Seibert, fake sincerity dripping off them both.

Marti tilted her head toward it like a cat catching scent of prey.

"Oh yes." Teli followed her gaze and softened her voice to cocktail-circuit charm. "That was the Paws For Caws fundraiser last spring. Dog walking fundraiser to support the crow population. I'm quite involved in animal welfare."

"I'll bet you are," Marti muttered.

Lori elbowed her.

Marti straightened up, shifting gears before Teli could bristle further. "Did your husband lend his car to anyone recently? Someone who might've been using it before his death?"

Teli paused long enough for Marti to count the seconds between truth and fabrication.

"Damian Kane," she said, chewing on her lower lip until it went pale. "Detective Kane has had it for a couple months now. Leo loaned it to him, said something about needing time... They never transferred ownership."

Marti felt Lori's stare meet hers again; this time it landed like impact rather than inquiry: Kane.

"Well, fuck me running," Marti whispered to herself.

"Pardon me?"

She straightened up and smiled. "I said 'luck be coming,'" Marti replied with a straight face. "Just hoping we catch a break on this case."

"That's all we need for now." Lori's voice was calm but her brain was already ten blocks away chasing down timelines and murder weapons. She nodded at Teli. "Thank you for your cooperation."

Teli folded her arms across tight designer black and didn't bother pretending anything close to warmth as she said, "Mm-hmm."

They reached the door before anything exploded. Barely.

Rosalyn appeared from the shadows of an expensive kitchen that smelled of cinnamon and rot, as if something sweet had spoiled just out of sight. She walked them out with a smile sharp enough to decapitate modesty.

As Marti stepped through the threshold, Rosalyn leaned close enough for perfume and heat and danger to blur together, and slipped something into Marti's hand with the discretion of sin under candlelight.

A scrap of paper folded tight enough to hide whole stories inside.

Her eyes flicked sideways toward where Teli stood watching them like a queen guarding secrets instead of treasure.

Marti clenched the paper in one fist as they descended the porch steps.

Outside, the world had gone full noir. Rain-slick streets, air thick with exhaust and leftover thunder, and Marti's boots squelching through mud that the city never bothered to clean up. She jammed the key into the ignition while Lori kicked something unidentifiable from the floor mat and climbed in after her. The scrap of folded sin, gifted by Rosalyn like a kiss with teeth, was still clenched in Marti's fist.

She handed it to Lori without looking, then slammed the car into gear and hit every puddle she could.

"Rosalyn slipped this to me before we left."

Lori didn't ask when or how. She just unfolded it like she was defusing a bomb and squinted at the scrawl inside.

"Good dog. FFCRosa781. Looks like a username. For an account on Falls City Friends."

"Falls City Friends," Marti repeated, as if tasting the words could make them useful. "Chat app?"

"Yeah. One of those ones where anonymity is king and everyone's either horny or lying. Why'd she call you a dog?"

"I am one." Marti drummed her fingers on the steering wheel, eyes scanning traffic like threats were hiding behind every sedan. "We'll poke around when we get back."

She barely got the last word out before cutting across two lanes as if God owed her right-of-way. Horns screamed. A flash of blue steel: a car she'd nearly sideswiped jerked into view in her rear mirror.

"Fuck," Lori muttered, gripping the oh-shit handle as if prayer would fix anything.

The other driver wasn't feeling spiritual. He floored it, muscled up alongside them like a domestic abuser on a bender, then swerved ahead to cut them off. Marti had to slam the brakes. Lori's bag spilled all over the floorboards.

"Oh Jesus!" Lori snapped, bracing herself against the dash.

The guy was out of his car before they'd fully stopped: a shrimp of a man with fists small enough to belong to a child's porcelain doll and a face red enough to fry bacon on. He stormed toward Marti's window as if vengeance came standard in his DNA. Each step scraped cheap leather against cracked asphalt. The streetlights caught the gleam of sweat on his forehead; droplets suspended like tiny urban stars against the crimson backdrop of his rage.

He banged on the glass with open palms first, then fists.

"You fucking cunt! Learn how to drive!"

Marti lit a cigarette with hands steady from practice. She cracked the window just low enough for her voice and other things to slide through.

"You done screaming yet?" she asked. There was no way this dude was breaking her window. Probably.

He leaned closer, spit flying as he shouted, "This ain't funny! I will end your life, you psychotic bitch!"

Marti smiled then: the kind that promised pain and meant it.

And drew her gun.

She didn't point it at him right away; just rested it against her hand like a casual suggestion from Hell itself.

He hadn't seen it or didn't care and punched the window again as if he needed to bleed.

Then she raised the steel.

Window still cracked an inch wide.

"I said," she growled, "get back in your shitbox car before I paint your fucking brains across my windshield."

The gun barked and the bullet flew, lodging itself in the innocent wooden bench across the street.

His eyes went wide so fast she wondered if he'd pissed himself. No fight left now; just wide-eyed panic as he stumbled backward, tripped over his own ego, and scrambled back into his shitty little sedan without another word.

He peeled off down the street as if fear came factory-installed in his tires.

Marti rolled up her window and took another drag off her cigarette, letting silence settle between them like ash.

"Asshole," she muttered.

Lori stared straight ahead, knuckles pale against her thighs but breath even. "That was... loud."

Marti smirked. "You're welcome."

They didn't say anything else until they pulled into their parking lot. The sky finally gave up and unleashed hell. Rain hammered down like punishment or absolution, depending on how guilty you felt walking through it.

Chapter 6

The rain had fucked off by sunset, leaving behind wet pavement slick as sex and twice as dangerous under streetlight glare. The city tried pretending at peace again: neon signs blinking half-hearted apologies above alleys full of secrets no one bothered to clean up after.

Marti took two steps up toward their office building and paused to shake water from her jacket collar before lighting another cigarette; the kind you don't bother trying to quit anymore because vices are loyal.

"Well look at that," she said between puffs. "The sun's playing peekaboo."

Lori tilted her head toward that brief sliver of orange against bruised clouds and snorted. "Don't get excited. It'll be pissing on us again by midnight."

By the time they reached their front door, both women were soaked enough for shirts to cling in all the best places. But neither of them commented on that part.

Not right away anyway.

Inside their office, with its comforting mix of stale smoke, broken blinds, and whatever haunted memories lived in coffee-stained carpet, Marti tossed wet keys onto her desk without ceremony.

Smoke curled through slats of dying sunlight while Lori booted up their computer system as if preparing for battle instead of social media sleuthing.

"Pull up Falls City Friends," Marti said around another inhale. "Let's see what kind of fucked-up treasure that username leads us to."

Lori signed in with a roll of her eyes and a flick of wet hair off her collar. Her fingers tapped keys as if trying to beat up the internet through sheer frustration. "It's just Rosalyn's account," she muttered. "Doubt we'll get anything besides tits and tantrums."

"Don't be such a cynic," Marti said, dragging on her cigarette. "She knew someone would come sniffing. Left a little message for the 'good dog.'"

"Woof," Lori deadpanned, clicking open the profile.

Rosalyn either had something to say, or she was dangling bait: just enough for the right kind of bitch to want to bite. Marti wasn't sure which game they were playing yet, but she'd play it better.

Kane's name surfaced in her brain like rot bubbling in a swamp. She wanted something, anything, that could crack his shiny, smug veneer wide open. Maybe that stupid-ass ThunderBlade he faked damage for could be useful. If there was an angle there, she'd crawl down it teeth-first.

Marti's hatred for Kane wasn't the sexy kind of grudge, the kind that turned betrayal into foreplay. No, it lived lower than that, down where blood boiled and fists clenched before reason had time to catch up. Just thinking about him made her jaw tighten and her skin itch as if she needed to peel it off.

"Scroll down," Marti said, leaning in until their shoulders touched. Their damp shirts stuck together for one too-honest second.

Lori hesitated, then started sifting through pastel-filtered selfies and duck-faced desperation. "She really knows how to sell absolutely nothing," Lori muttered. "It's just an endless swamp of vapid bullshit."

"Wait." Marti stabbed her cigarette toward the screen like it was a weapon. "That one. Click."

"Which? The one with the too-tight top and sad little caption about self-love?"

"That one." Marti's voice sharpened. "There's something behind her."

With a sigh that put all five stages of grief into one breath, Lori clicked and enlarged the photo.

They both bent closer, faces inches from each other, breathing in smoke and heat and the faint scent of wet skin.

"There." Marti tapped the screen just shy of burning it. "That red piece of shit in the background? That's the ThunderBlade."

"Could've been when her dad still owned it," Lori said, skeptical.

"Find out when this was taken." Marti's voice dropped low in that way that always made Lori feel like she'd die if she didn't listen right now.

A few clicks later: "Eight months ago," Lori reported flatly. "Still belonged to Daddy Dearest."

Which meant Rosalyn probably didn't know jack shit about Kane. She likely wasn't part of whatever shadowy mess he'd woven himself into this time. Lori breathed out and let herself feel relieved, and maybe just a little smug about how much that bothered Marti.

"Keep going." Marti waved smoke away from her own face as if clearing fog from some fucked-up crystal ball.

The glowing screen lit up their features with every click deeper into Rosalyn's curated hellscape: latte shots, thigh gaps, brunch plates carefully arranged for maximum thirst-trap efficiency.

Then.

"There," Lori said, pointing at Rosalyn standing like some lipstick prophetess in front of an old crumbling brick building.

Marti squinted at it like it had offended her. "Yeah, I know that place. Old warehouse down by the docks. So?"

"So nothing. Just familiar."

"Nah." Marti stubbed out her cigarette with force. "It's a shithole."

Lori shrugged but kept scrolling; martyrdom looked good on her when she wore it with tight jeans and determination.

Each new image brought another helping of spandex outfits over impossible curves or smoky eyes peering out under neon party lights. A who's-who of people nobody sane would ever want to know, but here they were all over this woman's feed like flies on sugar-laced garbage.

Then.

"Back." Marti hit Lori on the thigh, not enough to hurt, just enough for electricity to crackle between them as she pointed again.

Rosalyn posing with a group dressed in black: slick smiles, careful anonymity that screamed 'we do illegal shit but make it fashion.'

"Who are they?" Lori asked, not because she expected an answer but because silence felt heavier when people looked exactly like trouble should look.

Marti narrowed her eyes at the screen as if she might conjure names through sheer will. "Don't know yet," she murmured. "But I want to."

She pulled another drag from her cigarette while staring at Rosalyn like she was prey; beautiful prey with painted nails wrapped around secrets.

"Message her."

"What?" Lori froze mid-keystroke, hoping this was just another one of Marti's bad ideas whispered into smoke and forgotten seconds later.

"She knows something, or likes pretending she does." Marti grinned without humor. "Either way…"

"And if she's tied up with Kane?" Lori offered.

"All the better," Marti said as she leaned back in her chair like a wolf getting comfortable after picking which throat to bite first. "Maybe I can fuck them both and see who begs louder."

Lori groaned but typed anyway because no matter how much sarcasm coated those words, jealousy still curled tight somewhere under her ribs.

Marti: Hey there, Rosalyn. Got a few questions for you; I bet you've got answers worth hearing.

Rosalyn: Ooh hello Marti! What's on that beautiful mind of yours tonight?

Marti: That ThunderBlade GT your dad used to show off: when did he get rid of it?

Rosalyn: Ugh, cars? Really? You've seen my profile. I'm not exactly Miss Motor Oil over here. Pretty sure I tuned out every time he brought that thing up... Sorry babe.

Marti: Fair enough. Not my favorite fetish either, but work calls. So... what are you up to tonight?

Rosalyn: Just hanging around, soaking in the silence. Boring as hell, honestly. You?

Marti: Same dead energy over here. Quiet enough I can hear my own bad decisions echoing back at me.

"Why the fuck are you making me sound like a sad librarian?" Marti asked, arms crossed as Lori hovered over the keyboard as if it might bite her.

Rosalyn: By the way, those boots you wore today? Sexy as sin.

Marti: You think so? They're practically disintegrating from all the shit I drag myself through, but yeah; they've got some miles left in them.

Rosalyn: I like a woman who knows how to wear them dirty.

Marti fist-pumped like she'd just won a rigged game of Russian roulette. "Tell her I want to meet."

Marti: Maybe I'll show you how they come off... real slow.

Rosalyn: God yes. I've got some dirty ideas about that.

Lori stiffened in her seat, cheeks going crimson as she squinted at the screen as if it might rewrite itself if she stared hard enough. Rosalyn's messages kept slinking in hot and slick, and every word made Lori's jaw clench tighter.

"Keep going," Marti murmured, leaning in so close her breath ghosted across Lori's cheek. She didn't move away.

Lori swallowed and kept typing, fingers trembling like they wanted to be part of this little striptease masquerading as reconnaissance. She was half-witness, half-accomplice, and fully aroused against her better judgment.

Marti: Dirty ideas?

Rosalyn: Like untying those boots with my teeth while you squirm for me.

Lori's gasp was sharp enough to draw blood. "Okay, maybe take over now."

Marti did not.

"Tell her I'd kiss her anyway," she said, lighting a cigarette like this was a poetry reading and not explicit espionage foreplay.

Marti: I'd lean forward and kiss your filthy little mouth.

Rosalyn: Mmm... tease my nipples with your thumbs while your tongue keeps working that dirty mouth magic on my clit.

"Nope," Lori said as she sprang up from her chair as if it had grown spikes. "Nope nope nope."

She backed up two steps, arms crossed in self-defense against whatever Marti thought she was doing or getting off on doing. But Marti just slid into her spot as if she belonged there all along.

Marti: You'll be begging for more. I'd taste every inch of you until you forget your own name.

Rosalyn: I'll whisper the filthiest things into your ear right before you slam back inside me. You into Whispering?

Marti grinned like someone had offered her a loaded gun and full immunity.

"It's capitalized. What is Whispering?" she asked, dragging smoke into her lungs before grinding out the cigarette on Lori's stapler without shame or apology.

"This?" Lori whispered before regretting every molecule of air that passed her lips.

"Fuck it. Yes."

Marti: Hell yes. Tonight?

They both stared at the screen now: Lori strung tight between horror and something hotter, Marti calm but with eyes that gleamed like twin switchblades under moonlight.

Rosalyn: Tonight sounds perfect. Meet me at Falls City Best Hotel, 8pm sharp. Book the room and message me once it's done; I want to film it. You down?

There wasn't even a pause before Marti reached for the keys again.

Marti: Count me in. See you there, beautiful.

"Jesus fucking Christ," Lori breathed out, her eyes wide as if she'd just watched someone walk barefoot through fire and wink while doing it. "You're seriously going through with this?"

"Why wouldn't I?" Marti countered with that feral grin stretching across her face like war paint.

"Because it's a goddamn trap? It's being filmed! You don't know anything about this woman except she wants to suck your toes on camera!"

"She wants a lot more than that." Marti shrugged one shoulder and leaned back in the chair: the picture of unbothered corruption. "Besides... what if she's working with Kane?"

"That's exactly what I'm saying! What if this is Kane's girl? His bait?"

"Then we'll find out." She slid a glance toward Lori now, dangerous and reckless enough to get them both killed or off in ways therapy couldn't touch. "And maybe I'll fuck the truth out of her."

"This isn't you," Lori snapped, her voice tight with fury or fear or jealousy wrapped around fear pretending to be fury. Who could tell anymore?

"This is exactly me," Marti said as she stood and prowled toward the desk where Lori had retreated behind professionalism as if it offered any real protection anymore. "I'll be filming too."

"You what?" Lori blinked, arms folded now to brace or block or both, as if she'd somehow forgotten who she worked for after all this time.

"If Rosalyn spills anything about Kane mid-orgasm, I want it on record."

"Ah," Lori muttered as she hip-checked Marti out of the chair hard enough to earn a grunt of approval from deep in Marti's chest. "So noble of you to sacrifice your body for justice."

"Absolutely." Marti made herself comfortable on top of Lori's desk, legs crossed toward temptation and cigarette tucked behind one ear like punctuation on sarcasm incarnate. "I can't use the QuantumSpecs again: too risky."

Lori grabbed a folder from beneath Marti's ass and slammed it onto the table beside them.

"What else have you got for me?" Marti asked sweetly, halo nowhere in sight, and smiled when she saw that even now, even furious, Lori hesitated just long enough to prove she cared too much for either of their own good.

Lori leaned back in her chair, rubbed her temples as if she was praying for strength or a lightning bolt. Then she looked Marti dead in the eye.

"Alright. You want to be a dog? Wear a fucking collar." She grabbed her coffee, took a sip. "Go buy one. I'll gut the Specs cam and mount it in the tag slot."

Marti was already sliding off the desk, grinning like she'd just humped a leg and been praised for it. "Yessss," she hissed.

"Hold it, Fido." Lori waved her hand. "The bodega on 12th sells collars and leashes. Cheaper than pet stores and less questions asked."

Marti narrowed her eyes. "And you know this because...?"

Lori's smile started slow, then bloomed: sharp enough to draw blood.

"Some questions dig up answers you're not ready for," she said, tapping her screen as if invoking some kind of perverse oracle. "Let's just say, not all my surveillance has been government-sanctioned."

The air between them thickened with suggestion and secondhand smoke.

"Now fetch," Lori added, turning back to her monitors. "Before I decide to muzzle you instead."

Marti stared for a beat, throbbing heat radiating from every inch below her waistband, then spun on her heel and stalked out like she still had control of the situation.

Twenty minutes and two cigarettes later, Marti came storming back in and tossed a thin leather collar onto Lori's desk with unnecessary precision.

"Good enough?"

Lori picked it up as if it might bite or purr. Her mouth quirked sideways in approval. "Perfect." She rolled her chair back and got to work jury-rigging the Quantum-

Specs into the collar's tag ring with swift fingers. It took thirty seconds: show-off engineer shit.

She stood and strolled into Marti's office with the collar dangling from two fingers like an offering or a dare.

"Okay, Rover," she said. "Up."

Marti rose, eyes locked on hers as if they were gearing up for something far messier than espionage.

Lori stepped close, too close, and fastened the collar around Marti's neck with careful tension. She didn't break eye contact once.

Marti's breath hitched when the leather tightened; panties soaked through the moment that buckle clicked home.

"This clasp starts recording," Lori said, tugging the strap once more to make sure it held tight. "You've got two hours of footage max, so don't fuck her into next week."

A soft sound slipped from Marti's throat: half moan, half challenge. Lori just gave her cheek a light slap that landed softer than judgment but harder than affection.

"See you tomorrow," she said as she turned away.

"Tomorrow." Marti echoed it while she watched Lori's ass move toward the door like punishment wrapped in silk.

She grabbed her keys off the desk and walked out. The click of heels echoed through gray corridors lit by flickering fluorescents that hadn't been replaced since Henderson was in office.

Outside, Marti slid behind the wheel of her car and flipped the ignition. The engine roared to life, deep and guttural, as if reacting to the thing pulsing low in her gut. She lit another cigarette and tasted it like sin.

Neon signs smeared across wet pavement while traffic blurred past like ghosts trying to forget their stories. The whole city smelled like oil, and rain: a cocktail Marti knew too well by now.

She didn't rush. The streets cracked open around her as she cruised them, windows down, hoodie pulled up just enough to shadow that telltale glint of metal peeking from beneath her collar. Somewhere ahead: Rosalyn and answers that might come gasping between moans if Marti played this right.

Back at her apartment, she barely bothered locking the door before tearing through what counted as wardrobe: black T-shirt stretched tight across muscle memory and defiance; dark jeans slung low on hips that lied about softness; boots scuffed from too many exits gone sideways; leather belt looped with ease. Hoodie zipped halfway up because mystery made people talk faster and stare longer.

She caught herself in the mirror before leaving again. She tilted her head slightly so the collar showed just enough under shadow and gave herself a nod that said: yeah, bitch is ready.

Then it was back into the car. The city still spat secrets at every red light toward Falls City Best Hotel where neon buzzed like a migraine waiting to happen and pavement gleamed slick under rain that had no business being romantic but somehow was anyway.

Marti's apartment sat a solid twenty blocks from the hotel. Unless you were Martina Starova. A shortcut through The Kings District, past Sun City and a careful drive along the pedestrian paths around City Hall to the Longwood District, meant Marti got there in seven minutes.

She parked, reached for another cigarette she didn't light yet, took one last glance at that glowing sign above: FALLS CITY BEST HOTEL buzzing as if irony never existed. Then Marti muttered: "Showtime."

Chapter 7

The Falls City Best had been losing fights with time since disco died. It wore its decay like a bad habit: siding the color of smoke-stained enamel, parking lot pocked with oil bruises and cracks deep enough to swallow regrets whole. Marti killed the engine with a flick of her wrist.

The sky overhead held back rain, waiting for someone to flinch first. Marti stepped out, leaning against the door as she lit up. Nicotine rushed her lungs while wind combed cold fingers through her hair. Across the lot, the neon sign stuttered: FALLS CITY BEST, the S flickering in and out of existence.

She blew smoke at it and pushed herself toward the entrance.

Inside, the lobby's attempt at charm collapsed under buzzing fluorescents. Worn floorboards complained beneath her boots. A skeletal plant wilted beside a dead vending machine; both were abandoned relics from better times. Two guests shuffled past with collars up and gazes down, doing penance for whatever landed them here.

Marti kept moving. She was hoping to find out more about the car from Rosalyn, and if she didn't, she wanted an orgasm. She preferred both but would take either.

The kid working the desk couldn't have been more than nineteen: blonde, surly, gnawing on a thumbnail crusted with something Marti didn't care to identify. He kept tapping his screen, acknowledging her approach.

"One night," she said. "Second floor."

Without looking up, he tossed a keycard across the counter and jabbed a finger toward the payment terminal.

Marti tapped her wrist against plastic. Green light. Transaction complete.

"Pleasure doing business," she muttered, pocketing the keycard and heading for the stairs before the kid could pretend to care.

The stairwell smelled of industrial cleaner battling decades of cigarettes and lost weekends. Each step creaked promises of better accommodations that would never materialize. By the time Marti reached the second floor, lemon disinfectant had given way to the stale air of rooms that had seen too many temporary occupants.

The carpet beneath her boots might've been blue once. Now it was worn to submission. Sconces cast shadows that stretched and sharpened along the hallway. Marti's footsteps echoed against walls that had heard every lie whispered between these doors.

Room 212 rejected her first two swipes before the lock surrendered with a click.

She shouldered the door open to find twin beds positioned like estranged relatives at a funeral: close enough to acknowledge kinship, far enough to avoid conversation. The blanket on the nearest bed frayed at its edges, threads escaping like prisoners planning getaways. Marti dropped her bag onto it, claiming territory.

The desk beneath the window had been pushed against the wall as an afterthought. She tested the chair, which groaned in protest. Her spine echoed the sentiment. She abandoned the seat and moved to the window instead.

Outside, the first raindrops struck glass, tentative at first, then with growing confidence. Water traced jagged paths down the dirty pane, distorting the parking lot lights into trembling halos. Marti pressed her fingertips against the cool glass and watched her prints fade into nothing.

The fridge hummed despair in C minor, two half-drunk water bottles rattling against a solitary beer old enough to vote but not wise enough to know better.

Marti stripped with economy: shirt off, jeans peeled down inch by inch until they hit motel carpet soaked in the echoes of fucks past. The bathroom was cleaner than expected, which made it suspect, but she pushed the thought aside as hot water hit her skin. Steam followed close behind like shame on payday, wrapping around her shoulders and settling into her lungs.

She stood motionless under the spray, letting water cascade over tense muscles and fake flesh. The shower wasn't about getting clean; it was about getting armed again.

Back in the room, she slid into yesterday's clothes: jeans still warm from body heat, shirt clinging where old sweat mixed with new perfume. She didn't dare be naked when Rosalyn arrived. She might bring unwanted company. Marti's fingers trembled as she fastened the collar cam, the tiny device barely visible against the dark fabric. Just as she tapped it to confirm activation:

Knock-knock.

Marti's pulse quickened. She drew a deep breath, settling her features into easy neutrality.

Game time.

She crossed to the door, hesitating just a moment before opening it without ceremony.

Rosalyn stood in the hallway shaped like trouble and slicked-down weather: coat long and black, dripping wet from shoulders built for sinning upright or lying leftward. Their eyes locked for three heartbeats before Rosalyn stepped past her, filling the room with expensive perfume and dangerous potential. She dropped her coat onto a chair with more flair than some women give orgasms.

"What a night," Rosalyn said, running a hand through damp hair.

Marti leaned against the closed door, watching her through narrowed eyes. The cigarette taste lingered on her tongue as she offered a crooked grin. "Oh, it will be."

Rosalyn turned toward her, any pretense of subtlety abandoned somewhere back at street level. Boots climbed halfway up thighs meant for breaking hearts or necks. Denim skirt painted on tight enough to make decency beg. White crop top soaked through and proud of it. Those red lips could make you bleed without trying, eyes gleaming like high beams before impact.

Marti pushed off from the door and turned the lock with slow finality: the kind that says no turning back even if you wanted to lie about it later. The click echoed between them.

Rosalyn's bag hit the floor with a heavy thud. She crossed the distance between them in two strides, fingers fisting denim tight where Marti's hips met attitude. Their mouths collided without preamble, teeth clicking, tongues wrestling for dominance. Marti's hands traveled down Rosalyn's spine before grabbing her ass, thick and firm as bad decisions served hot on repeat.

"Hope you don't mind," Rosalyn whispered against her mouth, breath hot and uneven. "I brought toys."

"I love a good playtime." Marti pulled back, gaze dropping to the bag on the floor. Its odd bulges triggered warning bells that competed with the heat blooming low in her belly like arson left unchecked.

"You said we'd film." The words came out rougher than intended.

Rosalyn disentangled herself and kneeled beside the bag, unzipping it to reveal lighting rigs and enough camera gear to make porn stars nod respectfully. She handled each piece with expert familiarity.

"I said 'live.' You just skimmed my texts." She glanced up, challenge written across her features.

Marti's jaw tightened. The lie hung between them, obvious as a gunshot in church, but something about the way Rosalyn's fingers moved over the equipment made her pulse race anyway. She crossed her arms and legs, trying to ignore how soaked her panties were getting under these damn jeans.

Rosalyn continued assembling gear with professional detachment, the transformation from seductress to technician somehow making her more dangerous. From the bottom of the bag, she produced a mask: black leather half-face lined with something soft as secrets whispered too late.

"I brought protection." She held it up, light catching on its polished surface. "Stylish anonymity fit for shame-proof streaming sites." Her voice dropped an octave. "You still in?"

The mask dangled between them as if it were a question, a challenge, a promise. Marti stared at it, heart hammering against her ribs as desire and suspicion waged their silent war.

Marti ran fingers along its edge, considering destiny or damnation, and nodded once, sharp enough for both.

"Yeah," she whispered, voice vibrating through ribs beneath skin still tender from yesterday's adrenaline crash.

Rosalyn glanced up from where she knelt with the microphone. "No talking." Her eyes narrowed, professional and predatory all at once. "Only noise."

Message received. This wasn't dialog; it was soundtrack. Not words; no car confessions; just want.

A red light blinked awake on the camera tripod. The little electronic eye focused, adjusting itself to capture every detail of the bleached motel bedding and the two figures about to defile it.

Rosalyn slid into frame, microphone steady in one hand while the other worked Marti's buttons. Pop. Pop. Pop. Each snap surrendered something older than desire: restraint, maybe, or the pretense they were doing this for anyone but themselves.

Fabric peeled back. Marti's breath caught in her throat. Lavender perfume hit her nose, cutting through her senses cleaner than any pill or powder ever managed.

Rosalyn leaned close, lips brushing Marti's ear. "I'm gonna make you moan 'til screaming feels polite."

Reality fractured. Three seconds of pure nothing followed by everything at once. Marti bit down on her lower lip until she tasted iron, her self-control sliced clean through by lust sharper than logic.

The camera caught Rosalyn kneeling, fingers working Marti's jeans slow enough to build anticipation, quick enough to promise friction. Marti's mind flashed forward: herself alone tonight, replaying this moment on screens people pretended weren't bookmarked between banking apps and email inboxes.

Without warning, Rosalyn hooked her teeth into the waistband of Marti's underwear. Gravity betrayed Marti's knees before her brain could catch up, and she sat hard on the bed's edge, uninvited but unresisted.

Rosalyn turned her attention to Marti's boots first. Her tongue traced old scuffs, testimonies to past beatdowns and narrow escapes. She worked the laces loose one by one, using nothing but determination and spit-slicked patience. Marti clenched her jaw against sounds as Rosalyn tugged at knots that surrendered when persuaded by growled threats contained behind gritted teeth.

The boots slid free. Marti stared at them lying on the carpet. Not costume pieces anymore but artifacts of her life. The soles worn smooth where purpose had carried her, without apology, through streets that didn't forgive hesitation.

No words passed between them, but the microphone captured everything: cloth dragging across sensitive skin, the wet sound of Rosalyn's mouth exploring territory, the catch in Marti's breath when tongue met flesh. Heaven smelled like this, if God were queer enough to recognize holiness in acts performed for viewers hiding behind incognito browser tabs.

Rosalyn crawled up Marti's body, skirt bunched around her waist, thighs bare and demanding. She paused, hovering above Marti's face with a question in her eyes that required no voice to ask and no words to answer.

Marti's hands found Rosalyn's hips and pulled her down.

There were no introductions left worth giving.

Cunt lowered over hunger, and Marti's mouth opened wide before thought could catch up: before objection or please first.

The first touch of tongue against heat stole her breath.

Her nose filled with Rosalyn's scent: sex spiced with something darker, like vengeance cooked down to syrup. Her tongue worked in circles, then long strokes, her face soon soaked in wet that claimed territory without permission. Rosalyn ground down harder, her hips stuttering just enough to telegraph who'd been holding back.

Not anymore.

Somewhere above, the mic clipped to Rosalyn's hem captured everything. Gasps melting into the gurgle of spit and arousal, denim rasping against thighs that flexed like promises made in the dark. Marti lost herself beneath that filth made flesh, pinned and wanting more.

Rosalyn's fingers found the headboard. Knuckles whitening, rings biting into skin as she rode Marti's face. Each sound she released seemed torn from somewhere deep, too raw for the word "moan" to contain, bouncing back at them from motel wallpaper stained with decades of bad decisions and better orgasms.

The ache in Marti's jaw spread. Her eyes watered. Still she stayed locked in: tongue pressed against thick folds, teasing her clit with the patience of someone who had hours to kill and scores to settle. One hand gripped Rosalyn's thigh hard enough to leave fingerprint bruises that would catalog themselves under "evidence."

When Rosalyn threw her head back, the sound she released belonged to sins even God had stopped trying to forgive.

Marti smiled into the slick. Her tongue traced patterns of possession while Rosalyn's thighs trembled on either side of her face, power shifting between them with every stroke.

"Don't stop," Rosalyn hissed through clenched teeth. Her voice frayed like wire pulled too tight across rusted fenceposts.

Like hell Marti would ever stop.

Marti answered with action. She curled her tongue just right; sharp flick followed by suction that sent Rosalyn jolting forward as if electricity had found her spine. A boot heel slammed into the mattress. Denim scraped skin. The mic caught it all while Marti sucked pleasure from its source and slid a finger between folds without warning.

No buildup. Just raw entry.

Her finger curved up until knuckle-deep inside velvet heat that clenched without rhythm. Curling against flesh desperate for pressure that would leave ghosts long after climax passed.

Rain hammered the concrete outside, keeping time with Rosalyn's broken breaths, the soundtrack to pleasure verging on violence.

Inside: Marti fucked upward, tongue relentless, jaw working overtime. Her finger, now a second one, hooked deep and hard until Rosalyn collapsed forward onto her elbows, gasping into the mattress like air was punishment.

The slap came next: flesh on flesh, followed by a groan that cracked open something primal between them. It wasn't about elegance anymore. It was about endurance. About how far Marti could drive Rosalyn before she broke down crying or begging or both.

Marti withdrew her hand, slick and trembling, then dug into her bag beside the bed. Her fingers collided with silicone, cold despite the heat of the room. She lined it up without ceremony against Rosalyn's cunt and paused. Their eyes locked.

"Ready?" Marti mouthed.

Rosalyn nodded once. Messy curls fell over her cheeks, flushed deep crimson in the half-light.

Marti pushed in slow: one inch... two... three. Rosalyn's lips parted around a silent scream, swallowed by the damp bedding beneath them. The toy buried itself deeper while Marti's thumb found Rosalyn's clit, grinding circles with precision. Rosalyn's thoughts scattered across her face; concentration, surrender, desperation.

The red light of the forgotten camera blinked in the corner.

Rosalyn bucked once, twice, then froze mid-motion. Her climax hit hard. Her thighs shook before giving out, and she slumped forward across Marti's lap, gasping, shivering, unrepentant. Microphones picked up every thundering heartbeat, every ragged breath between them.

Marti yanked off her own shirt, her mask tossed somewhere between the nightstand and the floor. She leaned down close enough to kiss sweat from Rosalyn's shoulder blade. No asking permission. No need. Consent lived in every bruise, bite mark, and breathless sob they'd shared tonight under motel lights that flickered like dying stars.

"Your turn," Rosalyn muttered, voice hoarse against the crumpled sheets.

Marti grinned slow. She rolled her shoulders back and reached for what came next, knowing they were far from finished. Saints never survived these stories. And sinners?

Sinners got silent sequels.

Chapter 8

Rain slapped the window like an angry drunk. Neon lights bled through the glass, casting warped strips of color across the worn tile floor. Marti stepped inside, dripping and satisfied, her jacket slung over one shoulder and half a grin riding her lips.

Lori didn't look up right away. She didn't need to. The scent hit her first: heat, sweat, and a particular brand of afterglow that wasn't Marti's alone.

She tilted her head, eyes gleaming with something sharp. "Did you shower this morning or just let Rosalyn do the rinsing?"

Marti tossed her jacket over the back of a chair and dropped into it as if her muscles had stopped cooperating.

She lit a cigarette, took a drag, then blew smoke at the ceiling.

"No time," she said. "We wrapped up maybe an hour ago. If you want to call what we did wrapping up."

Lori's gaze flicked down to Marti's legs, sprawled at odd angles. "Walking like that... should I drive you to urgent care or just applaud?"

"She made me sore in all the best ways." Marti stretched her arms overhead and sighed as if she was remembering every thrust in high definition. "That woman fucks like she's been training for the Olympics."

Lori muttered something under her breath and reached for her phone. A few swipes later, Rosalyn's face filled the screen: grinning in some mirror selfie with one thigh cocked just so.

"She put this on her pay site?" Lori asked, scrolling deeper than necessary. "You're probably featured in the highlights reel."

Marti smirked around the filter of her cigarette. "Probably. But if you want collar cam footage, that's free real estate. Probably won't see much, but that woman makes sound happen."

Lori blinked. "Sound happen?"

"Oh yeah," Marti said, her tone purring now. "She's got a thing for sound, whispering into mics while squeezing hips hard enough to make them talk back."

"A symphony of sex?" Lori said.

Marti grinned wider. "Exactly that. Just add some moaning percussion and slap-based rhythm section; she's conducting a whole concerto out of my crotch."

Lori gagged and set down her phone as if it might be contagious.

"I'm serious," Marti said through another cloud of smoke. "I made noises I didn't know I was capable of. Like musical queefing." She wiggled her fingers in the air like jazz hands.

"That is not something I needed lodged in my brain." Lori stood. "Did she say anything relevant? You know: words not moaned into your skin?"

"Nope," Marti said. "Just sex stuff." She paused before adding, "Very effective sex stuff."

Lori turned toward the counter without replying, flipping on the ancient coffeemaker as if caffeine could bleach mental images from memory.

Marti groaned as she hauled herself upright, limbs protesting with every movement, and padded toward the bathroom.

The light buzzed overhead as if it wasn't thrilled to see her either. She caught sight of herself in the mirror: eyes half-dead but satisfied as hell. She smirked at her reflection while peeling off sticky layers one button at a time.

Steam curled up as hot water hit porcelain, fogging up everything except the part of her brain still tingling from Rosalyn's last bite.

She didn't have to do this. She was proud of how she looked, how she smelled, how she'd been fucked. But Lori had made that face again.

Maybe jealousy looked good on Lori.

Maybe Marti wanted to see more of it.

Maybe not.

She dipped her hands under the stream anyway and splashed water onto skin that still hummed from earlier performances.

Rosalyn had left marks: not bruises but fingerprints spelled out in sweat. Marti wasn't sure if washing them off felt like erasure or flirtation.

Either way, Lori would smell soap instead next time they stood too close.

A splash. Then another. Marti scrubbed her hands like she was erasing evidence, suds clinging to her fingers before slipping down the drain in streaks of white. Water scalded, but that just helped her focus. No ghosts of kisses left behind if you scorched the skin clean.

The mirror caught her eye and held it. She grinned: brazen, lopsided, cocky as hell. She winked. Not because she needed reassurance, but because she enjoyed the look of herself freshly fucked and scheming. A girl with soap under her nails and sin still drying between her thighs.

She shoved her pants down, quick and efficient, and grabbed the washcloth again. The coarse cotton scraped across her skin as she scrubbed: inside thighs first, then up her belly where Rosalyn's hands had clenched like anchors. The cloth paused at her crotch; just a heartbeat of memory between her legs before she wiped it away too.

Last came the ass crack because dignity was a luxury and Marti had better things to cling to.

She tossed the cloth into the laundry bin without ceremony, grabbed the faded office towel from its hook, and patted herself dry as if blotting ink off a secret love letter. That towel had cleaned up blood once. Today it just wiped away sex.

Pants back up. Shirt smoothed flat over anarchy. She stared into the mirror: hair wild, pupils dilated. She nodded.

Good enough for corporate espionage.

The bathroom door clicked shut behind her like a vault sealing off classified sins. She stepped back into the office smog of old coffee, cheap cigarettes, and paper cuts waiting to happen.

Lori was already seated on the couch with two mugs steaming between them like a peace offering. Marti cocked an eyebrow but took hers anyway.

They drank in silence; black coffee that burned on its way down and washed out whatever echoes were still bouncing around Marti's mouth from earlier moans.

And then.

"There it is!"

Lori shot up like she'd been tasered, mug nearly flying out of her hand as she darted toward the window with wide eyes and thudding boots.

Five floors below heaven, crouched on a rust-bitten fire escape as if reborn from the gutter, was a filthy street cat with amber eyes and an attitude problem.

"Hey baby," Lori called in that soft voice she used on Marti when trying not to spook her.

The cat twitched its tail and bolted down the stairs without a glance back.

Lori leaned out until half of her body disappeared through the window frame. "Goddamn it!"

Marti laughed: a single sharp bark. She flicked ash into an overflowing tray. "Yeah, I'm sure that mangy thing really wanted your love," she said. "Now get your ass back here before you fall out."

Lori pushed herself back inside with more dignity than deserved for someone abandoned by a street feline and flopped onto the couch with a scowl aimed skyward.

"That cat will come around," she muttered.

"Sure," Marti said around her cigarette. "Right after we finish unraveling this insurance clusterfuck."

She dug through a pile of files until she found what they needed: twelve pages stapled together with sarcasm and damning screen captures. She handed it off to Lori without ceremony.

Time to play nice with corporate overlords.

As Lori clicked open her laptop and loaded their report, Marti lit another cigarette and grabbed the phone receiver as if clutching someone's neck. She punched in Tobias West's number from memory; it was either that or she'd spent a few lost weekends staring at his number. She waited as it rang once, twice.

"This is West."

No hello. No pleasantries. Just sharp consonants on overpriced speakerphone static.

Marti smirked against the receiver. "It's Marti Starova."

Pause.

"I'm listening."

Of course he was.

Lori leaned closer to share mic space as if they were recording porn audio commentary instead of blowing open an insurance scam. Her voice had the warmth of fresh steel when she spoke: "We've been reviewing Claim 472, the one tied to that dashcam footage from October third."

She slid the full report across to Marti without looking away from the screen.

Marti flipped through it while talking: "Whoever pulled that job knew their shit inside out: deepfake overlays, timestamp warping. Someone who doesn't just dabble in IT but lives there."

"We're talking years of experience," Lori added, arms crossed now as if daring West to argue through satellite delay.

There was silence on his end; pure corporate processing time before he said anything else.

Marti lit another cigarette off the last one's embers while they waited for God or capitalism to respond.

They didn't mention Ari Stirling, not yet, and if West noticed that omission?

He wasn't stupid enough to say so aloud.

Chapter 9

Tobias West finally cleared his throat as if he'd just choked on a stock option. "Are you saying someone in my company brought in a hacker?"

Marti didn't flinch. She flicked ash into an empty mug and leaned back, legs sprawled like she was still drying off. "I'm saying your dashcam footage didn't get fucked up by accident. Someone who knew what they were doing, got in early and did it clean."

Lori slid a document out from the stack beside her keyboard. The paper whispered across the desk before she tapped it with one nail. "We pulled server access logs."

Marti adjusted her shirt collar, now damp with sweat or nerves. Hard to tell which. She kept her eyes on Lori's fingers instead of West's pixelated face.

Lori continued, voice sharp around the edges. "The first person to touch the footage was someone logged in as 'rm318.' Before it went into official investigative circulation, before anyone else so much as glanced at it."

West's silence stretched again; long enough for Marti to take another drag and wonder if he'd hung up or just died mid-call.

Then: "And that matters because...?"

"Because," Lori said, pointing at the paper as if stabbing it, "whoever rm318 is, they had first crack. No oversight. No witnesses. Just them and the raw evidence."

"Plenty of people would've looked at it after that," Tobias said, but his tone had shifted: less insurance guy, more cornered cat.

"Sure," Marti said. "But they saw a tampered file. Whole lot easier to swallow a lie when it's already been dressed up and fed through the system."

"And what exactly was changed?" Tobias asked.

"That's the real bitch of it," Marti replied, glancing at Lori again, not for confirmation but for tension relief. They both knew where this was heading.

"We can't say for certain yet," Lori admitted, pushing a strand of hair behind her ear. "But our guess? Someone wanted to exaggerate the damage before handing it off to you. Multiple claims, all doctored the same way."

"Make an oopsie look like a goddamn tragedy," Marti added. "And if someone's running this many altered claims through the system, they're not just padding one payout. They're running a fucking pipeline."

"Could be insurance fraud," Lori mused. "Or maybe whoever did this wanted the report to show no coverage at all; make it look like someone else was liable."

"Either way," Marti said, "we've got fabricated footage. And someone on your payroll, or someone with access, is playing tech wizard with criminal intent."

There was another pause.

Tobias let out that low, unpleasant laugh again: the kind that never reached his eyes even when you were in the room with him.

"You're not seriously suggesting Valenzuela had anything to do with this level of sophistication?" he said, voice dry as Arizona pavement.

"She on your suspect list or not?" Marti countered.

"She can barely log onto her email without IT walking her through step-by-step." He snorted. "Trust me. I've seen her reply-all chain disasters in real time."

"So probably not our hacker," Lori said, scribbling something just out of West's sightline.

"But still worth keeping an eye on," Marti added. "Even pawns get sweaty when someone's moving queens behind their backs."

Tobias paused again, probably realizing how little control he had over anything anymore.

Lori smiled at nothing in particular and flipped the document closed with a slap of paper-on-wood.

Marti leaned forward then, letting smoke curl between her fingers as she hovered near the mic as if she might bite it.

"We're circling in on rm318," she said. "That's where your secrets are hiding."

And for now?

Tobias didn't argue.

"You know John," Tobias said, like he'd forgotten they were still on the line, as if some shadow named John had just materialized next to him, probably holding a glass of scotch and bad decisions. "I think I might know who it was."

Marti flicked ash into her empty coffee cup. Lori arched an eyebrow so high it nearly hit her hairline. Neither of them had clocked another person in the room with Tobias, let alone someone who might actually have a fucking name.

A new voice sliced through the speaker: masculine, firm, and not from the Tobias they knew. "Rufus."

Marti froze mid-inhale, cigarette hovering just shy of her lips.

"No," Tobias said, even though it was already too late. His voice cracked around the word like it physically hurt. "It can't be Rufus. He used to work with the police; hell, that's why we brought him on board in the first place. We needed someone clean." A bitter laugh. "Honest, even."

"We have to consider—"

"No we don't," Tobias said. "Forget we mentioned Rufus."

Marti's gut twisted in recognition. Rufus wasn't exactly a unique name, but it also wasn't Bob or Mike or something innocuous enough to brush off.

"Rufus?" she whispered, voice low and tight.

Lori shot her a look. Marti shook her head like it might loosen something useful in her brain.

"Who?" Lori hissed.

"Shush. You sound like an owl."

"Oh please," Lori muttered under her breath, but she shut up anyway.

"We'll keep digging," she said to Tobias instead, cool professionalism sliding over her like lingerie under a trench coat. "You'll get updates as we have them. Please, whatever you do, do not act until we have all the evidence. I'll send over our payment info."

Tobias murmured something that sounded like half-agreement, half-resignation.

A dull ping announced his confirmation of funds about thirty seconds later. Efficient bastard. Lori tapped her screen a few times before sending over the evidence folder they'd pulled together. The green checkmark flashed: transaction complete.

"Appreciate your trust," Lori added, already halfway checked out of this conversation, fingers twitching for caffeine or home baked bread; Marti couldn't tell which. "You'll hear from us soon."

The line went dead with a soft click.

Marti leaned back in her chair but didn't relax. Her limbs went slack. That was different. They wouldn't—couldn't—pursue Juanita if she was connected to Ari. That was non-negotiable. But this guy...

Marti's gaze was fixed on something invisible and far away, as if trauma had a zip code she could still locate by memory alone. Then her eyes flared wide with recognition that slapped across her face sharp as thunder.

"Rufus," she breathed again, this time not as a question but as an accusation dressed up like nostalgia.

"Okay," Lori said, leaning forward now, chasing after that tremor in Marti's voice like it meant more than Marti wanted it to mean. "Who is he?"

Instead, the past sucker-punched her and dragged her under. One breath she was in the office, next she was knee-deep in anger, caffeine, and silence that reeked of old toner and older mistakes.

Central Division. Crusty homicide floors with asbestos flaking from the vents and grief baked into the drywall. That special blend of rot only fluorescent lights could highlight. Kane had yanked her down to the tech crypt after some dickless hacker nuked their servers mid-case.

And there he was.

Rufus fucking Montgomery.

Half-buried behind towers of monitors, wrist-deep in keyboards and coffee mugs stained the color of misery. His face flickering blue with code. Quiet as fallout dust.

Too quiet for a guy wired into everyone's secrets.

Just smart enough to vanish whenever things turned surgical.

The memory hit like blunt force trauma behind the eyes. Marti didn't want it clawing out of its grave, but trauma doesn't ask permission; it just shows up hungry.

She leaned back as if it might hold her together through this part. Shadow burned low behind her ribs, familiar as sin. She lit a cigarette with fingers that remembered more than they should.

"Kane introduced me," she said, voice flat like a chalk line. "Rufus Montgomery. Tech analyst. Surveillance pervert. The kind of bastard who could find cum stains in a snowstorm if they whispered to a traffic cam." Rufus never amounted to more than a stain.

Lori looked up from her laptop at that one, lips parting just enough to show tongue-tip pink against white teeth. Marti ignored it. Mostly.

"I was combing through Dalrymple's phone records, a case I had been working on," she went on, watching a roach scuttle across the floor instead of Lori's face or thigh or mouth. "Rufus had pulled them for us. There was a call logged at 4:28 a.m., three minutes long."

Her eyes drifted to the ceiling where an old water stain split into jagged branches like an arterial bleed in drywall.

"Except we had Dalrymple on camera at 4:28 talking to someone in person. No phone in sight." Her voice dropped lower now, as if it might shatter if she raised it too high. "I told Kane Rufus faked the logs. Maybe covering for someone, maybe something else."

She took another drag; felt it scrape down her spine like broken glass in syrup.

"That got me one enemy and zero answers."

She exhaled toward the ceiling crack and leaned into the part that still stung worse than withdrawals.

"Rufus pulled up footage from when I was interrogating Gomes." She flicked ash onto Lori's floor without apology. "Overhead angle. Shitty resolution but clear enough to catch my jaw twitch when I smelled something off."

Younger Marti stared up from that screen: leaner, meaner, all sharp edges and unslept nights. Across from her sat Gomes, sweating rivers while she played calm, and then.

"I stood up."

No warning. No cue.

"Just walked out," she muttered, words bitter as black coffee gone cold. And yes, her cup had gone cold again too because of course it had.

"Like someone else grabbed the strings and yanked."

And that was when Gomes made his move. He elbow-slammed the window open; shards flew everywhere like shrapnel made of bad choices. He climbed out into daylight as if he'd been waiting for curtain call all along.

Marti blinked hard.

"That video fucked me sideways," she said, soft but not gentle. "Torched my career. My pension. Paved me a one-way slide into Shadow."

She didn't say how many nights she'd watched that footage over again, trying to pinpoint what made her bail mid-interrogation without ever remembering making that choice.

She didn't say how sometimes she woke up with glass in her throat and Gomes still climbing out that window behind her eyelids.

Didn't need to say it.

Lori's fingers hovered above her keyboard now, not typing, not moving, just waiting for permission or maybe absolution or maybe something Marti didn't have names for anymore.

Marti didn't give her either one.

"Pull up those insurance files again," Marti ordered, sharp again. "Cross-reference Rufus's name with the altered claims."

Click-tap-click.

Time stretched thin until finally Lori spoke: "Found him... Holy shit."

Martina leaned forward so fast her hip cracked against the desk corner. She stared at Lori's screen as it swiveled toward her.

There he was.

Rufus fucking Montgomery.

Different job title, same rat-face grin hiding behind polished spectacles as if he wasn't rotting beneath them all along.

"Worked Falls City PD under Tech Division," Lori said. "Now he's at SecureGuard Insurance." She clicked through more files. "Jesus, Marti. Look at this. His ID's all over the claims with altered footage as supporting evidence."

Marti stared at the photo until spots danced in front of her vision; not even Shadow could smooth them out this time.

All those years ago...

And this little bastard was in her face again. Accessing, maybe altering the video.

Her heart kicked hard against her ribs as she muttered one word:

"Fuck."

Chapter 10

Marti had just said, "This could be—" when the door slammed open hard enough to shake dust from the ceiling tiles.

Both of them flinched. Lori nearly spilled her coffee.

A woman stormed into the office like a rich, panicked thunderclap: Francesca Stanfield, if Marti remembered her face right from news clips and charity gala photos. The suit she wore probably cost more than Marti's rent. Her heels clicked across the tile like war drums, eyes wide with some cocktail of fear and fury. Jewelry glittered on both hands, but even diamonds couldn't hide the tremble in her fingers or the way her breath snagged in her throat.

"Please," she gasped, her voice cracking like a bad hinge. "I need your help. My daughter's missing."

Marti hated drama before caffeine. She stepped out from behind the desk, jaw tight, trying to look as if someone who'd rather be electrocuted than emotionally engaged.

"I'm Marti Starova," she said. "That's Lori Harring. She actually knows how to use empathy without vomiting." That garnered Marti a death stare. Her first of the day.

Lori had already abandoned her coffee and closed the door behind their new guest with a quiet click; her eyebrow raised at Marti for the intro but otherwise unbothered.

"Francesca Stanfield," the woman said, softer now, as if saying it made her more real here, in this cluttered office that smelled like whiskey and ancient takeout cartons.

Marti gave a nod that could've meant anything: hello, sit down, don't bleed on my carpet. She gestured toward the mauve chair that had the fewest rips in the fabric.

Francesca collapsed into it as if her bones had suddenly been revoked. Her knees knocked together beneath the pristine pencil skirt, hands knotted in her lap as if she was trying to hold herself together manually.

"My daughter..." Her voice dipped into a whisper. "My little girl Serra is gone."

Lori moved first. She always did when someone cried. She crossed to Francesca and sank into a crouch beside her chair, hand brushing against Francesca's shoulder with practice: like touching a live wire too soft to bite back yet.

"Gone?"

Much to Marti's displeasure, Francesca nodded instead of explaining.

Marti watched their fingers touch, Lori's bare and sure, Francesca's covered in polished rings and desperation, and felt something spark in her gut. Guilt? Lust? Something equally inconvenient.

"We'll find her," Lori said, as if she was ordering fate around again. "We'll figure this out."

Marti shot Lori a death stare: her first of the day. Why the fuck would Lori say that?

Francesca sobbed once, sharp and sudden, and clung to Lori now as drowning people do; both arms clasped tight around Lori's wrist as if it were the last lifeline left in this city of broken glass and broken promises.

"I can't. I just want my baby back," she choked out. "Serra. Her name is Serra."

"We're here for you," Lori murmured, smoothing flyaway strands from Francesca's face without asking permission first. That was just how she touched people, as if they belonged to her care for exactly as long as they needed it.

Marti stared for another second before dragging herself back into functional mode. It wasn't like she hadn't seen worse; a mother begging wasn't new, but it still scraped at something raw inside her chest.

"Start at the beginning," Marti said. "No metaphors or spiritual awakenings. Just facts."

Lori slipped an arm around Francesca's shoulders as if holding her upright might anchor them both there longer than five minutes. Her voice dropped into that coaxing register that usually worked better than any threat ever could.

"Tell us everything about Serra," she said. "Start slow."

Francesca blinked hard and fumbled a crumpled tissue from her coat pocket, dabbing at one eye as if that might stop the flood. "She's seventeen. Loves stars more than people. Sleeps with a fucking telescope in her bed." Her voice cracked around the edges. "I always thought she'd die on Mars, not..."

The words slammed into silence. Her chin trembled, but she held it up as if that might count for something.

"She used my credit card to buy a movie ticket." Francesca's gaze locked on Marti. "Three weeks ago now. That was the last time anyone saw her."

Marti didn't blink. "Movie title?"

"Something French and depressing," Francesca whispered.

Figures.

"We're going to help," Marti said, grabbing the stack of papers Francesca had brought with her: phone bill, credit card statement, something folded so many times it barely counted as paper anymore.

Lori returned to the desk, brushing against Marti's shoulder as she took the documents and opened the top sheet. The faint scent of lavender clung to Francesca's paper trail: covering rot with perfume.

"Let's see," Lori murmured, sharp eyes scanning every column of charges as if each line might spit out a secret if she stared hard enough.

Marti crowded in beside her, their thighs pressed together under the desk without acknowledgment. She didn't say anything about how nice it felt or how wrong that timing was. She just looked.

Across from them, Francesca clutched her purse as if it had a heartbeat. Her breath stumbled out of her, rough and wet in the quiet room.

"Ms. Stanfield," Lori said without looking up, "we'll find your daughter."

Francesca's expression flickered; hope trying to exist next to grief and getting eaten alive. "My dad said you'd find her."

Marti raised an eyebrow. "Who's your dad?"

Francesca opened her mouth. She lost whatever name had been brewing in the back of her throat. Another sob hit her instead.

Lori slid the tissue box across the space with two fingers and didn't comment when Francesca took three at once.

"The cops tried," Francesca said after a moment, picking at her thumbnail as if nerves lived underneath it. "They went door-to-door. Dug through security footage until their eyes bled or whatever they do when they pretend they care." Her tone had teeth now, sharp and shaking. "But it all came up empty. They said Serra just vanished."

Marti met Lori's gaze over the paper trail, something unspoken sparking between them: old frustration dressed in new dread.

"Revue Cinema down on Troy Street," Lori said, tapping the credit card statement. "Purchased at 10:37PM on the...fourth of the month."

"And nothing since," Francesca sniffled. "Cops can't find shit."

Nothing ever just vanished.

"You're not wrong to be pissed," Marti muttered, dragging a nail down the side of the credit statement as if she was scraping off rust. "Cops are good at declarations and bad at delivery."

"Trust us instead," Lori said firmly enough to cut through Francesca's spiral. "We'll turn over every rock until something bites back."

Francesca nodded too fast to mean anything stable and reached into her bag again, this time pulling out a glossy flyer already soft at the corners.

Serra stared out from it: all cheekbones and defiant youth with a ponytail too tight for comfort and eyes like she knew secrets adults didn't deserve to hear. The unicorn charm around her neck didn't fit her esthetic.

"This is what I've been handing out," Francesca said as she passed it over like a relic.

Marti took the flyer and let herself study it longer than necessary; long enough to memorize Serra's smirk into muscle memory. "Serra's phone number," Marti said, not looking up, just flipping a pen in her fingers like it was loaded.

Francesca blinked, hesitated, then, "834573-11665." She reeled it off like she'd been rehearsing, which is all the cops had been. Across the room, Lori was halfway through typing before Francesca finished. Her fingers stabbed the keyboard with that chaotic grace she reserved for hacking into things they shouldn't have access to.

Marti noticed Lori's jaw set tighter than usual as she keyed the last digit.

"You aren't calling it?" Francesca asked, narrowing her eyes at Lori.

"If it's still on, we don't want it to ring and announce itself," Lori explained.

"We have other ways," Marti said, tucking the pen into her pocket only to pull it right back out again.

Then Lori cleared her throat, the sound small but pointed, and leaned forward so only Francesca could hear her next words even though Marti already knew what they'd be.

"You need to keep our involvement quiet," Lori said, surprising even herself with how firm her tone came out. "No police updates. No morning show exclusives."

"They're useless anyway," Francesca snapped, as if grateful someone finally said it out loud.

Marti exhaled smoke and stared at Francesca like she could reach into her brain and pull out all its dirty little truths.

"We'll find your daughter," Marti said. "Or we'll find whatever made her disappear."

Francesca turned to leave, sinking back into the rain-soaked night. It wasn't worry etched across her face anymore. It was relief filled with regret.

After Francesca's footsteps faded down the hall, Lori spun her chair toward Marti with a gleam in her eye. "I just deployed a lightweight phone worm called 'Boston Lace,'" she announced, tapping her monitor. "It'll take about an hour to stealth deploy and respond, but if Serra's still phone exists, we'll know. I'll activate the camera and mic if it has power."

Marti raised an eyebrow. "I love it when you get all illegal like that. Can you get a location?"

Lori shrugged. "No. It's an 8345 number: NetGhost. The kind we use. Can't be tracked. But I'll be able to turn it on. Use the camera to see where it is."

"I wonder who Francesca's dad is. Look that up, hmm?" Marti tapped ash into the tray without looking away from Serra's picture. "Wait! Did Francesca pay?"

Lori rolled her eyes in disbelief and grabbed the phone.

"Ha! Supergirl fucked up for once. Our standard rate for rich people. Get her to sign the contract. I don't want her ghosting us if we don't find the kid."

Marti flicked her cigarette butt into the tray and turned toward her partner, for work only, for now, and offered a razor-sharp grin that never quite reached her eyes.

"Okay, she interrupted us. Back to Rufus."

Marti shoved off the couch, Shadow still clinging to her muscles like a bad ex. She stalked over to Lori's desk, leaning in close enough to feel body heat and arousal.

"Rufus Montgomery," Lori said, tapping the screen as if it had personally insulted her. "Married. Three kids. Wife looks PTA-approved, probably bakes gluten-free cookies for the neighborhood watch."

"Bet she's got a ShowPin board dedicated to passive aggression," Marti muttered, squinting at the photo. Happy family. Matching outfits. A man-shaped lie framed in pixels.

Lori scrolled. "He likes casinos. Selfies with slot machines, blackjack tables, the occasional pissed-off dealer photobombing in the background. The Crimson Crown pops up a lot: shitty dive bar out near East 9th. Classy place to lose your paycheck and your teeth."

Marti leaned closer, eyes narrowing. "Something's off."

"You think everyone's off."

"No," Marti snapped, "I know everyone's off. But him? He reeks of wrong; we just don't know what flavor yet." She angled toward Lori, voice low. "Let me talk to him."

Lori tilted her head. "You're serious?"

"I can get him to spill his guts." Marti's grin turned feral: sharp teeth behind soft lips.

"Or you'll spill them for him," Lori muttered.

Marti didn't blink.

Lori sighed, rubbing her forehead as if she could scrape the stress out through skin. "Look, he's probably just a pawn in whatever this is. You're too." She hesitated. "You're too close to it because of Gomes."

Marti spun so fast the floor creaked under her boots. "Too close?" Her voice cracked on fury and something worse underneath it. "When that fucker escaped custody and carved up a little girl like confetti, who took the fall? Me! Who lost their badge? Their rep? Their fucking life?"

"Marti—"

"Don't fucking Marti me!" She shook now, not from Shadow but rage, and maybe shame riding shotgun.

Lori stood and grabbed her arm before she could detonate further.

Their eyes locked.

There it was again: that breathless territory where anger flipped into something else. Something hot and electric and too close.

"I'm sorry," Lori said quietly. "I didn't mean it like that."

Then she touched her.

Just fingertips on a shoulder, barely pressure at all, but it landed like a punch to the chest wrapped in silk. Marti jerked as if the contact burned, mouth parting around no words at all.

One second she spiraled inside her own fucked-up storm. The next? She stared straight into Lori's eyes, half-ready to crawl inside them.

The air between them crackled. Marti's pulse hammered against her throat while her breath caught somewhere between her chest and lips. That dangerous territory between fury and desire stretched before her. A familiar battlefield where she'd lost too many times before.

"You okay?" Lori asked, voice soft enough to cut.

Nope.

"Shadow," Marti lied without blinking. "Blame it on the Shadow."

But they both knew better.

That touch had hit harder than any withdrawal tremor or combat flashback. Clean electric hunger that made everything too loud, too bright, too goddamn tempting.

She dragged in air that tasted like Lori's perfume and stepped back just enough to keep her sanity. "I'll check the morgue for Serra," she managed, turning away before her tongue could betray what her mouth was already planning.

"Oh God, you think she's dead, don't you?" Lori's eyebrow arched like a dare, challenge dancing in her eyes. "So optimistic."

Marti didn't flinch. "You and I both know she probably just ran off. I still want to check."

Lori bumped her shoulder into Marti's. Playful, teasing, dangerous. "All business, all the time. You ever try being fun?"

"This is fun. My kind of fun," Marti said, the corner of her mouth twitching upward. "Wanna come?"

Lori blinked twice. Something flashed behind her eyes: surprise, interest, suspicion. "Seriously?" She tugged at her jacket zipper as if it had betrayed her. "Yeah. Fuck it. Never been to a morgue before. Might as well." Her fingers worked the zipper nervously. "Since this is business and not...whatever it is you and June used to do in broom closets."

"Ha-Yoon," Marti corrected, side-eyeing her.

Lori's grin spread slow and knowing. She'd heard Marti talk about Ha-Yoon more than once, always with that low, hungry tone reserved for whiskey and bad decisions. In Lori's mind, Ha-Yoon was thirty-five if you squinted hard enough, built like sex incarnate, with eyes that promised chaos and lips that sealed the deal. Hourglass curves and a face straight off a Z-drama poster.

Yeah. Lori was curious.

Chapter 11

The wind slapped at them as they hurried toward the coroner's office, each gust throwing accusations and carrying the scent of coming rain. Marti hunched her shoulders against the cold, boots splashing through puddles that mirrored a sky heavy with threats. Before them loomed the morgue, a blocky concrete monument to mortality with slit windows that glared down like suspicious eyes.

Marti paused on the cracked sidewalk, Serra's face flashing through her mind. Cold on a slab? Or halfway to Mexico with some dealer's cash? Either way, she needed to know. And that meant Ha-Yoon. Which meant...

Fuck.

"So," Lori said beside her, arms folded tight across her chest. Her eyes narrowed against the wind, but something else too, something sharper. "Ha-Yoon. What's she like?" A pause thick with implication. "Lemme guess: young, hot as hell, body built for sin?"

The edge in her voice could've cut glass.

Marti let a smile curl at the corner of her mouth but kept silent. Let Lori think what she wanted. The truth would hit harder. Funnier.

Lori clicked her tongue against her teeth and looked away, jaw clenched against whatever she was swallowing.

Inside, the building greeted them with the stench of bleach losing a long war with mildew. Their boots echoed across scuffed linoleum that hadn't seen love or maintenance since the last century. Fluorescent lights hummed overhead, casting everything in a sickly pallor that made even Lori's vibrant presence seem faded.

And there, behind the reception desk: Ha-Yoon.

Not what Lori expected. Not even close.

Sixty-three with black hair slicked back behind her ears and reading glasses balanced at the tip of a nose that didn't give half a fuck what anyone thought of it. Her face was a map of lines and stories; smile-wrinkles curled at the corners of sharp brown eyes that knew too much and probably liked it that way.

That wasn't wisdom in her gaze. It was vice.

Ha-Yoon looked up from her paperwork, and Lori felt something itch between her ribs: the sensation of being dissected by someone who'd already read your autopsy report and found it boring.

"Ahh...Marti." Ha-Yoon's voice poured like aged whiskey, her smile promising trouble older than both their sins combined. "It's been too long."

Marti strolled forward with ease, hands stuffed in pockets. But Lori caught it, the way Marti's shoulders relaxed, how her eyes brightened at the sound of Ha-Yoon's voice. Whatever existed between them still had gravity.

"Couple days at most," Marti countered, but warmth colored the edges of her words.

Lori stood frozen, mental images shattering around her feet. This was Ha-Yoon? This unflinching receptionist for death? No high heels or pouty lips or thigh gaps. Just confidence aged like scotch and laced with wickedness that made Lori's assumptions feel childish.

Ha-Yoon cocked an eyebrow at Lori, her gaze measuring, calculating. "And who's this?" The question hung in the air like smoke.

Lori stepped forward, extended a hand that hung unanswered for two painful seconds before she lowered it again as if that had been her plan all along.

"I'm Lori," she said, smile brittle. "I work with Marti."

"Is that so?" Ha-Yoon didn't blink. She leaned forward, resting her chin on the back of one hand, close enough that Lori caught the scent of something expensive and subtle. "Well. I hope you'll be around for some...after-hours strategy sessions."

Marti's jaw tightened. "She's heading back to the office," she cut in, the weight of Serra's disappearance suddenly visible in the tension across her shoulders.

"Pity," Ha-Yoon murmured, still studying Lori as if she were a puzzle she hadn't decided to solve or burn. "I always figured three hands were better than two."

Lori frowned, turned that over in her mind, then let it drop. She nodded once, cast Marti a look that flickered between hurt and anger, and headed for the door. Her footsteps echoed a little too quickly across the worn floor.

Ha-Yoon watched her go, appreciation lingering in her gaze. "Cute," she said, the word carrying weight beyond its single syllable.

Marti stepped closer to the desk, folded her arms. "Can we focus? I need to check if—"

"If any young men or women have come through recently. Who, specifically?" Ha-Yoon's eyes sharpened, reading Marti like a case file she'd memorized years ago. "You think I don't know why you're here?"

"Missing for three weeks." Marti pulled out her photograph of Serra and let Ha-Yoon stare at it for a moment.

"So?"

"No."

"Just no?"

"Marti what do you want me to say? No is the answer. Your girl is not here. You should be happy," Ha-Yoon said as she gestured at her computer screen.

Marti blinked. "Yeah, of course. But no Jane Does?"

Ha-Yoon shook her head. "None that look anything like her. Sorry, I thought you'd be happy."

"I am Ha-Yoon, I am. I don't know why I am being an asshole about good news. I'll let her mother know," Marti said as she dragged a hand down her face.

"Can it wait twenty minutes? I want you to fuck me. I found an interesting spot." Ha-Yoon said as she stood and slung a leather bag over one shoulder.

Marti's jaw tightened, muscles working beneath skin and she smiled. "Yeah, twenty minutes."

Ha-Yoon's heels clicked against linoleum as she moved toward the back of the office; confidence trailed behind her like perfume meant to confuse rather than attract. "You make it sound like a hassle. You want to skip it?"

"Fuck no. I need the distraction when everything goes to hell," Marti said as she followed unzipped her jacket.

"Good." Ha-Yoon paused at the door to the back rooms, one hand on the handle. "Follow me," she said, pushing through the door into the morgue's secrets.

The door creaked open: solid industrial steel. It slammed shut behind them with an echo that made Marti's nerve endings stand up and salute. The stairwell beyond was concrete and bad lighting, the kind of place for trading secrets or bruises.

Halfway down the first flight, Ha-Yoon stopped.

"I brought you something." She reached into her bag and pulled out briefs: black cotton with an O-ring stitched dead center like a bullseye on desire. "Put these on. Over the jeans."

Marti blinked. "Over?"

"I like texture," Ha-Yoon said with a shrug that dared argument.

Of course she did.

Marti slid them on. The waistband stretched high over denim, snug where it counted, absurd everywhere else.

Then came the toy: yellow silicone, thick base, smooth as smirked lies. Ha-Yoon handed it over like passing a torch.

Marti weighed it in her palm. Cool at first touch, soon slicked with lube she smeared on in quick strokes while holding it steady. She unzipped her fly and adjusted until the silicone base met panties and open air; not comfortable, but comfort wasn't the point here.

She didn't ask what came next.

Ha-Yoon answered anyway.

She bent forward until her hands touched cold concrete steps, ass angled up beneath the hem of a navy dress that clung as if it wanted in on the action too. "Fuck me," she said, voice velvet-wrapped command. "Make me remember this stairwell."

Marti stepped up behind her, lifted the dress slow to tease herself more than anyone else. White panties framed Ha-Yoon's ass like an invitation wrapped badly.

Marti kissed through fabric, low and deliberate, and dragged them down inch by inch while heat bloomed between them fast enough to burn oxygen.

She pressed the toy against slick folds already giving her permission.

"Jesus," Marti muttered as arousal coated silicone.

Ha-Yoon's body opened for her without complaint; hips rocked back as if she'd been waiting years instead of minutes for this exact geometry: denim-covered thighs braced behind bare flesh bent over stairs stained with mundane sins.

Each thrust pushed resistance into pleasure until both vanished.

Ha-Yoon moaned low at first, then louder as friction built rhythm from chaos, and sound bounced off concrete walls as if surveillance couldn't keep up.

Marti gritted her teeth against how good it felt; every push grinding the dildo's base against swollen nerves under denim-on-cotton layers. Absurdity turned into some grotesque kind of thrill.

This wasn't sex made for softness or storybook endings.

It was need weaponized by trust, shaped into something sharp enough to taste blood if you weren't careful.

And Marti? She was never careful with women who smiled like danger came easy in their mouths.

"More, Marti. Deeper." Ha-Yoon's voice cracked as her thighs squeezed, slick and glistening in the piss-yellow stairwell lights. Marti slammed forward, one hand gripping Ha-Yoon's shoulder, the other bracing against concrete. Ha-Yoon's cheek scraped the step she was folded over. "More."

Marti didn't need a second fucking invitation.

She drove harder: one brutal thrust after another, watching Ha-Yoon shudder every time the harness bottomed out with a wet slap. Her body jerked as if electricity had taken root in her spine, all muscle and noise and too much damn want. "Fuck," Ha-Yoon sobbed. "That's it, it's so fucking good, don't stop."

Her voice pitched up at the edges, curled into something raw, and Marti felt her own clit throb in protest at not being touched. Too bad. Ha-Yoon was unraveling fast, and Marti didn't believe in mercy mid-fuck.

Then Ha-Yoon shifted with knees together, feet still wide, which squeezed everything tighter like a goddamn vice. The sudden clamp made Marti grunt. She bit down on a curse as she adjusted her stroke to short, brutal pumps that punched into that slick heat.

"Jesus," she muttered into Ha-Yoon's shoulder blade.

Ha-Yoon moaned again: low, guttural, a sound too dirty for daytime and too honest to fake. It echoed through the stairwell as if it had somewhere to go. Marti chased it anyway.

Her free hand slid down to find that perfect curve of ass, tracing it once before cracking a slap across it hard enough to leave print. Ha-Yoon cried out but didn't flinch.

"You like that?" Marti asked between thrusts, breath ragged. She slapped her again; crimson bloomed across skin already flushed as she timed it with the rhythm of her hips pounding forward.

"Yes! Fuck, yes!" Ha-Yoon gasped between open-mouthed moans.

Marti leaned into it now; palm stinging from every strike, cock buried in cunt so wet she could feel slick coating the cheap nylon of the strap-on harness. The stairwell reeked of sweat and sex and something feral clawing its way to the surface.

"You want it harder?" Marti growled into the back of her neck. "You want me in your ass?"

Ha-Yoon nodded. Her words broke around panting breath: "Yes, please, please fuck me there."

Marti didn't wait for ceremony.

One more slap to make her squirm. Then lube-slick fingers shoved their way into tight muscle with zero patience for finesse. Ha-Yoon yelped, not quite pain but close enough to ride on, and Marti felt that ring twitch around her knuckle as if it was begging for more.

"Oh fuck," she hissed as she pushed deeper with one finger, then a switch to her thumb. The way Ha-Yoon clenched was obscene.

Back to pounding cunt while working her ass open. One push from behind sent both holes gripping around whatever they could take.

Ha-Yoon's face dragged against rough concrete with each thrust but she didn't try to lift it. Her mouth hung open in some twisted mix of ecstasy and surrender.

And then it hit.

Her body snapped tight as if a livewire had gone off inside her. She screamed, not delicate or romantic, but loud enough someone twelve floors up heard it through the walls. Her cunt convulsed around silicone. Slickness poured down Marti's thighs like spilled champagne at a crime scene celebration gone wrong.

The walls held their secrets but gave back echoes: hoarse cries, wet slaps, desperate pleas folded into concrete like confessions nobody would ever read aloud again.

Marti's clit sang with every grind of pressure; the base of the strap pressed down like a trigger. Every thrust she gave sent electricity crawling up her spine, a dirty symphony in her nerves. She was soaked, breath ragged, body pitched to snap.

"Ha-Yoon, fuck, I'm right there," she gasped, her voice catching like a match on dry tinder.

Ha-Yoon's moans spilled up the stairwell: broken things torn from her throat. That sound kept Marti going, drove her hips harder, deeper, until slick heat smeared fire between them. Marti felt herself unraveling. The orgasm crashed into her as if she'd hit a ten-car pile-up, chaotic, brutal, unstoppable. Her jeans were damp. Soaked. She didn't care.

She fucked through it, still chasing that last twitch in Ha-Yoon's thighs, that final clench around silicone as if Ha-Yoon was trying to keep her inside forever.

Then slowly, deliberately, Marti stopped. She drew back inch by inch until just one finger lingered at the edge of Ha-Yoon's body, trailing slick as it slipped free and curled down against her thigh.

The cock stayed put, strapped snug beneath the cling of briefs stretched over denim: bright yellow and shameless in the stairwell gloom.

Ha-Yoon turned, lashes heavy with the kind of afterglow that didn't wash off easy. She dropped onto the stairs with a thud, legs still shaking as if she'd been gut-punched by God herself, and tugged Marti forward by the belt loops.

Without flinching, she took Marti's slicked finger and wrapped her mouth around it; lips tight, tongue greedy.

Marti groaned in her throat. "You're fucking feral."

Ha-Yoon grinned around the finger and popped it free with a wet sound. "You love it."

She hauled Marti closer until they were crotch-to-face and eye-level with their mess: the dildo glossy with Ha-Yoon's come and sweat-slick friction.

"My dick looks good on you," she said, her voice full of filth and reverence both.

Then she leaned in and started sucking it clean with slow licks like melting ice cream off summer pavement, all sin and sweetness rolled into one obscene display of self-worship.

Marti could barely breathe. Her pulse throbbed behind her eyes; every inch of skin lit up like a Christmas tree wired wrong.

The stairwell stank of sex and stale smoke and something wild trapped between brick walls, as if this place hadn't seen light in years but remembered what heat felt like now.

"You're unbelievable," Marti said, watching that tongue work its way along silicone again and again until not even shine remained. Ha-Yoon could've been kneeling on an altar for all it mattered. Marti would've worshipped anyway.

And Jesus, she wasn't done yet.

Ha-Yoon sucked deeper now; slow pulls dragged saliva down Marti's faux shaft while she locked eyes as if she knew exactly what she was doing to her. Because she damn well did.

Marti's knees tilted inward under the pressure bubbling in her gut again. Her hips twitched forward without asking permission.

"Fuck," she growled. "I'm gonna come again if you don't stop."

Ha-Yoon didn't stop. She hummed around the plastic cock as if this was dessert and she wasn't leaving crumbs behind.

Marti bit down on her own knuckles to keep quiet this time, not out of shame or shyness, just because screaming again might bring someone running. No way in hell was she explaining any of this to building security.

Marti didn't get a warning: just raw heat and too much pleasure, all at once. Ha-Yoon's hand slid into her unzipped pants like it belonged there, fingers curving with intention. Then squeeze. Fuck, right there. Marti shattered.

Her second orgasm slammed into her like a truck doing ninety in a school zone. No ramp-up, no buildup: just full-body detonation. She grabbed the railing to keep from collapsing, knuckles white, legs useless. Her thighs trembled hard enough to knock teeth out. For a second, she forgot where they were: just stairs and sweat and Ha-Yoon looking smug.

"Jesus fucking Christ," Marti gasped. Her voice cracked. "You trying to kill me?"

Ha-Yoon pulled the slick dildo from her lips with a wet pop and a sigh that sounded both saintly and obscene. She wiped the back of her hand across her mouth as if she'd finished licking frosting off a spoon.

"If I wanted you dead," she said sweetly, "you wouldn't be standing."

"Standing is generous," Marti muttered, still clinging to the railing.

They both went quiet at once: footsteps above them, heavy ones. Marti tensed. Ha-Yoon froze, one hand still cradling Marti's thigh as if she couldn't let go just yet.

A door opened somewhere up the stairwell, then slammed shut again. The footsteps trailed off.

Ha-Yoon exhaled through her teeth and peeled her underwear off in one move, damp cotton sticking between her fingers before she held it out like an offering.

Marti took them without hesitation and tucked them into her jacket pocket while handing over the now-silent dildo, like this was any regular Tuesday morning meeting.

"I'm keeping these," she said.

"I figured," Ha-Yoon smirked. "You never used to sweat on stairwells," Ha-Yoon added, eyes dragging down Marti's body. "You getting soft?"

Marti rolled her eyes but couldn't stop grinning. "You're lucky I remember how good your tongue is or I'd have called this whole thing off."

"'Remember'?" Ha-Yoon arched an eyebrow as if she'd been insulted. "Almost forgot?"

"I said almost," Marti teased.

They both laughed, quiet but breathless.

Ten minutes later, they emerged from the stairwell looking almost respectable. Marti had missed a button, Ha-Yoon's lipstick was gone, but the security cameras would show nothing more scandalous than two women having an animated discussion about mortality statistics.

Marti leaned against the edge of the desk. The fun part was over. Reality had clawed its way back in. "Thanks," she said, quiet but heavy enough to carry the weight she'd swallowed.

Ha-Yoon turned in her chair, eyes soft again. "Good luck, Marti." A pause, then a crooked smile. "Try not to find her on my slab."

Chapter 12

Marti just wanted to get to the fucking Crimson Crown. From Judge's Hill to Eastwood should be a twenty minute drive. After thirty minutes, Marti was still in Faircrest Heights, and no matter how often she honked the horn, the overturned semi was not moving.

She finally got far enough to take the same alley everyone else was creeping through, and was spit out on 14th Street. Just a few more blocks to get to that shithole.

Ten minutes later, she pulled into the cracked parking lot behind the Crown, her hands still white-knuckled on the steering wheel. The neon sign flickered like a dying heartbeat. She sat there for a moment, engine ticking as it cooled, before slamming the car door and heading for the door.

The Crimson Crown looked exactly how Marti felt: soaked in regret and reeking of old nightmares.

Rain smeared the front window as if someone had tried to clean it with tears and whiskey. She stubbed out what was left of her cigarette against the brick wall outside, took a wheezing hit off her Shadow inhaler to level the playing field, then pushed through the door.

The air inside hit her like a punch to the gut: sour beer, ashtrays that hadn't been emptied since Bush was president, and desperation marinated in cheap cologne.

Marti peeled off her coat like old skin and shook it out with a snap; water flew everywhere. No one cared.

She was hunting.

Her eyes adjusted fast. Muscle memory kept them sharp even in gloom thick enough to hide a murder or three. The place hadn't changed: same broken jukebox sulking near the bathrooms, same bartender with his prison tattoos and bad attitude scrubbing glasses that would never get clean.

And there he was.

Rufus.

Corner booth under a flickering bulb that made his pockmarked face look more fucked than usual. He hunched over a glass as if he thought he could drown inside it if he tried hard enough. His thin shoulders curved inward like parentheses around nothing, shirt hanging loose on a frame that had never seen a gym from the inside.

Marti moved through the crowd, smooth and slow, slipping into a booth across from him but tucked far enough back to keep eyes on him without catching his attention.

She flagged down the bartender with two fingers and mouthed 'whiskey neat.' No flourish required.

She liked her whiskey the way she liked everything else: unapologetic and willing to make her throat burn.

The server slapped it down in front of her without ceremony; no garnish bullshit here. She curled her fingers around the glass as if it might hold answers instead of alcohol.

She threw it back neat in one go: a liquid punch straight down her throat that seared every inch of its path before detonating somewhere in her chest with nuclear heat.

Fuck yes.

Eyes watering, not that she'd admit it, she let the fire take over for a second. Let the pain feel good because at least that meant she wasn't numb yet.

The flavor lit up all kinds of receptors: dark smoke clinging to oak barrels soaked in sin, warm wood cradling ghosts of other nights just as bad as this one, and underneath it all… burn. Real burn. Not this artisanal 'hint-of-maple' crap bars tried passing off now.

Marti set the empty glass down like it was the period at the end of a sentence she didn't want to write. The burn still curled in her throat, a warm snarl of satisfaction sitting low in her chest. A flash of something close to contentment flickered through her nerves: booze-induced, temporary, toxic as hell. She signaled for another.

"Fucking Gomes," she muttered into her fist.

Surveillance footage? Too convenient, too much. Marti could smell Rufus on it: the kind of stink you couldn't wash out. Her fingers tightened around the fresh glass before she realized it was there.

"Jesus," she breathed, forcing herself to ease up before she shattered the damn thing.

"You look like you're ready to kill somebody," said a voice across from her.

Marti blinked. A woman had sunk into the opposite seat, half-drunk and unapologetic. Bloodshot eyes, smeared eyeliner that looked like war paint after a long night fucking or fighting; maybe both. Her perfume clashed with the bar's natural musk of stale beer and desperation. But her blue dress was tight. Very. Tight.

"That obvious?" Marti asked.

Tight Dress shrugged and stole a sip from her drink without breaking eye contact. "Just saying. You've got that 'I know where the bodies are buried' stare."

"Oh I do," Marti murmured, dragging her gaze past the woman and back to Rufus.

He was hunched over a slot machine like it would give back his money and respect, both of which he'd probably pissed away years ago. Cigarette hanging from his lips. Nicotine stains on his fingers like he'd been trying to erase evidence with ash. The cigarette trembled slightly, not from emotion but from the persistent shake in his right hand that three drinks hadn't cured yet.

"You keep eyeballing that guy," Tight Dress said, tapping her chipped nail against Marti's glass. "Ex-boyfriend? Fuckbuddy? Criminal mastermind?"

"None of the above." Marti didn't blink.

"Mmm." She leaned forward, cleavage catching the red light in a way that demanded attention; even Marti took notice. "He's bad news."

"Isn't everyone in this bar?" Marti asked, voice flat but not uninterested.

Tight Dress laughed like they were sharing secrets instead of surveillance. "You know Rufus?"

Marti turned to face her, slow and deliberate. "Who?"

"Oh come on." She tilted her head toward him. "Rufus, the shitty security guy who can't get it up and can't hold his alcohol?" She raised an eyebrow like they were swapping gossip over mimosas instead of whiskey and revenge.

"Nope." Marti lied so smoothly she almost believed it herself.

"Well," Tight Dress said, swirling the last dregs in her glass before knocking them back, "he just got fired. The shit has no money."

Marti let one corner of her mouth curl up: not quite a smile, more like the satisfaction of hearing someone else brake their car too late on black ice.

"Yeah?" she said. "Why you telling me?"

"I hate the little fuck. And I mean little. If you're going to fuck him, you should know. Little," Tight Dress said as she pinched her fingers together.

She leaned closer, voice dropping. "Six months ago he convinced me to help him move some merchandise. Said we'd split everything fifty-fifty. Next thing I know, cops are at my door with a warrant while Rufus is across town counting my half. I spent thirty days in county lockup while he bought that fancy car. Some kind of fake AI video of me doing shit. Figure you deserved a warning before he does the same to you."

Marti wondered how desperate Rufus might be for money. She leaned back in the booth, heat curling behind her sternum unrelated to booze this time. If Rufus knew why he was unemployed, he wasn't showing it. Maybe that could work in her favor.

Tight Dress exhaled through lipsticked lips and drank the remainder of Marti's whiskey. Marti waved for another. The woman shoved her empty glass aside with theatrical flair. "Anyway," she sighed, standing with the wobble of someone who'd made three bad decisions tonight but still had room for one more, "not my circus."

She paused beside Marti's shoulder just long enough to drag one manicured finger along the vinyl booth edge and smirk. "But damn... I hope your monkey throws shit."

Then Tight Dress sauntered off, hips swinging like bait on a hook, and left Marti staring after her with half a hard-on and full intent to bleed Rufus dry before sunrise.

Alone with her thoughts. Alone with her target. Marti lit a cigarette with the flick of a manicured nail and dragged deep until the smoke settled something mean inside her.

The Crimson Crown was half-empty but fully depressed; its regulars slouched around sticky tables like discarded thoughts. A slot machine wheezed in the far corner, lights coughing off its screen and into Rufus Montgomery's smeared glasses. He sat hunched, one elbow perched on the bar as if it carried the weight of every drunken mistake he hadn't yet confessed to. Marti watched him from her shadow-soaked booth, fingers tapping ash into a pile that never quite reached the ashtray.

He didn't know she was here. Didn't know she had him in her sights.

She stubbed the cigarette out under her boot with deliberate pressure, ignoring the lonely glass dish nearby. Places like this didn't deserve courtesy or cleanup. The smell alone warranted an arson charge.

She slid out of the booth and moved toward him, hips loose, steps careful. The floor stuck underfoot in places where beer had fought gravity and lost. She passed two tables of passed-out dreams and one guy who hadn't blinked since 2009.

Then she was there, pressing close enough to feel the heat coming off his hunched, defeated frame.

"Rufus Montgomery," she said, letting his name curl off her tongue as she dropped into the stool beside him. "Well fuck me sideways, you look exactly like I pictured, but greasier. We went to school together."

He turned toward her with the sluggish glare of someone deciding whether to bother pretending he gave a shit, the motion making him grip the bar edge like it might buck him off. His eyes were red-rimmed, pupils swimming in liquor. "Who's asking?" he asked, taking another swig.

Marti tilted her head, waiting for any sign of recognition. Nothing but confusion on his doughy face.

No spark, no flicker, not even a twitch.

Didn't remember her at all. Of course, the fucker wasn't wearing his glasses, so he probably couldn't see past his nose.

She leaned back, caught her reflection jittering across a slot machine screen behind the bar, a fractured version of herself haloed in neon cherry symbols and bad karma. Her hair was shorter now. Lips darker. Eyes harder than they used to be when she still thought justice meant something besides revenge ratios.

Still. How could he not recognize her?

She looked back at Rufus and decided that would work.

Chapter 13

"Name's Bertha," Marti said, letting it land between them like a dropped knife. "Bertha Tinkledorp."

One beat passed.

Two.

Nothing but blank stare and stale whiskey breath leaking from his mouth.

"I heard about your little career hiccup," she added, nodding toward where that sultry disaster-in-heels had exited moments ago. "Tough break."

Rufus snorted: half laugh, half phlegm. He scrubbed one grimy hand through limp hair that hadn't seen shampoo this decade. The gesture left him slightly winded, as if even that small movement taxed whatever passed for his cardiovascular system.

"Fucking tell me about it," he grumbled. "One day you're top dog on security protocols. Next day you're ass-out because some bitch decided I was too good at my job."

Marti curled one leg over the other and smiled like sin wrapped in silk. "Must've been quite the bitch."

His eyes narrowed as if he'd just noticed how close their knees were under the bar.

"What do you care?" he asked sharply, more bark than bite, and slammed his empty glass down hard enough to make it cry for help, though the force was more theatrical than threatening, his wrist too thin to deliver real violence.

"Heard you might need a job," Marti murmured, voice smooth as bourbon on bare skin. "A quick one? Cash. Off the books."

He stared ahead at nothing with angry nostalgia clouding up his face.

"My brother always said I was too trusting," he muttered, almost to himself. "Said people like you would come around eventually."

Something dark shifted across his features, raw and unfinished.

Marti let silence stretch between them as if it were foreplay for something much bloodier than sex.

"Oh honey," she whispered, her voice barely audible over the clatter of bottles and the low thrum of bad decisions echoing off the bar walls. "You have no—"

"Fuck you!" she screamed.

Tight Dress was in Rufus's face, her words slurred but sharp as broken glass. Spit flew. She stabbed a red-lacquered nail in his direction. "You leave my friend the fuck alone."

Her hand settled on Marti's shoulder as if branding her.

Friend? Marti didn't flinch, but she bit down on the word.

"You owe me, you little fuck," Tight Dress snarled, her voice caught between rage and performance. "And I want you to pay up. I wanna buy... wanna buy..." She waved toward Marti, fingers fluttering as if she'd forgotten how sentences worked.

"Me a drink," Marti said.

Rufus blinked. His jaw went slack before his usual smugness tried to claw its way back. He glanced between them: Marti steady as stone, Tight Dress swaying like flirtation itself. The math didn't add up in his head. Something shifted behind his eyes.

"Pay me what you owe me you little shit."

He opened his wallet with apparent pain, fingers fumbling with the leather like they'd forgotten how joints worked and slapped crumpled bills on the bar.

"That cover it?" he muttered.

Tight Dress snatched them with precise fingers. She counted the bills slow enough for nearby ears, folded them into her clutch with a neat snap that echoed over the music.

"It's a start," she said, sobriety slipping through her voice like a stiletto under silk. Her fingers squeezed Marti's shoulder once, firm and warm. She leaned close.

"Some of these assholes only understand theater," she murmured against Marti's ear, breath warm and whiskey-sweet. She delivered a wink so slow it felt obscene.

She adjusted her dress with one tug: an unnecessary move that managed to hypnotize. She flashed Rufus a smile that could've frozen boiling water, then turned on her heel and walked away, hips swinging like punctuation marks at the end of a sentence.

Marti watched her go. The tight dress vanished into the crowd like smoke through cracked glass.

The game had played out on martini-soaked parquet floors, but Marti still couldn't tell who'd been bluffing; she wondered if she'd just been roped into somebody else's long con with cleavage and claws.

Rufus stared at Marti as if trying to solve her face: familiar but like too many washed up whores to be trusted.

"So, no job?"

He let out a laugh so dry it could've been sand in a casket. "Bertha, you're alright," he said, voice coated in leftover bitterness. "Don't worry about me. I got an ace in the hole."

Marti's mouth had just parted to ask what the hell that meant when the server dropped off another round of rotgut. The glasses clinked like bones on a morgue tray. The place reeked of sweat-pickled wood and sour booze, a flatlined memory of better nights. Marti lit up a cigarette with the precision of a priest preparing last rites, pumping nicotine into the stale air until her lungs burned and her nerves stopped screaming.

She leaned in, close enough for Rufus to see every smudge of kohl around her eyes. "This ace," she whispered through a curl of smoke, "is it enough? You got enough money left after my friend just cleaned you out? It's risky but I can get you a crisp."

He took a sip of his whiskey like courage came by the ounce. Ice rattled against glass as he leaned back, sizing her up as if he thought she'd steal his secrets along with his lighter. "That's shit money for me. I don't wipe my ass for less than five crisp."

Marti tried not to gag into her drink.

"Old pal from the force," Rufus said. "Still owes me for some freelance work I did. Guy's been climbing the ladder real steady-like. Amazing how much smoother things run when you got the right connections."

Marti raised an eyebrow with the kind of disbelief that belonged under stadium lights and applause tracks. "And it's better than ass-wiping money?" she snorted. "What you've got must be nuclear if it's worth that."

Rufus grinned: jagged thing, all teeth and ego. He laughed again, this time with more whiskey than wit. "Let's just say some old favors compound interest real nice," he said. "Might be luck's finally decided to suck my dick tonight."

He meant Marti, but all she did was take a drag of her cigarette and throw it in his drink. He was too drunk to notice.

"Imma check it out." He slid out with too much swagger for someone still bleeding career wounds, steadying himself against the table edge for a heartbeat before his legs remembered their job. He wandered toward the lone slot machine tucked in the corner as if it owed him money. His gait had the careful precision of someone who'd learned to hide how much effort walking in a straight line required after midnight. He fished coins from his pocket like they were relics and shoved them into the slot with greedy fingers.

A burst of pixelated fanfare exploded across blinking screens; cherries aligned like planets deciding to quit fucking around.

The machine screamed: JACKPOT!

"Holy shit!" Rufus shouted loud enough to startle a drunk two tables over. He turned back toward Marti, arms high like he'd conquered Vegas itself. "Bertha! You're goddamn good luck!"

Coins clattered into the tray in a sad metallic drizzle that sounded richer than it was.

He stumbled back to their booth clutching maybe eighteen dollars in quarters and pride thick enough to choke on. His grin stretched wide enough to crack molars.

"Drinks on me!" he crowed, throwing his arms open like he'd just saved democracy.

Marti blinked at the tiny heap of winnings. What a sad little fuck he was.

Rufus kept talking: some babble about fate and fortune. She wasn't listening anymore. The bar had sunk deeper into itself as night wore on; darkness curled around edges, whiskey breath turning syrupy in the heat between bodies and mistakes.

She reached across and patted Rufus's hand with deliberate slowness, a gesture balanced somewhere between mockery and foreplay.

Depending on how drunk you were, it might've even looked affectionate.

He leaned closer, breath warm against her cheek now, perhaps desperate under all that masculine bravado, and murmured, "We should do this again sometime, Bertha."

His voice dipped lower than necessary.

"You're quite the lady."

Marti smiled without showing teeth.

Marti gave him a slow, sultry smile: the kind that promised nothing and denied everything. "I'm married, Rufus." Her voice dripped with smoke and sin. Then she stood up, peeled herself off the sticky leather booth as if it had tried to keep her, and walked toward the exit with the sway of someone who knew exactly how much attention her hips stirred when they moved.

Chapter 14

Outside, the rain was doing its best impression of biblical vengeance. Neon signs bled pink and green over wet pavement, and the next bar and the next one blinked their open legs down the block. People loitered under flapping awnings, trading smokes, spit, laughter: whatever currency meant something in this part of town.

Marti tugged her coat tighter around her ribs and stepped into the noise. The sidewalk pulsed with bodies. Familiar chaos. She felt safer here than in silence.

Then she saw him: college age if you were being generous, drunk enough that his mouth ran faster than his brain could steer it. Shaggy hair sweat-slicked to his face, beer bottle swinging in lazy arcs from one hand while he yelled obscenities at passing strangers as if he thought it counted as foreplay.

Marti ducked her head, paced her stride. Don't engage, don't invite.

"Hey!" he slurred. "What the fuck is this? Some tranny cosplay shit?"

She kept walking.

"I said," louder now, chasing after her with words first, "are you a man or a woman? Doesn't matter; you'll suck my dick either way!"

The crowd laughed: some nervous, some eager for blood.

"Fuck her up, Zach!" someone yelled from behind him, too excited for their own good.

Zach didn't need encouragement. He lunged like a bad idea in motion, swinging a wide right that might've broken a nose if it landed somewhere useful.

But Marti wasn't built for losing fights to wasted frat rejects pretending to be men. She stepped into him and snapped an uppercut under his chin so clean it skimmed past his ear and tore it. Flesh unzipped just enough to make him scream.

His punch hit her shoulder instead of her cheekbone: lucky break. It sent her sprawling backwards into a puddle that splashed up around her as if the gutter was trying to swallow her whole.

She rolled through the wet like she'd been born in it, twisting away as his boot came down for her skull with enough force to crack concrete if it connected.

She spun up onto shaky feet and drove forward, head-first into his chest, which knocked him off balance just long enough for him to jab at her face like a cornered animal. His thumb grazed skin just above her eye and ripped it open. Blood blurred half the world red.

Marti hit pavement with a wet slap she didn't feel until later. Her hand landed on something slick: a bottle someone had left like an omen. She grabbed it without thinking.

Zach charged again, too stupid to notice what was in her grip until the base of the glass bashed against his jaw with all of Marti's fury behind it. The bottle didn't break, but the sound it made was dull and unforgiving, like a body hitting cold tile.

He howled, more dumb animal than man, and staggered back.

Marti followed him fast, swinging now. Not elegant. Not trained. Just full of rage and broken glass breathless in her hands.

The bottle exploded against the side of Zach's skull when she found bone harder than recycled glass.

He screamed; the sound cracked air. He punched her square in the ribs hard enough to send Marti flying straight into a wall plastered with club flyers advertising nights no one would remember sober. She hit hard enough to knock wind from lungs but not fight from body.

Garbage lined the curb: half-open boxes and used condoms piled in broken plastic bags. Marti swept her arm out as she stood again, flinging trash into his path like confetti at a fucked-up parade.

It worked enough to trip him up for half a second. Long enough for Marti to duck under his next swing. That one missed and hit brick. The impact made Zach cry out as if he'd broken something he didn't know how to use right anyway.

Marti swung again despite vision gone red and wet, right hand dripping blood now, but this time missed as pain zigzagged through muscle and nerve like lightning looking for ground.

Zach dropped low, and Marti pounced. She grabbed two fistfuls of his over-gelled hair and yanked his head down just as her knee shot up. Cartilage crunched. Blood sprayed. Not enough force to put lights out, but fuck it: his nose would never look the same again.

He screamed as if someone had canceled his trust fund, and shoved her back. Marti slammed into the wall with a thud that knocked the air from her lungs. She slid down the brick like bad graffiti, sucking wind, ribs shrieking. Then came the boot, close enough she could hear it slice through air toward her skull. She rolled, barely dodging death by douchebag.

Marti clawed upright, pavement spinning beneath her feet. Zach reeled in with a wild haymaker just as she drove her fist into his kidney as if she was punching rent money out of him. Flesh smacked flesh. Nerve endings screamed. They both hit the ground like dropped meat.

Her ears howled with static. The alley tilted sideways. Reality spun like a broken ride at an abandoned carnival. Across from her, Zach curled around himself and whimpered like a kicked puppy. Marti grinned through blood-stained teeth. That jab had saved her life.

She dragged herself up using fury and ruined joints, legs stumbling until they remembered what running felt like. She ran, harder than she had in months, maybe years, down alleys soaked in piss and moonlight, bruises blooming across her skin like dark flowers. Her lungs felt scraped raw with sandpaper, vision fogged with tears or sweat or smoke; who knew anymore?

Her boots splashed through puddles, each step sending lightning through her ribs. Two blocks. Three. The sounds of the fight faded behind her, replaced by her own ragged breathing and the distant wail of approaching sirens.

She didn't stop until her legs buckled and walking turned to limping, then to crawling through someone's forgotten shortcut behind a dead sushi bar. Marti collapsed in a shadowed corner between two dumpsters that smelled like rot-funk and meth vomit.

Gasping, bleeding, twitching from adrenaline fallout, she fumbled through her pocket until fingers closed around cold plastic salvation. She jammed the inhaler into place and hit it hard.

The hit kicked in slow: first pressure lifted from her chest; then everything softened. Edges dulled. Pain retreated to corners she could ignore. She slumped against the wall, head resting on brick still warm from sun long gone down.

Eyes shut tight now, not quite sleep but the closest thing available without dying first, Marti tensed every inch of herself: fists clenched so tight her nails bit skin, toes flexed until they cramped in worn boots sticky from old blood and alley sludge.

She breathed deep and fast and again: inhale, squeeze everything like one last fuck you to the world, and then let it all go in one long hiss that made no sound but stole everything sharp away for a second or two.

Somewhere in that quiet dark between bruises and sanity, sirens wailed, long and high-pitched, slicing through whatever peace she'd scraped together on this piss-stained ground.

Her eyes flew open.

"Shit," Marti muttered as reality slapped back into focus.

One last inhale for courage, or whatever passed for it these days, and she was moving again, slipping between buildings like a rumor no one wanted to admit they'd heard, city grime sticking to sweat-slick skin until it felt less like dirt and more like armor.

No one stopped her. No one saw her go.

Just another ghost bleeding through shadows with cracked ribs and stolen breath, and none of it stopping her yet.

Always knew how to make a scene, didn't you, Marti? She thought to herself, a bitter chuckle escaping her lips. As she stumbled deeper into the concrete jungle, memories of past fights and narrow escapes resurfaced. They reminded her of the price she often paid for her impulsive decisions.

Her key slipped once, twice, then jammed hard enough to make her knuckles scream. "Don't start with me," Marti growled at the lock before the door groaned open as if it resented her reappearance. The hallway inside wasn't much better: dim light, peeling paint, and that faint smell of damp misery she couldn't quite scrub out. Home sweet fuck-all.

"Made it," she muttered. Her voice barely carried above the door slamming shut behind her. Still breathing. Still standing, kind of. That counted for something.

The adrenaline had worn off somewhere between the alleyway and the stoop, and now the real party started: the throb in her temple pulsing in sync with her heartbeat, ribs aching as if someone had taken a crowbar to her side just for fun. She staggered to the freezer, grabbed two icepacks; cold enough to numb something, if not everything. She pressed one against her neck and used the other to brace herself down the hallway.

The bathroom light flickered as if it was waiting to start some amateur horror show. The cracked mirror didn't disappoint.

"Fuck me," Marti said, staring back at herself as if she'd found roadkill with her face. Purple blooming across her cheekbone, a cut above her eyebrow still leaking down into her lashes. She leaned closer. "Why's it always gotta be the fucking face?"

The sting in her hand refused to be ignored any longer: tiny glass souvenirs embedded in raw skin. Icepack forgotten on the sink, she yanked open the medicine cabinet; outdated painkillers, half an old toothbrush, no antiseptic worth shit.

Perfect.

She clicked on the shower and let it heat while peeling off bloodstained layers that stuck like bad memories. The water hit her like an accusation: scalding first, then melting into familiarity as she scrubbed grime and guilt from every scrape and split-lip souvenir.

No moaning over sore muscles here. Just hisses through clenched teeth as soap met wound. She didn't bother washing her hair; luxuries were for people who hadn't clawed their way out of bar fights and back alleys twenty minutes ago.

Wrapped one towel around her hand, another around whatever dignity remained, then limped back to the bedroom with a fresh icepack pressed against her collarbone.

She dropped onto the bed hard enough to make springs squeal but didn't move again.

"Bar fights at thirty-five," she muttered toward the ceiling fan spinning rust-flecked circles above her head. "Living my best fucking life."

Her fingers flexed around the towel-wrapped hand as pain throbbed its steady rhythm beneath bone. "Guess some things never change."

Chapter 15

Marti walked into the office looking like a crime scene that tried to pass for human and failed.

"Jesus Christ," Lori blurted from behind her desk, half-standing by instinct before she remembered Marti hated being coddled. "What happened to you?"

Her eyes scanned from swollen jaw to that angry gash slicing through Marti's eyebrow like punctuation on a bad night out. Purpling bruises were settling in as if they owned the place.

Lori's face twisted: worry first, then frustration, exhaustion pulling at tired features as if this wasn't new but never got easier either.

Same loop they'd danced before: bleeding woman walks in like nothing happened; woman behind desk tries not to scream or cry or drag bandages across skin she wants to taste instead of tape shut.

She didn't ask again. Not yet. The worst stories weren't told; they bled out across office carpet and awkward silences at 9 a.m.

"Sit down," Lori ordered, rising from her chair. "I'll get the medkit."

Marti collapsed into a nearby seat, lighting up a cigarette. As the smoke danced around her, Lori returned with the medical closet's contents in tow.

"Rough night with Ha-Yoon?" Lori teased, attempting to lighten the mood. "You need someone with a softer touch."

Marti just laughed, shaking her head. "Got into it with some college punk." A stream of smoke escaped her lips as she exhaled. "Didn't know when to walk away."

"Him or you?." Lori dabbed BioBuild into Marti's cuts. The sting made her flinch, and the room hummed. "Really, Marti? Street brawls at your age?" Lori scoffed. "You aren't Dorian Gray, you know."

"Who?" Marti furrowed her brow.

"Never mind." Lori sighed, finishing up her gentle ministrations. She returned to her desk, the shoulders slumped.

"Anyway," Marti said, the excitement returning to her voice. "You should have seen me at The Crimson Crown." She stubbed out her cigarette and leaned back. "I got close to Rufus."

"Montgomery?" Lori raised an eyebrow, clearly intrigued.

"Yep," Marti replied with a satisfied grin. "Sat right next to him while he drowned his sorrows. Turns out he got fired because of that fraud we uncovered."

"Good riddance," Lori muttered, sharing in Marti's triumph. "Too bad you're too hungover for a victory drink."

"Tell me about it," Marti groaned, rubbing her temples. "But Rufus mentioned something interesting. Said he had an old colleague who was good for twenty grand."

"Who? Kane?" Lori asked sharply, catching on to Marti's agitation.

"Can't be sure," Marti admitted, a bit hazily. "But he said the guy had to pay him to keep his mouth shut."

She chuckled, remembering the alias she'd given Rufus. "I told him my name was Bertha Tinkledorp. Funny thing is, he didn't even recognize me from our days in Falls City Police."

"That's a good thing," Lori mused.

"Sure hope so," Marti said, tapping her fingers on the desk, her thoughts turning inward. "But why the fuck didn't he recognize me? It's only been a few years. More than a few. I mean, I knew him on sight."

"Maybe it's because you've changed a lot since then," Lori offered. "You've lost, what, thirty pounds? And your Shadow use... It's showing on your face."

Marti froze. Her fingers stilled mid-tap.

"Jesus, Lori." She didn't bother keeping the edge out of her voice. "Thanks for the pep talk."

But the words hit harder than they should've. She could feel them worming under her skin, settling into that place where doubt had been nesting lately.

Her reflection in the office window caught her eye: hollow cheeks, new lines carving their paths across worn-out skin. "Past her prime" would be generous. She looked like a rough draft someone forgot to polish.

"On the Serra case, I've got something," Lori said, beckoning Marti over to her screen. "PingLace is showing the phone's active."

Marti leaned in, watching as Lori tapped into the phone's camera remotely. The image that appeared was dark and distorted, showing what looked like an alley wall with graffiti partially visible in the frame.

"The screen's cracked," Lori noted, frowning as she adjusted settings. "That's why the image is so warped. Can't make out much else besides that brick wall. Does it look familiar?"

"A brick wall in God knows where? Familiar?"

"Well, back alleys are kind of your thing," Lori said with a side-eye.

"Fuck," she muttered, dragging both hands through her hair as if she might pull herself together by force. "I need a mid-life crisis before I actually hit mid-life."

"Maybe you should take up knitting," Lori chirped from across the room, too chipper for someone who'd just insulted her boss's face.

Marti snorted. "I'd rather fuck a twenty-three-year-old and regret it immediately." She stood and stalked toward the desk. "What's the password for Falls City Friends again?"

Lori blinked, caught off guard by the sudden pivot from spiraling to sexcapades. "Uh... hang on." She rummaged through a battered notepad by the monitor, flipping past doodles and old grocery lists. "Here we go: NoirNights23."

Marti entered it without ceremony. "Of course it is."

A few swipes later, she was buried in photos and bios; all fake smiles and desperate captions. But then: Rosalyn.

"Hot damn," Marti said under her breath. Black leather jacket, raspberry lipstick, dark hair twisted into something sleek and sharp-edged. The kind of woman who looked like trouble on purpose.

"Marti," Lori began cautiously, but she never finished.

"Shhh." Marti waved a hand at her as if she was swatting away a bug. "Found my crisis."

She tapped through screens with precision, message box open, fingers flying: Wanna meet? Upper west side? Now?

Before she could scowl at how ridiculous that sounded out loud, a response lit up her screen.

"Oh fuck me," Marti grinned. "She's fast."

"You say that like it's a bad thing," Lori deadpanned.

"It's not." Marti grabbed her coat and slung it over one shoulder with flair stolen from an old noir film reel. "Wish me luck. I'm off to make terrible decisions."

"Good luck," Lori called after her, already regretting it.

The quick drive to the Gemund was all red lights and second thoughts. Marti cranked the radio to drown out the voice in her head asking what the fuck she thought she was doing. By the time she pulled into the hotel's parking garage, she'd convinced herself this was exactly the kind of bad decision she needed.

The place was beige-on-beige business-class boredom. No concierge tried to flirt or offer help when she sauntered inside alone, which suited her fine.

Anonymous enough for sins of opportunity.

The guy at reception handed over the keycard as if he was dealing blackjack: completely dead behind the eyes with just enough politeness to pretend he wasn't judging her.

She liked him immediately.

In the elevator, she checked her cuticles, wondered if she still remembered how to flirt without using Shadow as social lubricant, then told herself to shut up and just get laid already.

Upstairs, she tossed her bag onto the motel-grade comforter and texted Rosalyn the room number with zero foreplay: 407.

Then sat back on the edge of the bed as if her phone might bite her. Her heart thudded, impatient and unreasonably hopeful.

"This is stupid," she whispered aloud as if hearing it would slow things down inside her chest.

But stupid was better than numb.

A minute passed.

Then two.

Then ping: "On my way"

No punctuation. Of course not. Cool girls never needed punctuation.

She didn't mean to fall asleep, but maybe adrenaline had nowhere else to go once confirmation came in. Her head dipped forward; drool threatened mutiny; dignity slipped just far enough for dreams to creep in about goddamn knitting needles chasing her down alleys.

The knock hit like gunfire against wood.

"Shit!" Marti jolted upright with a burst of pure panic-turned-lust-turned-self-loathing in under two seconds flat.

She stumbled into the bathroom with toothpaste crust still clinging to the faucet from whoever stayed here last and splashed cold water onto her face until she could almost pass for awake or alive.

In the mirror: damp hair clinging to temples, eyeliner smudged into something borderline seductive or criminal depending on context.

"I can't believe you fell asleep," she murmured at herself as she ran wet fingers through tangled locks. "Maybe you are getting old."

But she winked anyway, a cocky little gesture of defiance aimed squarely at time itself, and opened the door half-expecting Rosalyn to ghost before things even began.

Instead:

"Well hello there," said Rosalyn, voice richer than expected and thick with mischief as she slid into the doorway as if she'd been practicing all day for this one moment.

Marti opened her mouth for something slick or clever or filthy, but Rosalyn beat her to it.

"What happened?" Rosalyn asked, stepping closer with slowness, fingertips rising toward Marti's face as if they had every right in the world to land there.

Marti didn't flinch this time, not from touch or time or truth creeping around between them like old smoke curling under locked doors.

She let Rosalyn touch her cheek and smiled back as if maybe tonight wasn't such a terrible idea after all.

"Walked into a door," Marti said. "And hello to you too." She grabbed Rosalyn by the belt loops and pulled her in as if gravity had finally decided to do her one good thing today. Their mouths crashed together with enough heat to make the curtains blush.

Rosalyn didn't waste her breath on pleasantries. She leaned in, her voice low enough to qualify as a sin. "I want you to enjoy every second of this, Marti."

She peeled Marti's shirt away like it was a barrier, Marti assisting with a breathless eagerness, stripped bare beneath Rosalyn's hungry gaze.

"Bruises. I like," Rosalyn murmured, pushing Marti onto the bed, her body eager and electric.

"Lie down," came the command as Rosalyn undressed with fevered urgency. "Let me fuck you."

Marti complied, stretching out like an offering; skin against rumpled sheets, tension crackling in the air.

Rosalyn climbed on top, straddling her with a raw possessiveness. She dove down, teeth sinking into Marti's nipple. Pressure, then tongue, then a fierce suck that had Marti gasping into the sheets.

"More," she urged softly.

Rosalyn's mouth descended southward with purpose, fingers trailing Marti's stomach to her navel before lapping at it reverently. Each caress ignited goosebumps along the way.

"You can talk now," Rosalyn said against slick skin.

"Tongue fuck me," Marti breathed, alive with need.

Rosalyn grinned, diving in with abandon, her tongue swirling before zeroing in on Marti's clit. Fingers joined in the dance, teasing open folds until they found wet warmth.

Pleasure spiraled as Rosalyn devoured her. Each flick of her tongue sent Marti spiraling closer to ecstasy.

"You're fucking beautiful when you fall apart," Rosalyn whispered breathlessly against Marti's thigh before kissing downward. A path of obsession along every soft inch of flesh.

Marti gasped as Rosalyn took her toes into her mouth, teasing them as if they were forbidden fruit. Each gentle bite ignited fire within her core.

"Oh god... that's... oh fuck," she panted, lost in a haze of sensation as Rosalyn worshipped every part of her foot.

With each stroke and suction, tension built to unbearable heights until Rosalyn reined it in, slowly savoring every reaction from Marti's shaking form.

When their eyes locked again, lust swirled thickly between them. Rosalyn paused before renewing her assault: thrusting two fingers deep inside while her tongue worked its magic.

"Don't stop!" Marti choked out as waves of pleasure peaked and crashed over her again and again.

"Not stopping," Rosalyn growled back before burying herself deeper into Marti's slick heat. Wet sounds filled the air—raw and primal—as the world around them faded away.

And when that final wave hit like thunder. Marti shattered completely, body arching as everything inside twisted and snapped apart under Rosalyn's relentless mouth.

Breathless and ruined on the couch cushions, Marti finally blinked up at her lover who emerged glistening and unapologetic from between her thighs.

"You're welcome," she said playfully.

Marti could barely muster a defiant glare. "I'm still not buying you lunch."

Eventually, Rosalyn peeled herself off and padded toward the bathroom on silent feet. Her bare ass swayed with every step. The cruel thing knew exactly what gravity could do with hips like that.

She paused at the doorway under flickering fluorescent light, glancing over one shoulder with an expression equal parts smug and saintly.

"You coming?"

Marti didn't answer right away. She watched the swing of those hips disappear over tile.

But yeah. She was halfway off the bed before she realized she hadn't blinked yet.

Chapter 16

Rain slammed the pavement like it was pissed. Fat, angry drops ricocheting off cracked concrete, soaking Marti's boots and mood in equal measure. Falls City didn't do gentle. It did bleak, loud, and mean. Neon signs buzzed overhead, trying to stay alive. One hiccupped and blinked out as she passed beneath it: fitting.

She'd wasted the whole goddamn day with Rosalyn. Naked limbs, breathless grins, her nails dragging down Marti's spine as if she owned her. And she did, for a few hours anyway. Lori would've been thrilled to know she played secretary, paralegal, and probably janitor while Marti got railed across Rosalyn's high-rise bed like a woman with nothing better to do.

Whatever. That's what payroll was for.

Her phone buzzed loud enough to make her jump, slicing through the wet night like it had claws. She ducked under the rusted awning of a liquor store that probably hadn't been open since Bell was in office. Half the storefronts on Main Street stood empty, their 'For Lease' signs faded and ignored. The banks had foreclosed on them and left the corpse to rot.

"Yeah," she said into the receiver, voice raw from cigarettes and guilt.

"Marti?" The voice on the other end was tight, controlled in that way people got when they'd been awake too long with their thoughts. "It's Francesca Stanfield."

Marti pressed her back against the brick wall, rain dripping from the awning onto her boots. "Mrs. Stanfield. It's late."

"Early," Francesca corrected, and there was something bitter in her laugh. "I haven't slept. Haven't really slept since—" She cut herself off, and Marti could hear the drag of a cigarette, the slow exhale. "Tell me you have something. Anything about Serra."

The desperation underneath the composure made Marti's chest tighten. She'd heard it before from other parents, but this was different. This woman wasn't just scared, she was carrying something heavier.

"I'm following leads," Marti said, which was true enough. "These things take time."

"Time." Another drag. "You know what my dad once told me about time? That it was the only thing you couldn't buy, steal, or take back."

Marti shifted against the wall. There was something in Francesca's voice: a weight that suggested she knew more about running than most people.

The rain was picking up, turning the street into a mirror of neon and headlights. Marti watched a car crawl past, its tires hissing on wet asphalt.

"I left the city years ago with Serra, put it all behind us. But here I am, right fucking back in daddy's back pocket." Francesca's laugh was hollow now.

Marti wondered about Francesca's daddy issues.

The pieces were starting to form a picture Marti didn't like. "You think maybe your father's involved in her disappearance? Who is he?"

"I think my father is a lot of things, but he's not stupid. And he's not careless. And he sticks to women his own age." The cigarette crackled again. "But if people found out she was his granddaughter... I need to know if she's alive, Marti. I need to know if trying to protect her from him all these years just ended up delivering her right into trouble."

The line went quiet except for the sound of Francesca's breathing and the rain drumming against the awning. Marti could feel the woman's fear, the guilt she'd been carrying around like broken glass in her chest.

She knew that feeling.

"Mrs. Stanfield—"

"I keep thinking about this bedtime story I used to tell her when she was little," Francesca interrupted. "About a princess who lived in a tower to keep her safe from a dragon. But the dragon was family, and the tower was just another kind of prison." Her voice broke completely then. "Maybe we should have spent more time with my family."

"Family can be helpful," Marti said. Non-committal, simple.

"Yeah? Well, look how that turned out." The bitterness was back, sharp enough to cut. "Find her, Marti. Find who took her before I do. My daughter doesn't need to grow up with a mother who is in prison for murder."

The line went dead, leaving Marti alone with the rain and the growing certainty that this case was going to get a lot worse before it got better.

Flicking her cigarette into the street, she pushed herself off the wall and slid back into Falls City's gleaming rot. The rain didn't let up; it never fucking did. Every alley whispered Serra's name as if a ghost was trying too hard to be heard.

She cut past Ridley Park, past rows of shuttered shops and broken dreams gone cold. The city breathed beneath her boots: wet asphalt pulsing under neon veins.

By now the photo of Serra had creased along every edge but Marti kept showing it anyway: habit or hope or both.

"Seen this girl?" she asked a sex worker who'd planted herself against a mural of smeared saints and cartoon dicks.

The woman looked up, eyes rimmed red beneath lashes caked in cheap mascara. She eyed the photo as if it might bite her before shaking her head once.

"Nah," she said.

Marti nodded without expecting anything else. Still held out hope that next time would be different; because if she didn't believe that even a little bit, what was left?

"Be careful out here," Marti offered because saying nothing felt worse.

The woman chuckled without smiling. "In Falls City? Honey... no one gives a fuck."

Marti offered nothing back: not pity, not platitudes. She drifted back into the dark where people disappeared for good if they weren't careful.

The rain kept falling like vengeance was personal tonight.

The marquee at the old Rialto flickered like it couldn't decide whether to stay alive or die spectacularly. Marti stood across the street, cigarette tucked between her lips, watching soaked moviegoers laugh their way into cabs and rideshares. Bright lights spilled across the slick pavement like some dumb promise of joy. She crossed anyway.

Inside, the lobby reeked of artificial butter and damp carpet. The kid behind the glass box office was all zit-pocked skin and apathy, as if he was one bad review away from swan-diving into nihilism.

Marti tapped on the glass with Serra's photo. "Three weeks ago. This girl come through here?"

He squinted like it hurt, scratched his scalp under his headset. "Maybe? I mean, I dunno. Tons of people come every day."

She stared, hoping irritation would beam into his brain. It didn't. "Fucking helpful," she muttered, sliding the photo back into her jacket and stepping out into the rain again.

Falls City swallowed her up: chewing neon into shadows, laughter into silence. The deeper she went, the louder everything unsaid became. Voices murmured from alleys, doorways, under broken umbrellas and over dented trash bins that nobody had bothered to empty all week.

At near 6th and Main, a guy with a tray full of discount Holotabs and half-dead burner phones nodded in acknowledgement when their gazes met hers. His trench coat had seen more winters than he had birthdays, and when their gazes met, he gave the kind of nod that said he knew why she was walking these streets at this hour.

Marti pulled out the photo. The vendor glanced at it, then away, like looking too long might burn his retinas.

"Yeah," he said, voice scratchy as old vinyl. "Few weeks back, I think. Girl wanted a tablet, but then she gets all twitchy, starts looking over her shoulder." He shifted his weight, the tray rattling softly. "Asked me if I saw the guy following her."

"What guy?"

"That's what I'm telling you: there wasn't one." He finally looked back at Marti, eyes sharp despite the fatigue. "Street was empty as a politician's promise. Just her and the shadows. When I told her that, she got this look."

"What kind of look?"

"The kind that says she knew something I didn't." He shook his head, pulled his coat tighter. "Smiled and walked off without buying jack."

Marti studied his face. Street vendors didn't usually remember customers who didn't buy anything.

"She say anything else?"

"Just thanks." He paused, considered. "But she kept looking back down Main Street, like she was expecting that ghost to catch up."

"Did it?"

"Nah. No ghosts. But she seemed normal, you know? I mean, not the kind who sees people following her," he said.

They both knew what he meant.

Marti took a drag from her Shadow inhaler and gestured in solidarity. He declined when she offered it over.

"Can't afford to see colors that ain't there," he said. He vanished behind a curtain of garbage bags swaying in the wind.

Four more blocks in: a woman huddled beneath an awning stitched together with duct tape and hunger pangs. Hood up, hair thin as cobwebs on one side of her scalp but defiant everywhere else.

"Nah, not that chick," she snorted when Marti asked. "Bitch prolly dead." Her laugh was wet and bitter. "Feels like even the sunlight's dead."

Marti handed over two cigarettes without ceremony.

"You need a light?"

The woman pulled her own Zippo with surprising flair, floral etching along its side, and lit up like it might be her last pleasure before death made its move.

Every step took Marti deeper into rot dressed up like routine: cops who wore ski masks now, gangs who wore badges, whispers about raids that never ended or maybe never began depending on who you asked.

Her phone pinged. A message from Lori.

"Serra's phone hasn't moved."

Too bad. Or good. At least it still had signs of life.

Like Marti.

Rain slapped the pavement, slicking the streets into a mirror of neon blurs and oily runoff. Under the overpass, Frank had gone full cryptid: wrapped in a patchwork of mylar blankets and scrapped circuitry, his augmented reality glasses glowing faintly in the dark like some urban legend spawned from the intersection of desperation and discarded tech. The interface ports stapled to his head, long rumored to have been put there by himself during a really bad Comadrine trip. A self-made golem.

"Frank," she muttered, spotting the familiar silhouette. He was curled like a dog against the chill but still smoking something that steamed in the wet.

"Marti," he said without looking up, voice shredded by decades and whatever he'd just inhaled. "Didn't think I'd see your ass again."

"Trust me," she said, crouching beside him so the rain only half-hit her coat. "I didn't plan on it."

His beard was more mold than hair now, eyes cloudy and knowing at once. "You got that look again," he said. "Like death's sitting on your shoulder but you ain't asked why yet."

She pulled a photo from her inner pocket, damp around the edges. "Her name's Serra. Seventeen. Missing three weeks or so."

He adjusted his cracked glasses as if they made any difference and squinted at the picture until his eyes turned glassy in a way that had nothing to do with sentiment.

"Cute kid," he said. "Never seen her." He hesitated, and Marti caught it.

"What?"

"Just... there's been talk. Bodies showing up more often lately." He rubbed his hands together as if it would help warm what was dead inside him. "Not old-timer overdoses; young ones. Too many for coincidence."

"How many?"

He shrugged under layers of filth-soaked wool. "Ten? Twelve? Depends who you ask."

Marti rocked back on her heels and swore under her breath. The kind of dread that wrapped around your spine like barbed wire started tugging.

Frank cleared his throat and leaned forward, hopeful as a dog watching someone unwrap foil.

"You carrying Shadow or Lumina? I'm dry."

Marti fished into her coat, pulled out a half-spent inhaler, and handed it over without blinking.

"You're an angel," he said.

"I'm enabling your slow suicide," she replied.

"Aren't we all?" He coughed into his sleeve and went back to his world without another word.

Chapter 17

Marti stood up and kept moving. The street swallowed her boots in puddles so deep she might've drowned if she stopped walking long enough to notice.

It wasn't just guilt or duty anymore. Serra's face had burrowed somewhere behind Marti's sternum and set up camp there with glitter stickers and hopeful eyes.

Near the bus terminus, she cut through an alley where rot bloomed from trash-stuffed gutters. Someone called out from a shadowed doorway: young woman, early twenties if you gave her benefit of the doubt; Marti never did.

"Hey," the woman rasped, voice frayed from too many late-nights and not enough water. "Got smokes?"

"Last pack," Marti said, flicking one loose and handing it over anyway.

She lit up with shaky fingers as if it might be the last good thing to happen to her this year. She took a drag deep enough to count as prayer.

"You're a lifesaver."

"Don't count on it." Marti pulled Serra's photo again and held it close enough to get smeared by raindrops running off her sleeve. "You seen her?"

Shaky Fingers looked hard, too hard for someone whose pupils didn't quite match, and shook her head as if her neck couldn't hold regret anymore.

"Nope...but the cops were looking for her a couple weeks back. Maybe a month. Sure that's the same picture."

Marti was shocked the fuckers might have actually done their jobs.

Shaky Fingers shrugged into herself like a folding chair collapsing mid-use.

"You heard anything from other people? Once the cops got them thinking?" Marti asked, hoping this one still listened when things went down around her.

"Not about her," she admitted between drags. "But I guess yeah... less kids around here this week than last." A pause. "More cops though."

Marti lifted an eyebrow. "That supposed to be comforting?"

Shaky Fingers offered a crooked shrug-smile and Marti left without another word because what else was there to say?

She hit the sidewalk again; rain slid down every crevice and into every crease without consent.

Serra's smile hovered behind her eyelids every time she blinked: a glittery ghost asking why.

Marti didn't have an answer for that.

But she walked faster anyway.

The neon cross outside St. Mary's Hospital flickered like a dying heartbeat, casting pink shadows across the cracked sidewalk. Marti had walked in a thousand times when she was a cop. Beat cop, Major Crimes, Homicide. They all led here. The busted letter 'M' in the sign made her think about...Maddison? Madeline?

When Marti was a cop, she thought she mattered. Thought she could sweep a broom through the filth and make this city less of a goddamn hellmouth. That illusion lasted about two precincts and a dozen corpses. Madeline had vanished into MethLumina, leaving behind three underfed kids and a husband who couldn't name their birthdays. Last she'd heard, rehab had taken her in. Marti hoped it took her forever, because anyone who ran like that needed more than twelve steps.

At least she hadn't killed her kids. Not like Lennon Hayes, who slit the throats of his two kids while his wife watched, then gave himself a hot shot and died puking while his wife screamed so loud her brain blew a vessel and she stroked out on the kitchen floor. Now she couldn't say a word, couldn't write, couldn't remember anyone's name but his. And even that came out slurred.

She'd learned fast that what families got wasn't justice; it was paperwork soaked in blood and a funeral they couldn't afford. She'd sat on too many couches pretending the truth didn't sound like screaming through drywall.

The drug dealer? Shot three other dealers because they charged ten credits less per pill. Didn't blink when Marti cuffed him, just asked if he could keep his shoes. The doctor? Poisoned his wife for reasons he never admitted. Marti figured it was either sex or money or some combination that ended with her bleeding out onto Egyptian cotton sheets.

None of them gave anything close to closure. Just scars for collection.

Serving both sides, badge and black-market, meant Marti knew how the city bled. She wasn't proud of it, but pride didn't keep you warm at night anyway.

Shadow did.

She hit again. Burn slid down her throat like molten razors dipped in honey, slicing up her nerves just enough to make the night tolerable. Reality softened, angles sharpened. Lights screamed too bright. Paranoia curled around her ribs, slick and intimate, like an ex with unfinished business. A hit was a coin-flip loaded gun. You pulled the trigger and hoped you liked what came out the other side.

Rain slicked the pavement like spit on a confession. Marti moved with boots heavy from miles and regret, the kind of tired that didn't show unless you knew what to look for. Down the alley, narrow and sour with engine oil and old piss, a woman stood half in shadow, half in neon. Legs bare to the thigh despite the cold, a thin mesh top clinging to high breasts and hard edges.

Marti clocked her in one glance: working girl posture, twitchy eyes, mascara smeared like warpaint on someone who'd seen too many midnights. Pretty, though. Asian maybe. Skin pale enough to glow under streetlamp flicker.

"You alive?" Marti asked, voice low and rough as gravel after rain.

The woman's laugh cracked sharp. "Only when they pay extra."

Marti stepped closer, pulling Serra's laminated photo out of her coat. "You seen her?"

The hooker hesitated. Then leaned in slow like it hurt to move that way. She sniffed once, looked at the picture with something deeper than recognition.

"Yeah," she said finally. "Fifteen, sixteen days ago. Running like hell near the ATMs off Granger." She tapped the photo with a nail cherry red. "Dropped this while tearing past."

She pulled something from between her tits, a delicate silver unicorn tangled in sweat and cleavage, and held it between two fingers like an offering or a trap.

Marti stared. Not at the necklace, not at first. Her gaze lingered on full breasts pressed tight by wet mesh, on skin glistened from rain and survival instinct.

"I kept it," Unicorn Chick said, watching her watch her. "Figured someone might come looking."

"You got a name?"

"No."

Marti raised an eyebrow but said nothing as thunder cracked somewhere distant behind skyscrapers bleeding light through fog.

"How much to buy it back?" Marti asked, already pulling bills from her coat pocket.

Unicorn Chick's smile slipped crooked across her face. "Depends if you're paying for the necklace or the view."

Marti glanced down once more, lingered deliberately this time, and met Unicorn Chick's eyes when she said, "Two-fifty if I want an hour?"

"Mmm." Unicorn Chick stepped closer, heat rolling off her like secondhand sin. "Special rate for dames in leather jackets who look like they fuck better angry."

Marti slid the bills into a waiting palm. Their hands touched longer than necessary.

She pocketed the necklace and reached for her phone just as voices echoed behind them, low and cruel and familiar in all the worst ways.

"Shit," Unicorn Chick hissed. Her hand shot up fast, grabbing Marti by both lapels and yanking her close enough to kiss or kill.

"What—"

"Trust me," she whispered before dropping low between Marti's legs.

Marti barely had time to brace herself against the alley wall before Unicorn Chick had her zipper down, fast and brutal, and shoved nose-deep against her groin like she meant it.

Which Marti totally hoped she did, but honestly knew she didn't.

Chapter 18

It wasn't pleasure but performance: filthy theater beneath sodium lights where cops didn't ask twice if they thought you were sucking or being sucked. And sure as hell, boots slammed puddles close behind them.

Laughter followed. The wet kind that smelled like rot and badge polish.

"Well fuck me," one of them jeered, "Tough guy likes 'em wild."

"She deepthroating yet?" another barked out through cigarette breath.

"Smack that bitch if she bites!"

Every word scraped Marti's spine raw while Unicorn Chick kept up the act: hands gripping hips like lifelines, mouth pressed close enough for heat but not touch.

They passed by laughing. The city's finest predators moving on without realizing they'd missed their prey entirely.

When silence returned thicker than blood clots, Unicorn Chick stood up slow and shakily zipped Marti back into herself with fingers that trembled under dirt and desperation.

"Sorry about that," she muttered without meeting her eyes.

Marti didn't speak right away. Her heart was still kicking bone trying to get out, but not from fear. Not entirely.

"They see me standing around not working..." Unicorn Chick shook her head hard enough to send rainflakes spinning off hair bleached too long ago. "Last week? They broke some girl so bad she stopped screaming halfway through."

Marti shoved an extra twenty into her hand without ceremony. "Keep it," she said.

Unicorn Chick curled fingers tight around cash like bruises hurt less than gratitude ever did.

"Ten percent for them," she whispered bitterly. "Rest goes to my pimp."

"No one protects girls like you anymore," Marti murmured as she lit a cigarette with hands steadier than they should've been after all that adrenaline bullshit foreplay they just pulled off together.

Unicorn Chick jerked her forward suddenly by jacket collar and kissed her hard, tongue sharp with want and whiskey breath sweetened by fake promises sold hourly to people who didn't deserve them. The kiss was filthy prayer wrapped around intimacy neither of them could afford but needed anyway; not comfort, just confirmation they were still here, still warm-blooded beneath all that ash and armor.

Then it ended as fast as it started: lips retreating with grace while rain needle-tapped rooftops above.

"You're good at pretending," Marti said quietly as she adjusted herself back upright.

"I'm better at surviving. My name is Naomi," Naomi replied just as softly. She turned slowly into shadow again where no blue light dared follow.

Marti watched until there was nothing left but puddles where heels once kissed concrete.

Marti walked anyway, grit in her step, and as soon as the street noise softened: snap, click, tap.

"Francesca, is this Serra's necklace?"

Two beats later her phone exploded with truth.

"Marti! That's hers! That's Serra's necklace! Do you have it? Please tell me you have it!"

"Yeah, some woman had found it. Kind enough to turn it over," Marti said. No point in telling her about the fee. She would just add the price to Francesca's final bill.

"Does she know where my baby is? Are you finding her?" Francesca sobbed through static.

"She doesn't know," Marti admitted while pushing between dumpsters that reeked of rot and cheap sex perfume mixed into rain-sour air. Her favorite. "But I'm getting closer now."

"You are," Francesca choked out between tears that echoed even over bad signal lines. "I knew I could trust you..."

Marti hung up before guilt could fuck anything else inside her chest.

Maybe this was all Francesca would ever get back from Serra: a silver memory that still smelled faintly of street musk and perfume. But right now it was something real in a world built on ghosts and rot.

And that would have to be enough. For now.

Marti kept walking. Between the rain, the dark, and the goddamn city clinging to her boots like a crying ex, progress felt like wading through molasses laced with cigarette ash. She passed flickering lamplight and busted storefronts: the kind of places that whispered promises and gutted you for believing in them.

Then came the voice.

"Hey, watch your back."

It slithered out from the shadows as if something wet and sharp. Marti pivoted, hand reflexively brushing her hip where a gun used to be. Just muscle memory now.

The speaker leaned against a graffiti-tagged brick wall, face half-lost in smoke and streetlamp shadow. Male, maybe. Hard to tell beneath the layers of grime and paranoia.

She didn't slow down. "Appreciate the sentiment," she shot back, dry as fuck. She must have heard that ten times already and she still hadn't grown eyes between her shoulder blades.

"Seriously, lady." The rasp followed her down the sidewalk. "Shit's not what it used to be."

What the hell did that mean? Was this guy giving cryptic warnings or auditioning for a cigarette ad? Marti grunted and kept going, wiping wet hair off her forehead with a hand that trembled just enough to piss her off.

The bank loomed ahead: cold glass and sterile corporate misery still glowing like it had something important to say.

She paused by the ATM. The screen blinked blue into puddles turned mirror-sharp by rain. Shadows stretched long across the concrete as if trying to trap her ankles.

Nothing.

No sign of Serra. No blood trail or scribbled warning note or desperate clue left in lipstick on the glass. Just more fucking silence layered over more fucking rain.

It had been weeks, after all.

She let out a breath and leaned against the wall, cold steel against soaked denim. Her brain throbbed behind her eyes as she tried, again, to put this fragmented puzzle together while everything inside her screamed she was too late.

"Damn it."

Not loud, but final, like stepping on something buried just beneath the surface and realizing it's a body.

Marti pressed her palm against her forehead, gauging whether she still felt human under all this static. No luck there either.

Every second wasted here was another Serra could be locked up or strung out or worse: hooked into someone's nasty little empire like all the other bodies Marti hadn't saved yet.

She pushed off the wall, flexed wet fingers numbed by cold and calloused by guilt.

Marti started walking the opposite direction, boots slapping wet pavement, thoughts chewing themselves bloody over Serra and this city that rotted under every light pole.

It had rained for seven and a half fucking hours, and nothing was washed clean.

Up ahead, shadows shifted wrong. A half-dozen men in piecemeal cop uniforms milled around as if they were bored and looking to kill something about it. None of their patches matched: fractured precincts turned gangs with sirens.

Marti ducked behind an overturned trash barrel just as someone pulled the trigger.

The shot cracked through the air as if it wanted applause. It was louder than it should've been, too loud for nerves already frayed raw. Marti dropped, shoulder slamming into wet concrete.

Not her turn to bleed tonight. But someone else's was ticking right on time.

She peeked around the rusted edge of cover and saw them: four of them on one man, a civilian maybe, or just someone who'd looked at them wrong while breathing.

Coated in blue-black armor with smiles like broken glass, the cops circled him before another gunshot rang out.

The guy screamed once before everything inside him splashed onto the streets like spilled wine at a funeral no one's attending sober.

They laughed. Loud and cruel and delighted with themselves as if they were boys playing King of the Hill with real bodies this time.

Marti pressed herself tighter against brickwork that stank of old battery acid, heart thudding fast enough to bruise ribs from the inside out.

"Fucking hell," she whispered under breath she'd been holding since Naomi walked away. She slid behind a dumpster coated in layers of graffiti and dried regret.

Out there, maybe ten yards off, the man twitched his last few steps toward nowhere worth getting to. His arm moved. Then didn't again.

"This city…" The words came sharp inside her mouth as if they'd been waiting all night to get out.

She stayed crouched there longer, watching blood turn puddles dark beneath streetlight halos, wondering how many more cracks had to split open before everything worth saving just slipped through.

The cops peeled off like they had better people to kill, and Marti unclenched for the first time in what felt like hours. No one saw her move. No one ever did when she didn't want them to. Ice water and adrenaline pulsed through her as she ran toward the man bleeding out on the pavement.

"Hang the fuck on," she muttered, dialing emergency services thankful for her burner phone. No need to tie her to killer cops, or to saving their target. Her voice cracked when the dispatcher answered, barely a whisper over the riot pounding in her chest, but she got the words out. Male, gunshot, unresponsive but not cold yet.

She kneeled beside him. Warm blood soaked into her jeans as if it belonged there, steam rising around them in the chill. He didn't have much left; his breaths were thin and slow, little gasps scraped against silence. She cradled his head in her lap as if maybe that meant something, as if pretending to care could anchor someone here.

"You're not dying on me," she said, low and firm, even though it sounded like a lie the second it left her mouth.

His eyes fluttered once. Then nothing.

The world pulled taut around her for half a second and then snapped clean through.

Marti heard the sirens before she saw lights bounce off glass and steel. Time to vanish again. She slipped into shadow as if she'd never existed at all: one more ghost in a city allergic to witnesses.

By the time she got back to her office, rain had turned her hair into wet ropes plastered to her neck and soaked through every inch of clothing. Marti shoved open the door with elbow and hip, too tired to care about mud boot-printed across the floor or blood crusting where denim met skin.

Dawn smeared light across cratered buildings outside: the kind of sunrise that couldn't bother showing up on time. Her coat peeled off in a wet slap against linoleum, revealing more red than she'd noticed before, down one side of her shirt like finger paint on cotton.

"Fuck me," she muttered and collapsed onto the couch as if gravity had been waiting for this moment all night.

She dug out her inhaler from under bloodstained folders and pressed it to her lips. The Shadow hit fast: a prickle under skin, quicksilver pulling at her spine until everything blurred enough not to matter.

Color came back too bright on grimy ceiling tiles, heat flooding behind her eyes like tears she wouldn't let fall. The couch breathed under her as she sank deeper with a groan that might've been grief or just withdrawal.

Her hand slid beneath damp fabric. Sometimes survival wasn't about saving people. It was about salvaging pieces of yourself before they stopped feeling anything at all. She moved slowly, chasing sensation so sleep wouldn't eat her alive.

By the time unconsciousness took hold, a siren howled in the distance. No one bothered answering.

Chapter 19

"Wait, seriously? You got off in the rain. In front of cops?" Lori blinked once, then shook her head, lips curving into something between horror and admiration. "Who even does that?"

Marti took a slow pull from her coffee, eyes glittering over the rim of her cup. "Technically, I was just the auxiliary participant. She started it."

Lori snorted. "Started it. Jesus, Marti. You could've said no."

"I could've," Marti said, dipping her spoon into the foam and swirling it. "But that would've involved self-control, and I like to keep my vices nicely balanced."

"Balanced?" Lori echoed.

"Sure. Sex, whiskey, unresolved trauma; like a fucked-up food pyramid."

The café wasn't fancy: chipped tile floors, sticky tables, WiFi that worked just often enough to pretend they cared, but there was an honesty to its grime. Everything smelled like scorched espresso and eighteen-hour shifts. The booth's cracked vinyl stuck to Marti's thighs through her jeans.

Lori leaned in across the table, hair brushing close to the condensation on her glass. "You usually tell me everything. In detail. Why the difference?"

"That's because it really kills the afterglow," Marti lied. She didn't want to see that hint of betrayal in Lori's eyes again.

Lori held her gaze. "And you didn't sleep again last night."

Marti shrugged one shoulder without denying it.

"Something more than just guilt rattling around up there?"

Marti set down her coffee with a clink that drew glances from two tables over. "Rufus was confident as hell last night."

"You said he's got something on someone. Who?" Lori asked.

"I think it's Kane," Marti said, leaning back against the booth like she had all day to explain this shit and not a single fuck left to give. "This is something worth tens of thousands. It's either career ending or life ending shit. My guess: career. Kane's career."

Lori raised an eyebrow.

Marti went on anyway. "I think he doctored the Gomes footage."

"Oh come on," Lori scoffed, "you're building conspiracy castles out of bar crumbs right now."

Marti sat forward, elbows on the sticky table top, voice low enough not to carry but sharp enough to cut. "If Kane pulled something shady, and Rufus backed him, then we're not just chasing our tails anymore; we're targets."

A phone ping got Lori's attention.

"Marti!" Lori's voice carried a note of excitement as she stared at her screen. "The phone's moving!"

"Your phone is moving?"

"Serra's phone, dumbass. Look," Lori said, turning the screen.

Marti watched the feed from the phone's camera: a hand, a blur, darkness. "Someone must have picked it up," she said, leaning closer.

"Looks like it's in someone's pocket" Lori agreed. "We should call it, offer a reward."

After a few rings, a young male voice answered.

"Yeah? Who's this?"

"Hi there, my name is Lori. I'm trying to reach the owner of this phone."

"This is my phone," the voice said defensively. "I found it, so it's mine now."

"Actually, it belongs to a missing girl," Lori explained, keeping her tone friendly. "We really need to get it back. Would you be willing to return it? I could pay you for your trouble."

The kid went silent for a moment. "How much?"

After a brief conversation, she covered the microphone with her hand. "Some kid found it. Says he'll give it to us for a hundred bucks."

"Done," Marti nodded immediately.

Lori uncovered the phone. "Meet me outside the Neiman-Costi Hotel in ten minutes," she told the caller, already reaching for her coat. Then she stopped.

"Can't," the kid said. "My mom's expecting me home. I got school tomorrow. I could meet you before school, though, same place."

Lori frowned slightly but nodded to herself. "Alright, tomorrow morning outside the Neiman-Costi. Eight AM. Don't be late."

After hanging up, she turned to Marti, unable to contain her excitement. "This could be our first real lead. We can check her call logs, text messages, something that might tell us where she went."

Marti stirred her coffee absently, watching steam curl up from the cup. Around them, the café hummed with its usual evening rhythm. A couple arguing quietly over a shared laptop, the barista with prison tattoos wiping down the espresso machine, someone's phone buzzing against a wooden table. Normal. Peaceful, even.

The bell over the door chimed behind them: the shrill kind made for gas stations and twenty-four-hour bail bonds offices, but neither of them turned.

Then everything stopped.

Not literally. No divine pause button slammed reality into slow-mo, but close enough: voices strangled mid-conversation; silverware froze mid-clink; even the espresso machine gave up its hiss as if it didn't want trouble either.

Three men walked in dressed like discount movie villains: black hoodies, gloves, ski masks that barely covered their beards, and fuck if one of them didn't look familiar from somewhere deep in Marti's memory where bad shit lived rent-free.

The leader stepped forward as if he owned air now and snapped his arm up so fast half the café ducked before he opened his mouth.

"Nobody fucking move!" His voice cracked with nerves or drugs or both. It didn't matter much which when you were staring at a nickel-plated revolver gleaming in your face under flickering fluorescent lights.

Bang.

One shot into the ceiling, not at anyone specifically, but still loud enough to make someone scream across by the pastry case and plaster dust rain down as if God had dandruff.

Marti didn't flinch. Her body language read bored-to-death with a side of ready-to-kill, but inside? Her pulse slammed against her ribs fast and dirty as nightclub bass.

She met Lori's eyes across the table, brown locking onto blue, and in that shitstorm instant they said everything:

Run if you can.

Fight if you have to.

Don't get dead for nothing.

A fucking robbery of all things. It was a coffee shop. What were they going to steal? Beans?

Behind Marti and Lori, a second armed man vaulted over the café counter as if he practiced that move in front of a mirror too many times, knocking over a stack of ceramic mugs as he landed beside the barista: a wiry kid whose whole body vibrated with panic as he raised trembling hands skyward.

The cash drawer popped open with an offensively cheerful ding.

Like this was just another transaction in some fucked-up loyalty program where frequent fear earned free trauma points.

"Wallets, phones, jewelry: on the tables, now!" Robber Number Three strutted between tables as if this was Broadway and he was starring in Murder: The Musical, swinging a canvas bag in one hand, brandishing a switchblade in the other. His breath came hot and horny behind the mask, like the whole thing gave him a semi.

Marti slid lower in her chair. "Stay calm," she muttered, voice razor-thin. The wooden seat groaned under her as she shifted. She'd seen too many bodies on too many slabs because people thought bravery was an immunity charm. "Do what they say."

Lori didn't answer. Her fingers locked around the edge of the table hard enough to make her knuckles scream white, mouth pressed shut like letting out even one sound might get her gutted. A little kid with glasses behind them broke into sobs and his mother clamped him to her chest with both arms and all her fear.

Then: "You!" One of them barked it at the next table over. Gun leveled.

Chapter 20

Of course some jackass had to play cowboy. He grabbed for his waistband as if this was his big fuck-you moment.

"Oh fuck," Marti hissed.

And then hell dropped.

Gunfire cracked through the air like fireworks at a funeral. Screaming tore out of people's throats in ragged bursts and metal howled against tile as chairs flipped and tables scattered. Customers hit the floor. Someone slipped in spilled coffee and went down hard near the pastry case.

"Move!" Marti snarled, grabbing Lori's arm and yanking her sideways just as a bullet punched through the potted plant they'd been hiding behind.

The café turned war zone in half a blink; glass blew out of windows sharp enough to slice gods, smoke curling thick across the room with that sulfurous stench of scorched powder and panic sweat. It caught in Marti's throat but she didn't stop.

She pulled her piece from under her jacket.

Because Falls City didn't let her take lunch without packing heat anymore.

They ducked under overturned chairs, dodging a line of fire that had no fucking regard for direction. Bullets bit into walls and sent splinters flying like angry confetti.

"She's gonna get clipped," Marti thought. But then: "There!" Lori shouted, arm outstretched toward a shadowy exit sign glowing above the back door as if it couldn't believe it was still working during all this shit.

They bolted. Alarm screamed when they shoved through, the kind that flattened eardrums and announced their escape with too much enthusiasm, but Marti didn't care. Out was better than dead.

The door slammed behind them into silence so sharp it hurt.

Narrow alleyway.

Wet pavement.

Smell of piss and old grease frying on bricks soaked by too many storms. But most importantly: no bullets.

"Go!" Marti barked again, pushing Lori ahead as sirens wailed somewhere nearby, too far to matter yet but closing fast. Her lungs burned like she'd swallowed half the gun smoke inside, feet pounding against broken concrete with every muscle screaming for relief she wasn't gonna get anytime soon.

Behind them: more shots, less frequent now, less wild, but still close enough to mean don't fucking stop running yet.

Lori stumbled once but kept moving, hair clinging to her face in damp strands, shirt ripped along one side where a chunk of flying debris must've grazed her on their way out. It exposed just enough skin to send Marti's brain veering off toward thoughts that had zero business existing mid-firefight.

Focus, fuckhead.

By the time they hit the mouth of the alleyway two blocks over, Marti's hands were shaking hard around her gun but she didn't let go; not yet; not until she could be sure no one was coming after them wearing ski masks and hard-ons for destruction.

And still: What the fuck was this?

Some robbery gone sideways? Maybe. But instinct curled cold in her gut like something meaner had taken root there. This wasn't random. Not even close.

She glanced over at Lori, eyes wide but still sharp, and yeah... They were alive.

Marti barely registered the crowd: just shapes and shadows that screamed a split-second too late. She yanked Lori behind a delivery truck, her boots skidding on broken glass. "Keep moving!" she snapped, though her lungs clawed for air.

"Can't shake them!" Lori's voice cracked around the words, more breath than sound. Her head swiveled as black-clad bastards closed in like wolves, faces blank, eyes hungry.

Marti didn't hesitate. "Split up!"

Lori's mouth opened as if she wanted to argue, but only a sharp inhale came out. She veered left down a piss-reeking side street littered with discarded umbrellas and the sins of the city. Marti bolted right.

The panic spread behind her like smoke: thick and choking, coating everything. People screamed without knowing why. Somewhere nearby, a woman dropped her groceries and ran into traffic. Marti didn't have time to wonder how many would die because of her shitty luck.

Bullets cracked the air beside her head.

She ducked low, heart slamming against bone, and slid into the nearest storefront: a nail salon with glitter-slick posters plastered over its windows and the sour tang of acetone in its walls. A bullet punched through the doorframe as she crashed over the counter, sending curlers and brushes flying.

The shopkeeper shouted something that might've meant get the fuck out or come back later. Either way, Marti didn't slow down. She barreled through a curtain of bead strings and shoved open the back exit.

It stank back here: wet dumpsters, old onions, something dying beneath cardboard boxes. At least it wasn't a fucking kill box.

Still not safe.

Still not sure if this was about her or just one more miscalculation in a life scrawled in bad math, but that cold curl in her gut said yeah... someone had marked her name with blood today.

She bolted through alleyway after alleyway, legs burning, lungs roaring.

"Where are you?" she whispered between gasps, not because whispering made sense right now but because anything louder might break something inside her.

Lori had better be alive.

She scanned every shadow like they might attack.

"Marti!" A low hiss near a dumpster, sharp and familiar.

She spun toward it so fast she nearly ate concrete.

"Lori." The name fell out of her mouth before she had control over her throat. The gorgeous idiot crouched behind rusted metal as if it was reliable cover while death rained from above.

Marti dove toward her as another round zipped past their heads and buried itself in old brick. They slammed down beside each other behind the dumpster like lovers interrupted mid-thrust; this honestly wasn't far off when it came to their usual level of chaos together.

"Down," Marti ordered between clenched teeth, pressing close enough to feel Lori's frantic heart beating where their shoulders touched.

"We're fucked," Lori muttered.

"Get your ass up," Marti hissed, fingers latching tight around Lori's arm. "We move now or we die here."

No time for romance; shame. They barreled from behind the dumpster into the alley, bullets stitching the air as if some asshole's idea of modern art.

"Left!" Marti shouted over the noise: gunfire, shouting, the pounding in her skull that never quite left these days. They burst into daylight and chaos, swerving through gawking tourists and disoriented city folk who couldn't tell a hit squad from a flash mob.

Marti yanked Lori back by the hand when she veered toward traffic. "Stay on me," she snapped. "Unless you're feeling real cozy with death today."

Behind them: footsteps amplified by adrenaline and pavement.

"This is bullshit," Lori gasped, hair wild where sweat clung to her temples. "Why are they chasing us?"

"No fucking idea," Marti spat, eyes darting for exit signs that didn't exist. Sirens wailed somewhere nearby. Back-up? Or just another set of cuffs waiting to ruin their day?

A door, half off its hinges and hiding behind a smeared window display of dead mannequins and mildewed sale signs.

"There!" Marti jerked Lori toward it as if they were late to brunch. The store sucked them in with a gust of musty air and broken glass underfoot.

"Back door," she barked before her lungs could catch up.

Lori pointed like a kid caught stealing cookies: shaky but accurate. Emergency exit glowing dull red at the rear.

They vaulted a tipped-over display rack that had once bragged about half-off lingerie. Something snagged Marti's jeans. Fuck it, fashion was for survivors.

When they reached the door, Marti braced herself against it. Hand on the handle, eyes locked on Lori's for half a second longer than necessary. "You ready?"

Lori nodded; not confidently, but enough. Marti kicked the handle down and slammed through as if they'd been evicted from hell itself.

Alarm blared overhead, shrill enough to peel paint, and then they were outside again, in another alley that smelled like piss and french fry grease.

"Run!" Marti shoved Lori ahead just as another shot cracked through the air beside them.

Something hot kissed Marti's arm. Pain bloomed like fire beneath her skin.

"Fuck!" Her voice came out ragged as she clutched at torn fabric slick with blood. No time to fall apart.

Behind her came Lori's scream: a sharp, gutting sound that cut deeper than any bullet ever could. She went down hard but crawled back up like she was fueled by spite alone.

Marti's stomach sank as she saw red spreading across Lori's side. Not deep, but bloody enough to make her want to kill whoever dared touch what was hers.

"Down!" she growled, planting herself between Lori and incoming death like some deranged guardian angel with a vendetta and shitty aim. Her gun barked once, twice; missing wide from pain but forcing their predators behind cover long enough to buy seconds.

Marti turned fast, bleeding, furious, and grabbed Lori again. "Move your pretty ass or bleed out in an alley."

"I'm trying!" Lori hissed through gritted teeth, stumbling forward while tears made tracks through soot and fear smeared across her face.

Sirens were louder now, closer, unforgiving in their pitch. Cacophony wrapped around them like a net: cops with itchy trigger fingers or bounty hunters with badges? Either way, not good news.

"We go where?" Lori choked out as they rounded another corner into more shadows that offered no safety.

Marti paused just long enough to press her hand tighter over her own wound before glancing back at Lori with something close to desperation cloaked in defiance.

"The office." Her voice cracked despite itself. "We always make it there."

Whether that was hope or delusion didn't matter now, as long as they kept running before fate decided otherwise.

Chapter 21

Marti and Lori crashed through the back end of Falls City's gutter line, lungs on fire, shoes slapping wet pavement slick with sewer stench. The alleys didn't care who bled where; they just soaked it up like everything else in this goddamn city. Somewhere behind them, gunshots had sputtered out like a dying engine, but the ringing still clung to Marti's skull.

Her arm screamed every time she moved. She didn't stop.

"There." Her voice was rough, raw as rust. A door swung open on rusted hinges, half swallowed by graffiti and shadow. It could have led them straight into a Wunk den or hell itself. It didn't matter. Marti shoved it open with her good shoulder and yanked Lori inside.

They hit the floor together in a breathless heap. Concrete scraped her palms. Lori's body trembled against hers, every sob a jagged spike in Marti's chest.

Marti pressed two fingers to the bullet wound along her bicep and hissed through clenched teeth. The blood was warm and slick between her fingers, pulse humming loud enough she thought it might echo off the damn walls.

"You're not dying," she told herself first. Then, turning toward Lori: "We're safe now."

Which wasn't true in any real way, but it settled Lori for a second.

Lori curled tighter into herself, arms wrapped around her side where the bullet had kissed skin. Her shirt was streaked red: enough to scare anyone not used to seeing their own insides on cotton, but not enough to kill her tonight.

Still, her eyes were wide and glassy as if they might break right out of her skull.

"I wanna go home," she whispered, voice shaking like a drunk during detox.

Marti leaned close enough to smell blood and fear and citrus shampoo under it all.

"This is home," she muttered. Then shoved herself upright with a grunt. "Let's move before someone decides squatters make for easy target practice."

Outside again, the rain bit harder than any bullet sting had managed yet. Their clothes were ruined: blood-slick and stiff with sweat, sticking to skin in all the wrong places. Marti's hand left little red fingerprints wherever it steadied her against walls or doorframes.

She flagged down a cab with the same arm that'd been shot three blocks ago. Because what the fuck else was new? Pain was just another accessory in Falls City; like lipstick or piercings or a loaded gun in your sock.

The cab stopped.

The window rolled down.

"Well, look who decided to bleed all over my backseat again," came that dry drawl from behind mirrored shades.

Cab Guy.

"Jesus." Marti blinked at the driver, then let out something between a laugh and an exhausted groan. "You still working nights?"

"You still getting shot?" he countered with a grin.

They slid into the back seat fast and low. Lori collapsed against Marti as if gravity gave up on her halfway through the motion.

"Trouble at Java Joe's," Marti offered when he raised an eyebrow in the mirror.

"That new café on 9th? Radio says it turned into a war zone: four dead, seven injured. Baby, too."

"Great," Marti muttered, one hand hovering near her wound as if that'd stop it from pulsing like live wire under her skin. "Just wanted a fucking espresso."

Lori made a sound next to her, half laugh, half sob, and buried her face into Marti's torn hoodie sleeve.

"You know," the cabbie said as he took a turn too fast for comfort, "this whole city's gone septic. People shooting each other over piss-stained corners nobody even wants anymore."

"Welcome to Falls City," Marti deadpanned without opening her eyes.

There was silence for one long beat, the kind that dared you to believe you were out of it, and then:

"Hope you've got good health insurance."

Marti cracked one eye open and lifted an eyebrow at him in the mirror. "I don't even have dental."

He barked a laugh just as they pulled up outside the office building that somehow hadn't been blown up yet this week. Maybe tomorrow.

They tossed him some crumpled bills, probably enough, and slammed the door shut behind them without waiting for change or thanks.

Inside smelled like dust and old betrayal. It was home, give or take ten stab wounds' worth of memories.

Marti dropped the deadbolt with shaking fingers and leaned hard against what passed for safety around here: a steel door and stubborn paranoia.

No shadows moved inside except theirs.

No bloodstains besides their own. Yet.

She let out a breath through clenched teeth and glanced over at Lori slumped by the couch as if someone had unplugged her.

"Welcome back," Marti said. And then softer: "Try not to bleed out on the rug."

"Guess they don't know who we are yet," Lori muttered, voice raspy like sandpaper dragged across asphalt. "Or they'd be here already with something loud and automatic. Either that, or Cab Guy was right. Drug shit. Wrong place, wrong time."

She moved toward the med closet, steps uneven but jaw set like steel. Pale as the moon and twice as pissed.

"Being shot sucks," she added, almost as if she was blaming Marti for it. "You've done this before? And just what? Shrugged it off like a bad hangover?"

Marti shrugged again, because of course she did. One shoulder lifted and winced its way back down. Her leather jacket peeled off slow, as if tearing a scab from concrete skin. Hoodie followed, stiff with drying blood.

The shirt underneath? Absolutely ruined, soaked through with a dark smear that clung to her arm where the bullet had kissed her too close. Lori's own shirt didn't qualify for date night either: torn along the side, blood blooming like some fucked-up corsage.

She stepped closer, squinting at Marti's wound. Just a graze, but deep enough to paint everything sticky red.

"I've got you first," Marti said through grit teeth. She sucked down a hit of Shadow; her head tipped back as the warmth spilled through her veins like honey laced with fire.

"Marti."

"You first." Her voice dropped lower this time, slower, softer as her fingers curled around Lori's buttons. "Let me."

She undid each one, eyes never leaving Lori's face as if daring her to object. Lori didn't flinch. Not from the touch. Not from the heat curling beneath it.

The graze traced just along Lori's ribs: a long weeping line that looked more like a slash but sent Marti's stomach twisting anyway.

She wiped at it with the edge of Lori's ruined shirt, dragging fabric across flushed skin in slow circles that felt more deliberate than medical. Blood peeled away in streaks.

Lori shifted under her touch. "Wait, what about you?" A hand came up to stop her but didn't quite connect. "You're worse."

Marti pressed a finger to her lips, not hard, just enough to make Lori go still beneath it.

"Shadow," she said again as if it answered every fucking thing: pain management, psychological avoidance... maybe even love if you squinted sideways on a bad day.

From the med closet she grabbed what they needed: ViaRevive in its unassuming tube and a blister pack rattling with pills she wasn't planning on using today.

Lori let her work in silence except for a sharp intake when the medication hit raw skin. Marti smoothed it over like paint on canvas and watched Lori's breath ease out after the burn passed.

"Fentafill?" Marti offered one up between two blood-crusted fingers.

Lori gave her the kind of look that could set glass on fire and shook her head.

Marti grinned without smiling and nodded once: fair enough.

Then it was her turn, which meant watching Lori hesitate for five full seconds before reaching for what was left of Marti's shirt.

Hands shaking, she dragged it upward over Marti's shoulders and throat and scars; more of those than anyone should collect by thirty-five. Finally off with a grunt of effort and incidental intimacy.

Her eyes flicked down, lingered on bare chest and bruises bloomed purple beneath skin left over from a street fight. Or street fuck. When she looked back up at Marti's face there was nothing but business between them. Mostly.

Lori pulled gloves over shaky hands and tore open a BioBuild pack with her teeth before Marti could say anything smart about it.

"This is gonna suck."

"No shit," Marti muttered just as the paste met flesh and sizzled like bacon in hellfire.

"Oh fuck," she hissed through clenched teeth as chemical stink filled the room: the kind that made your eyes water and your stomach lurch if you were sober enough to notice either.

She wasn't sober enough.

But she noticed anyway.

Still didn't make a sound beyond that initial curse. Just sat there while Lori pressed healing into skin too tired to argue anymore.

Marti didn't flinch, didn't scream. Just clenched her jaw and stared ahead like pain was a language she'd grown bored of. Lori dabbed more ViaRevive into the ragged trail carved by the bullet, trying not to linger but also not rushing. The stuff smelled like peppermint and formaldehyde. Between that and Marti's blood, it was a cocktail strong enough to knock your liver sideways.

Lori kept her focus on the task, even though her fingertips kept slipping across heat-soft skin. It was ridiculous how calm she sounded, how careful she was with each touch, even as her chest buzzed as if she'd swallowed a battery.

Marti swallowed a Fentafill dry: no water, just grit in her throat and a grimace that barely registered on her face.

"You should lie down," Lori said, tugging her toward the couch.

The office couch was shit for comfort but better than the floor. Both of them shed shirts during triage. Lori still had her bra on; Marti didn't bother. The leather was cold enough to punish them for every decision they'd made that day. Nipples tightened on contact, nerves prickling to attention. Neither of them mentioned it.

They collapsed side by side, breath slowing but never relaxing.

"Who do you think wanted us dead?" Lori asked, voice sharp around the edges.

Marti flexed her fingers as if she wasn't sure they still worked. "Take your pick. Someone pissed about us digging into Serra's disappearance? Could be the insurance scam. Some old grudge."

She hesitated until it became obvious.

"Or maybe," Marti said, "it's the cops I watched gun some poor bastard down in an alley."

Lori sat up as if she'd been slapped. "What?"

"I said maybe it's the police gang I saw murder someone," Marti repeated.

"The fuck?" Lori blinked. "You saw cops kill someone and didn't tell me?"

"I'm telling you now," Marti said, shrugging one bare shoulder as if this whole conversation bored her.

"That doesn't count!" Lori barked back, vibrating with fury. "Jesus fucking Christ, Marti."

Marti rolled onto her back, staring up at the ceiling tiles as if they might offer better company. "It didn't seem relevant."

"Not fucking relevant?" Lori spit the words out as she sat upright on the couch, tension rippling through her spine. "You watched a man get executed by cops and kept that shit to yourself?"

"Not like it's a new thing," Marti muttered.

Lori opened her mouth to argue. She closed it again as disgust twisted across her face.

"What happened?" she asked.

Marti exhaled through her teeth. "Saw 'em kill a guy is all."

She paused. Memory cost energy she barely had left. Silence settled over them like ash after a firebombing.

"Jesus," Lori whispered.

"I called emergency services," Marti added after a breath no one needed to hear. "Told 'em there was a body behind Primary Foods Distribution. Didn't mention uniforms or badges or anything else that could get me killed."

"You think we got caught in their crosshairs?" Lori asked, hands curled into fists against her thighs.

"Could be." Marti didn't sound convinced. "But those shooters peeled off before we crashed out near Benton Street. They were after us like hounds, and then...nothing. Maybe it was just some kids jacked up on Fentafill. Crashed before they found us. Maybe."

"So what then?"

Marti shrugged: more exhausted than evasive this time.

"I don't know," she said.

Lori lay back down beside her, staring at nothing while every worst-case scenario took root behind her eyes.

"I really hope you're right," she murmured, no less afraid.

The silence came back then, not awkward or heavy but worn-in and tired.

Marti blinked slow as heat bloomed under her skin from somewhere deep in the Fentafill haze. Limbs loose now. Breathing softer.

She shifted deeper into the couch cushions without asking permission. She never did. She let gravity take care of whatever posture remained between conscious thought and oblivion.

After a minute, Lori stood and padded over to Marti's desk chair near the window: the one with fewer bloodstains. She sat down cross-legged as if she planned to keep watch all night if necessary.

Neither said anything else, not because there was nothing left but because too much still hovered between them in static-charged air waiting to break apart again tomorrow morning with bullets or confessions or both.

Marti had passed out in a sprawl of bare skin and bruises, mouth parted as if she was halfway through telling the world to fuck off. Typical. Even unconscious, the woman demanded attention.

Lori watched her, arms crossed, jaw tight. Brave wasn't the word. Reckless maybe. Suicidally bold if you were being generous. But that kind of fire, that heat: it lit up something deep in Lori's chest she tried like hell to ignore.

She got up anyway.

Careful not to wake her, Lori snagged a thin blanket from the chair and draped it over Marti's torso; just enough to cover the worst of the cuts and the best of the view. Regret bloomed. The way Marti's ribs rose and fell under it made Lori's throat tighten. Vulnerable wasn't supposed to look like this: defiant while sleeping, legs tangled in a blanket she hadn't asked for, arms flung wide like a dare.

Fuck.

Lori turned away before her self-control failed her. She rifled through Marti's duffel until she found what she wanted: a black t-shirt with one sleeve half-torn and the hem crusted with god-knows-what from their last job gone sideways. She tugged it over her head anyway.

It hung off her shoulders like permission.

The fabric clung in spots where sweat had dried into salt stains; it smelled like stale cigarettes, cheap motel soap, and something deeper: Marti herself, soaked into the cotton like a claim no one had written down but everyone else could smell on her skin.

Lori sat back down in the chair and let herself sink into it. Her thighs stuck to the leather; Marti's scent stuck to her collarbone.

They needed supplies.

Not aspirin-and-Band-Aids supplies either. Real shit, stuff you couldn't walk into a pharmacy for unless you wanted a tracking number and federal attention tomorrow morning. She opened Marti's old laptop (keys sticky with what might've been blood or coffee or both) and typed fast.

The dark web offered its usual cocktail of overpriced trauma kits and sellers who thought encryption was optional. She didn't bother reading the full descriptions; just sorted by reputation and paid extra for discretion.

Another click submitted the order: field sutures, adrenaline ampoules, burn cream laced with lidocaine strong enough to make your teeth buzz. Enough to keep Marti alive next time she got cocky around someone holding steel instead of compliments.

Lori closed the lid.

Marti murmured something unintelligible in her sleep and curled tighter under the blanket without waking up.

The room held still.

Just breath, rustling fabric, and the low electric hum of secrets neither of them had said out loud yet.

Chapter 22

The morning air chewed on her cheeks like it had something to prove. Lori parked in the roundabout outside the Neiman-Costi Hotel and killed the engine. Marti was just five minutes away, sprawled out back at the office, asleep and stitched together well enough that Lori had given her a pass to stay horizontal for once. Which left Lori out here, pre-caffeine, hunting down a teenager with a cracked phone and just enough balls to put off the $100 reward.

7:55 AM. She checked her watch again like it might spit out something more useful than time, then scanned the front of the hotel. The place looked freshly waxed and too fucking smug about it, towering glass like polished teeth grinning at its own wealth. The doormen were burgundy-clad automatons, opening car doors with synchronized precision, while bellhops steered luggage carts as if they were auditioning for Swan Lake.

Old money didn't just stay here. It bled into the walls: discreet luxury, scented with expensive cologne and old scotch regrets.

8:03. There he was.

Lanky kid sidled up to a decorative pillar as if he'd been told "look casual" by someone who'd never seen casual outside. Maybe fifteen or sixteen, if you squinted past the attitude and acne scars. He wore a navy hoodie that had seen better weeks and jeans that sagged from poverty, not fashion. A beat-up backpack clung to one shoulder as if it knew better than to touch him too much. His sneakers were scuffed beyond redemption, and his eyes flicked between his phone and the hotel entrance like he expected security to descend any minute.

Lori crossed toward him, keeping her posture loose but her gaze sharp. "You the one I called about the phone?"

He jerked upright, defensive already. His face was thin, all cheekbones and tension, with dark eyes that held more weight than his age should've earned. Hair buzzed short on the sides but left longer on top: poorly dyed blue fading into natural black roots like a forgotten protest.

"Yeah," he said, voice cracking mid-syllable before he cleared his throat hard enough to try again.

"I'm Lori." She offered her hand more as performance than courtesy.

He stared at it for a second before giving her two fingers in a quick shake. "Tyler," he said. Not convincing.

"You got it?" she asked.

Tyler nodded once and reached into his hoodie pocket as if drawing a weapon; not fast enough to spook but slow enough to make her flex in anticipation. What he pulled out was a girly-girly phone: a pastel-pink case with silver stars, a unicorn sticker, a smear of nail polish and a cracked screen glittering with a spiderweb of damage where something had gone wrong.

His fingers were long and elegant, as if they belonged on piano keys instead of tucked into alleyway deals. For half a second Lori wondered what else those hands could do in life before she reminded herself not every stray boy needed rescuing.

She handed over five twenties without fanfare. No point haggling with someone who didn't expect honest pay in the first place.

Tyler's eyes widened at the stack before vanishing it into his jeans pocket as if it might get reclaimed if he blinked wrong. "More than I coulda sold it for," Tyler said with a grin. Relief hit his shoulders like warmth. Tension drained out of him fast enough for Lori to clock just how high-strung he'd been playing it.

"Where exactly did you find it?" she asked, now flipping the phone over in her hand as if it might start whispering secrets if she held it right.

"Alley behind some bar," Tyler said. "The Crowd or King's Clown or something dumb like that."

"Found at random?" she asked.

"Yeah." He shifted on his feet, jittery energy leaking through his soles onto rich-people pavement. "Yesterday. I cut through there sometimes; it's faster."

"And nobody else around?"

He shrugged, almost apologetic. "Couple people smoking outside the bar but nothing weird."

"Except a beat up phone sitting in the middle of an alley?"

"Near the wall. It was smashed when I found it. Looked like it had been there a while." Tyler gave another shrug, the universal teenage answer to everything from math tests to murder scenes, and looked away toward the hotel doors as if they might offer salvation.

"I thought maybe someone dropped it," he added.

"They did," Lori said. "Weeks ago."

His shoulders twitched. "I just found it yesterday, but could have been there for a while."

Silence stretched between them until Lori broke it with a business card pulled from her pocket: clean lines, black ink, no bullshit.

"You did right, Tyler," she said as he turned away, already retreating into whatever version of school would be his hell for the next few years.

She watched until his shoulders disappeared around the block before looking down at Serra's phone again, the glint off broken glass catching sunlight like an omen or warning or both.

Either way they had something real. Maybe if luck stopped being such a vindictive bitch, they'd find where Serra went when everything broke apart.

* * *

Sunlight tried like hell to claw through the office window, but the grime won. It always did. Dust streaked across glass thick enough to qualify as sediment, and whatever light survived was immediately swallowed by stale cigarette smoke and Marti's personal brand of apathy.

She slouched in her cracked leather chair, one boot kicked up on the desk, the other braced against the armrest. Shadow hissed from a slim inhaler between her lips. Sweet poison filled her lungs: burned sugar and control. For a second she forgot she was supposed to give a damn.

"Anything?" Marti asked, moving slowly toward Lori's desk as the latter scrolled through Serra's phone.

Lori shook her head, swiping through apps and messages. "Nothing connecting to the kidnapping. Last text was to someone named Jade at 12:43 AM." She held up the screen so Marti could see. "Says she was going to grab some money and hail a cab home."

Marti slumped against the edge of the desk. "So we're no closer."

"There's nothing else here that seems relevant," Lori confirmed, setting the phone down with a frustrated sigh. "Another dead end."

"Let Francesca know we have Serra's phone. She's going to want it," Marti said as she slunk to her office. She shut the door, unwilling to face how Francesca would react when she heard.

Giving mothers hope was fucking brutal. Marti had learned that the ugly way, back in her rookie year, when she still thought empathy might be part of the job description.

She sank into her chair and let her head fall back, eyes shut tight. Of course her brain picked now to spit up the Sanderson case like a hairball she couldn't cough out. Ellie Sanderson. Eight years old. Blonde. Missing front tooth. Disappeared on the way home from a friend's house in broad daylight as if the world didn't give a single shit.

Three days in, they'd found her backpack dumped in a drainage ditch like trash: pink nylon with glittery panda patches, some of them hand-stitched by Mom. Janet Sanderson had sewn them herself in what probably felt like an act of love at the time; something sweet and maternal and safe. Turned out to be a fucking breadcrumb trail to horror.

Marti could still see Janet's face when she'd broken the news, not the news, not yet, but close enough to gut someone. That flicker in her eyes when she heard about the backpack. Not horror. Not despair. But hope. Tight, desperate hope clawing its way back up like a rat from a sewer.

"She must still be alive," Janet had whispered. "If they only found her backpack..." She clawed at Marti's shoulder, desperate to hang onto something.

Marti had wanted to slap that delusion right out of her mouth.

The stats were clear, the scene even more so; the position of the bag, the lack of other signs. It all screamed dead kid. But Janet clung to that ratty hope with both hands for nine long fucking days while Marti and crew dug through every ditch and culvert within twenty miles.

Three days of calls at all hours. "Did you find anything? Did someone see something?" Her voice had gone from brittle politeness to frantic manic within seventy-two hours, clinging to each new clue like it was gospel.

They'd found a child's shoe three miles from the ditch, wrong brand, wrong size, and Marti remembered how Janet's whole face brightened as if it meant something good instead of absolutely fucking nothing.

"She wouldn't have walked that far barefoot: see? She must be out there."

It was mental gymnastics at Olympic level, watching that woman twist facts into fairy tales, fold agony into hope like origami knives.

And then they found Ellie.

And Janet broke. She crumpled right there on the dirt beside her daughter's shallow grave. She'd bought a police scanner and had been listening in. But worse than that was whatever shattered behind her eyes, like part of her brain just stopped accepting reality altogether.

Hope hadn't saved her; it had stretched the pain into something unrecognizable: drawn-out suffering dressed up in pastel daydreams. Torture with glitter on top.

Marti yanked herself back before it spiraled further. She opened her eyes and reached for what used to be hot coffee but now tasted like regret and cold ash water. Maybe if she could control this shit from drifting into her brain, she wouldn't need everything else to distract her.

Chapter 23

Fuck this day already.

Serra's phone was sitting out there with Lori, and Francesca would be hopeful.

Marti couldn't do it again.

Not when she'd seen what came after false hope got its claws in you. Not when every part of her already knew what Serra's phone meant.

Clue my ass. It was a goddamn gravestone with Wi-Fi.

She stayed behind her door while Lori ran interference outside, playing optimistic lesbian miracle-worker while Marti pulled disappearing acts behind paperwork and cold caffeine.

Evidence didn't lie. Evidence didn't smile at grieving moms or whisper maybe-maybes into shattered psyches.

Evidence was brutal and clean and cruel in its honesty: everything hope never fucking was.

The only other thing this brutal and clean and cruel was Shadow. It was just what Marti needed right now.

* * *

"Bingo," Lori said, slapping Marti back into reality with a stack of papers smacking her cheek. "Speeding ticket. Look at it. The fucker was driving."

Marti didn't flinch. She reached out, took the paper as if it might bite her, and squinted through the haze at the image printed on it.

Not Serra.

"Kane," she said, flat and final, the name like battery acid on her tongue. "Of course it's fucking him."

Lori leaned against the desk, arms crossed tight under her chest as if she was holding herself together through sheer spite. "He was behind the wheel when LaLoLa got smeared across the hotel walls."

Marti stared at the grainy timestamp on the citation. "Why kill her? What did she know that made her dangerous?"

"Probably something she wasn't supposed to say out loud." Lori's voice had that darkness creeping in again; the one that came out after too many nights spent listening to dying girls whisper their last regrets.

Marti clicked through files like they were land mines. "We've got surveillance footage from that intersection."

"We already looked at it," Lori said, but moved anyway, pulled up the video and hit play as if maybe this time magic would happen.

They watched in silence as headlights cut across security cam grain. The killer moved fast, hood up, face turned. There he was: tall frame, heavy boots. You could smell the arrogance off him even in black-and-white pixels.

Still no face. Still no proof.

"Fuck me sideways." Marti raked both hands through her hair, Shadow still burning sweet behind her teeth.

"I'd rather not do it sideways," Lori muttered as she typed into her phone.

Marti arched a brow without turning to look at her. "You flirting or filing?"

"Anonymous tip." Lori's thumb hovered over SEND before tapping it with conviction. "We tell them Kane did it again. Mention footage this time."

"They won't believe shit without a clean shot of his jawline in mid-confession." Marti peered at the frozen screen; paused right where death arrived in three frames per second.

"Maybe not," Lori said, slipping her phone back into leather pants that fit too well for someone who claimed to be 'just here for justice.' "But it's still worth trying."

"You're such a fucking idealist sometimes," Marti said, but there wasn't heat behind it: just tired affection wrapped in sarcasm and nicotine breath.

The silence returned like an old friend with bad news. Marti stayed with the screen while Lori watched her instead.

"Goddamn Fehr," Lori said. "We missed that one hard."

"He fooled everyone." Marti's gaze stayed locked on ghost-images of violence rendered in grayscale. "Corrupt piece of shit played hero until his mask slipped."

"He destroyed lives." Lori's voice wobbled now; the way it did when someone crawled inside and rearranged her version of morality without asking first.

Marti didn't look up when she spoke again. "You asking if I feel sorry for him?"

Lori hesitated before answering. "I guess I'm asking if Gardner went too far."

Marti snorted into a laugh so humorless it scraped bone. "Too far? Kane unleashed bloodlust with a badge and called it order. Fehr cooked poison and sold redemption packaged in blue polyester." She turned then, meeting Lori's gaze across the room's cluttered battlefield of half-empty coffee cups and broken ethics.

Lori leaned forward, resting one hand on Marti's thigh without realizing: or maybe fully realizing.

The room felt warmer.

And Marti? She breathed in Shadow again just to keep from kissing all that vulnerability off Lori's mouth right then and there.

Lori's brow furrowed, her hand still on Marti's thigh like she'd forgotten it or didn't care. "But don't you feel anything? Guilt, maybe? About Fehr?"

Marti gave her a look sharp enough to cut glass. "I don't care about Fehr," She huffed, rolling her eyes. "I didn't pull the fucking trigger. He dug his own grave by challenging the big dogs."

"That doesn't mean we shouldn't have tried harder," Lori said, the hand still warm against Marti's jeans.

"I did try." Marti stood, brushing Lori's hand off with a motion that was only half-hearted. "We told him to stop. He laughed, remember?"

Lori crossed her arms, but the fight in her had softened into concern. "It just feels wrong."

Marti lit a cigarette she didn't need and exhaled smoke toward the cracked ceiling tile above. "You want to assign blame? Start with the department that let him keep working while he poisoned half the South End. The falls aren't what kill people in this city; it's cops protecting each other while bodies pile up."

The silence that followed settled heavy between them, thick enough to chew on, bitter with unsaid things.

Marti grounded out her cigarette on an old case file and went still. Lori watched her with something like pity, which angered Marti more than anything.

Lori sighed first. "But that still leaves Kane."

Now there was a name worth staying angry for.

Marti turned back toward her desk as if rage alone could map a plan forward. "We need hard proof: evidence, motive, bloodstains clear enough to tattoo his goddamn face with in court." Her nails drummed against lacquered wood in a rhythm that had nothing to do with fear and everything to do with addiction.

Then it clicked, like a lightbulb wrapped in barbed wire.

She grabbed her phone without another word and hit speed dial.

The line picked up after two rings.

"Poppy Hendrix."

"Poppy, it's Marti Starova."

A laugh crackled through the line. "Hey you little whore, how are you?"

"Doing fine, you pervert." Marti leaned back in her chair, one boot propped against the desk edge. "Need a favor."

"Quid pro quo," Poppy fired back without hesitation. "What you need, baby girl?"

"Working a case for a friend. Woman named LaLoLa Henderson. Died in a motel a while ago. Need a rundown on whatever evidence you've got."

A low whistle. "You're going to owe me big for this."

"When have I ever not paid up?"

"Oh, I know you're good." Something in Poppy's voice shifted: professional interest overtaking the banter. "Gimme a second."

Marti counted. One Mississippi, two Mississippi. By the time she hit 231 Mississippi's, the line crackled back to life.

"Got the Henderson file." Poppy's voice had gone desert-dry. "Sealed but not off-limits yet. Ready?"

Marti's jiggling leg went still. "Go."

The sound of paper shuffled across the connection. "Victim's clothing bagged at scene. Shirt, skirt, under-things. All blood-soaked." A pause. "One heel had trace of something on the toe: still unprocessed. No transfer from the other shoe."

Marti closed her eyes, building the scene in her mind. "Keep going."

"Standard body swabs. Dried blood, nail scrapings, cheek saliva. Dermal scans of all external injuries. Bio-Prints too." Poppy's clinical tone never wavered. "Bruising shows a pattern: repetitive impact from something flat. Belt, maybe. Or a book spine, but nothing like that found on scene."

The silence between words felt heavier than the words themselves.

"No sexual trauma indicators, but we ran the panel anyway. Protocol." Poppy continued without pause, years of practice evident in her steady rhythm. "Room gave us 56 partials. Fucking motels. Most are smudged, half cleaned by lazy maids. So far, untraceable. Hair and fiber from pillowcase and carpet, synthetic, short strands. Could be a wig, could be from 2025."

Her breath hissed through her teeth. "Air particulates showed nicotine-heavy vape residue, plus burned resin: cheap street opiate, nothing high-grade. No surveillance from the motel."

The silence stretched for a beat.

"And the bullet," Poppy added, her voice dropping.

Marti's eyes snapped open. "Stop."

Silence hung between them.

"I need a copy," Marti said.

When Poppy spoke again, her voice had dropped to a whisper. "You want the bullet?"

"No. A copy. Exact dimensions. Striations, profile, base deformation." Marti stared out at Falls City's jagged skyline. "Unofficial."

A full second of silence followed. "You realize that's the kind of favor that doesn't come free."

"Nothing in Falls City does." Marti's voice remained even, betraying nothing.

Fabric rustled, followed by a muted curse as Poppy returned to her terminal.

"I'll give you a cast. Won't flag any logs." Keys clicked in the background. "Come by around 10 PM."

The line went dead before Marti could respond.

Chapter 24

9:56 PM. Machine oil and algae scented the wind off the river. Marti pressed deeper into the shadow of the Forensics Lab's loading dock, hood up, hoodie zipped to her chin. Nothing moved except the distant shimmer of neon advertisements overhead and the rhythmic buzz of a rooftop vent. Metal groaned against metal.

Poppy emerged like a creature from the deep: cobalt-dyed hair cropped close to her skull, lab coat bearing the ghosts of chemicals past. Behind thin lenses, her eyes darted, taking in the surroundings before settling on Marti. She beckoned without a word, and the metal door sealed them inside with a resonant thud.

"This way." Poppy's fingers zipped across a recessed panel, entering a code. A narrow service corridor opened before them: beige walls, low light, floor gritty with the boot prints of people who existed in the shadows of science.

"So," Marti broke the silence, "what's the price?"

"Your cunt."

A grin spread across Marti's face until Poppy added, "Not like that."

The grin collapsed into a frown.

"Going to cast your crotch." Poppy didn't look back as she led the way deeper into the building. "Keep a copy for myself."

"You want a copy when you can have the original?"

"Mmm-hmm. Always available, any flavor."

Marti narrowed her eyes, studying the back of Poppy's head. "You okay about this?" Poppy asked.

"Didn't think you'd even ask."

"What would I be, a real friend?" Poppy snorted as she pushed open another door.

The overflow room greeted them: an annex of forensic purgatory. Sterile air hung heavy with solvents and the latent heat of halogen lamps. Cabinets lined the walls like repositories of violence: scraps of denim, blood-slick blade fragments, all tagged and waiting. A container labeled M94-CARBON TRACE sat centered on the main table.

Above a vinyl exam table, a surgical lamp cast knife-sharp shadows.

Poppy glanced at a box of slip drives on the counter. "You know, we've been seeing a lot of video evidence come through lately. All pristine, all damning. Homicide Division. Kane's cases mostly. His conviction rate's through the fucking roof these days."

Marti's attention sharpened. "Yeah?"

"Makes you wonder," Poppy said, turning back to her kit. "How one detective suddenly gets so lucky with his evidence."

Poppy turned, eyes glinting behind those smudged lenses. "Pants off. Ass on the table."

"You've ruined my fucking mood," Marti complained.

"I think I can help you with that," Poppy said as the snap of latex gloves echoed through the room.

Marti stepped out of her jeans and underwear with efficiency. The vinyl table greeted the backs of her thighs with a cold kiss as she climbed up.

Poppy's half-smirk appeared. "Spread for me."

Thighs parted. Poppy leaned in, all business now.

"Want you swollen." Her touch was clinical but knowing, fingers working with the precision of someone who understood anatomy beyond textbooks. A few strategic strokes, just enough to achieve the desired effect.

"Beautiful lips," Poppy murmured without looking up. Then she did look, face to face, adding, "The scars suit you."

The touch disappeared. Poppy turned to her kit and began prepping materials with calm efficiency.

"Slip-X," she explained, swabbing Marti's labia with a thin gel that smelled of mint and antiseptic. "Stops adhesion. Otherwise I'd be ripping skin and hair when I pull this off." She glanced up. "Though maybe you'd enjoy that."

"I just might."

Poppy opened a small tub of BioFill marked with a violet stripe. The plaster inside caught light like oil on water.

"This one's chromatic. Turns pink as it cures so I can see my layers."

The first touch made Marti flinch: cold at first contact before settling into something like static sliding beneath skin.

"It drinks heat," Poppy murmured.

"What is this shit?" Marti's fingers curled against the table edge. "This isn't like the stuff in my cabinet."

"Banned version. If left too long on living tissue it burns right through."

Marti's entire body tensed.

Poppy's eyes crinkled at the corners. "I'm kidding."

"Fucking psycho." Marti exhaled. "I like it."

The second layer went on thicker: cool at first then warming under Poppy's touch.

"This layer keeps it intact when I pull."

"How considerate."

Poppy tapped something on her wristband. A UV emitter pulsed low across Marti's skin, making the BioFill flicker pale pink before hardening.

She counted under her breath, then slid two gloved fingers into position. Bracing against Marti's inner thigh, she pulled slow and smooth until the mold released with a soft sucking sound.

Marti exhaled sharply.

Poppy held the mold up to the surgical light. "That," she said, "is fucking art."

Sliding off the table, Marti pulled up her pants. Heat radiated from her skin.

"You're getting off on this."

"You think I'm pretending not to?" Poppy placed the mold into a scanner bed and keyed in capture parameters.

A laser grid washed over negative space: cunt rendered in data points while Poppy leaned back against the counter.

"Going to do obscene things with this," she said without blinking.

Marti zipped her fly. "The real one's coming home with me."

A grunt: that low-throated sound Poppy made when amused. Then she pulled something from inside her coat pocket, a glassine baggie crinkling between latex fingers.

Inside lay a 3D printed bullet replica so white it looked ghost-made.

"Why is yours pink," Marti nodded toward the mold, "and mine looks like chalk?"

"Crime scene bullet had full carbon trace; they print white at high density." She handed it over with precision. "You could fire this one again if you wanted."

Marti held it up to the light. "Wait: will my cunt turn rock-hard too?"

Poppy snapped off one glove. "Only if you're lucky." She turned back to the console. "The mold's hard so I can make soft copies later: FlexSil-9 resin blend. Smart memory polymer."

"Fuckable?"

"Oh yeah." Poppy keyed in batch parameters without looking up. "Hyper-realistic thermal flexure curves."

"Can you make copies?"

"I can, but don't worry," Poppy's voice remained dry, "won't start selling 'Marti Originals' until I need bail money."

"Want one for myself." Marti ran a finger along the edge of the table. "And maybe a second, gift-wrapped for my secretary."

That pulled genuine laughter from Poppy. She smacked Marti across the shoulder.

"Take your bullet and run," she said, voice softening just enough to notice.

Marti held the replica slug at eye level. The spiraled grooves caught the halogen light like fingerprints frozen in time. Her gaze met Poppy's: something unspoken passing between them. She turned toward the door.

The bullet felt light in her palm, but the weight of what it represented settled deeper with each step. Whoever had killed LaLoLa Henderson was part of Marti's story.

And she hated sharing the spotlight.

Marti pushed through the loading door and hit the street. Rain had been here recently; that weird wet smell clung to everything: cement, rust, and whatever hope smelled like when it was halfway drowned.

The city wrapped around her like a bad habit she couldn't kick. Neon lights flickered off puddles that pretended to be portals if you stared long enough. Marti didn't stare long enough.

She tapped her phone and brought it to her ear before it finished connecting.

"Lori? Got something extra juicy," Marti muttered without waiting for a hello. "I'll be back in thirty."

She hung up before Lori could reply; it was safer that way. Less room for questions.

The slow walk back gave her time to think, which was dangerous on stomach half whiskey and half nothing. Everything felt too quiet, as if the city's pulse had dropped just low enough to make you worry it wouldn't wake up again.

The office door creaked open under her hand.

Lori looked up from behind her desk with an expression between anticipation and suspicion: her usual baseline when Marti headed to the morgue. "That didn't take long. You bring me something good?"

Marti slid into the chair across from her and gave a quick nod. "Maybe."

"Oh fuck off with 'maybe.'" Lori snatched the baggie out of Marti's hand with ease and held it up to the light. "This is from LaLoLa's scene?"

"Yeah. A copy." Marti leaned back in her chair and started drumming against the tabletop with two fingers as if she was trying to summon patience or spirits.

Her face said shock, but her eyes said pay dirt.

"You got an actual copy?" Lori asked, staring at the bullet. Even empty rooms had ears in this line of work.

Marti nodded, taking the bag back. "My contact at Forensics made it for me. Said it's so strong, it can be fired again."

"Marti."

"What?"

"Did you just say that your contact—"

"Poppy."

"That Poppy," Lori corrected herself, "just gave you a bullet from a crime scene that could be fired again? As in, used in a second murder?"

"Lori."

"Marti."

"Look at this fucking thing. It's strong but it isn't fire-able. Look at this shit," she said as she pulled it out of the bag and held it up between her fingers. Without the gauzy look of the glassine, Lori could now see how misshapen the bullet was.

It could never be fired again.

"Okay, I'm an idiot," Lori laughed. "Not like I see that many bullets that have been through bodies."

Marti ignored that lie and tossed the bullet to Lori, then reached for her cigarettes.

Lori pulled out her phone, entered into camera mode, and zoomed in, studying the detail. "This is good. Really good." She set the phone down. "But useless without something to compare them to."

"Which is why we are going to compare it to Hitchcock's bullet," Marti said, her gaze drifting to the medical cabinet behind Lori's desk.

Frederick 'shoot me in the head' Hitchcock was found dead in Kransten Park, officially ruled a suicide, which was bullshit.

Hitchcock dealt spice and had history with Kane. Hitchcock was involved with LaLoLa, a dealer who'd been complaining about poisoned drugs killing clients before she was shot and killed in a motel room. Marti's working theory was Leo Fehr shot and killed LaLoLa over bad drugs—his, not hers—but now, she was figuring out a new theory. And Hitchcock's brain bullet was the key.

"Hitchcock?"

"Can you get the bullet please?" Marti asked.

"Hitchcock?"

"Lori."

"Hitchcock?"

"Fuck me, let's do this without arguing, please," Marti smirked.

The office hummed with the sound of the ancient air conditioner fighting a losing battle against the summer heat. Outside, a siren wailed, then faded. Someone else's tragedy in progress.

"Fine. Boss," Lori said, tossing the copied bullet onto her desk. "When haven't I been your servant?"

"You do know that you're my secretary, right? That I'm the boss and you are the one who follows my orders. Right?" The drumming of her fingers against the table intensified.

Lori exhaled slowly through her nose, studying Marti's face. "Why do I let you do this to me?"

"Because deep down you're as obsessed with me," Marti replied, not a hint of humor in her voice.

"That's what I'm afraid of," Lori muttered, but she was already turning toward the cabinet behind her desk.

The cabinet clicked open, and Marti felt her focus sharpen despite the strain fog clouding her brain. Whatever was in that cabinet would either confirm her suspicions or send her back to square one.

Chapter 25

They stood in front of the cabinet like it might confess under pressure. No words, just that low hum of dread vibrating between them, louder than any siren.

Inside: one plastic baggie, sealed and sweating under the fluorescent light. Inside that: what was left of the bullet that killed Hitchcock. And stuck to it like some macabre garnish, bits of something once called a brain.

Marti plucked it up with latex-gloved fingers, delicate as if it were jewelry instead of gore. She held it to the light like a priest with a communion wafer. The grooves in the metal caught the glow, tiny spirals etched by force and precision. Her eyes narrowed. "Ridges like fate lines," she murmured. "Except this palm only predicts death."

Lori collapsed into her desk chair without checking: a mistake. A pen stabbed her in the ass. She winced and threw it into the garbage.

Marti tossed the bagged bullet onto her desk like it was a chewed-up toy left by a very bad dog.

Lori rifled through her desk. "Here, you put on the Auggies," she said, handing over the pair of augmented reality glasses.

Marti slid the Auggies over her eyes, the world suddenly overlaid with glowing interface elements that made her head throb. "Fuck me, this is like having a migraine with benefits." She flexed her fingers into the haptic gloves Lori shoved at her, feeling the subtle vibration of the actuators coming online.

"You'll get used to it," Lori said, settling into the chair beside her. "Try not to punch anything virtual."

"No promises." Marti reached for the evidence bags, her gloved fingers registering the weight and texture through synthetic feedback. The Hitchcock bullet looked like someone had put it through a blender—deformed, flattened, barely recognizable as ammunition. The LaLoLa bullet wasn't much better, twisted metal that told the story of its violent encounter with bone and concrete.

She held them up, and the Auggies immediately began mapping their surfaces, tracing what remained of the land

and groove impressions with thin blue lines. "These are fucked beyond recognition."

"That's why we have the reconstruction," Lori said, fingers twitching over her keyboard. "What ammunition type?"

She felt the familiar twist in her gut. Since Fehr killed LaLoLa, and the same gun killed Hitchcock...that was too fucking easy. "BlueBullets," Marti said. Department issue for boys who wanted their blood hot and their trails colder than Mars at midnight.

"Loading BlueBullets dataset," Lori announced.

The mangled fragments in Marti's hands suddenly bloomed with ghostly overlays: perfect reconstructions of what the bullets had looked like before impact. The AR system filled in the missing metal, completed the shattered grooves, turned twisted scrap into pristine ammunition.

And there it was. Clear as daylight and twice as damaging.

"Son of a bitch," Marti breathed, rotating the bullets in her hands. The groove patterns lined up perfectly, the digital reconstructions highlighting every matching scratch and ridge in pulsing green. "Same gun. Same fucking gun killed them both."

The haptic feedback let her feel the phantom grooves, her fingertips tracing impressions that no longer existed in reality but lived on in the digital reconstruction. Two murders. One weapon.

"Well," she said, pulling off the glasses and letting them dangle from their cord. "That's gonna complicate things. Except I'm a fucking genius," Marti said, not bothering to explain as she turned her back and walked into her office.

Marti rummaged through the crap on her desk while Lori watched, as she always did, with bemusement from the doorway.

Then Marti held up something that looked as if it belonged in a spy film or a very niche sex club.

"Stole them from Falls City PD on my way out the door," she announced as she held out the PulseSpec Scanner: sleek, dark, and just phallic enough to make its point. She flicked the micro-display open with the grace of someone who'd done this too many times and never for pleasure.

"What is that?" Lori stepped closer like she couldn't help herself.

"Something they don't teach in whatever civilian bullshit passes for training," Marti murmured. Her voice went low, velvet wrapped around razors. She aimed the device at the bullet on her desk and tapped it on.

The emitter lit up in ultraviolet violet, the kind of glow that made secrets nervous. The copper Hitchcock casing answered back with tiny specks that sparked like imprisoned starlight trying to escape through metal.

The micro-display blinked alive. Bright-dim-bright... pause... bright again.

Old school Morse code and Spectra-Shift particles. A cop's invisible fingerprint if they were dumb enough to fire department-issue rounds and sure enough that no one would use the device intended to catch corrupt murder cops.

Marti felt Lori watching, breath held like confession before climax.

"Spectra-Shift," Marti said, tapping one fingernail against the pulsing screen. "Every set of bullets has a signature, and every signature is assigned." She gave Lori a glance sharp enough to cut fabric.

"Well," Marti said, smiling slowly enough to worry angels, "someone's been busy."

She didn't say Kane by name yet; it hung there like smoke between them anyway.

Marti didn't take long to give in to the impulse.

"Kane used to call these his 'signature sends.' Like signing your work in invisible ink."

"So Kane killed Hitchcock?"

Marti drew a deep breath. "Same gun killed LaLoLa. Fucker's been a busy little boy."

"You know what else Kane's been doing?" Lori's voice dropped. "Getting rich off insurance fraud."

"It's a goddamn shell game," Marti growled, pacing between her desk and the window, cigarette burning down between two fingers. "Rufus hacks the digital shit—video feeds, documents, timestamps—makes them say whatever the fuck they need to say for an insurance payout. Then Juanita runs it all through her little magic bureaucratic meat grinder and—poof—the money lands in Ari Stirling's greedy lap."

She flicked ash onto a plate already crowded with butts and half-melted gummy bears. Her eyes were sharp, feral.

"And fucking Damian Kane? That asshole is balls-deep in every part of it. He gets a cut of the cash, sure—but he's also the common thread stitching together two bodies that got too fucking close. LaLoLa Henderson. Frederick Hitchcock. Both dead. Both could've taken down the whole goddamn operation."

Marti leaned against the windowsill, watching rain smear streaks across dirty glass.

"Rufus used to be some half-broke Falls City PD tech monkey," she said, voice tight. "I bet that asshole did some gigs for Kane back when I was still trying to play nice with court subpoenas instead of baseball bats. No wonder that fucker had such a good arrest record."

She spat out a humorless laugh.

"Guess who got fucked over by Rufus's work?"

She tossed her cigarette into a cup of old coffee where it hissed and died.

"Me." Marti landed on the edge of Lori's desk with a thud, the way a cat lands when it knows it owns the whole damn room. Cigarette between her lips, she sparked her lighter and dragged in smoke like it owed her rent. Her eyes were sharp, glassy from too much stimulation or too little sleep, maybe both. "Kane's fucking filthier than I thought," she said without preamble. "Like, trash-fire-in-a-dumpster-behind-a-clinic filthy."

Lori didn't look up right away, fingers tapping at the keyboard like she was trying to ignore the chaos that had just floated in. But Marti's tone yanked her attention fast. "Filthier how?"

Marti exhaled slow, smoke curling toward the ceiling tiles like it was trying to escape this conversation. "He's got his greasy hands in every pie from here to fuck-all, but it wasn't his fake claims bullshit that got LaLoLa and Hitchcock killed." She flicked ash into her coffee cup—a sad little graveyard of caffeine and regret. "LaLoLa was raising hell, calling out batches of poisoned Shadow killing her regulars. That wasn't about forged policies or inflated car damage reports. That was about shutting down an operation that brings in real blood money. Putting Kane in the line of fire."

She could still see LaLoLa's body in those crime scene photos, her mouth open like she'd been screaming when death came fast and final. "You don't whack someone over a bad windshield claim," Marti muttered. "That girl was threatening Kane's main drug line."

Lori blinked slowly, processing every word like they were bricks being laid around them.

"And Hitchcock?" she asked carefully.

Marti crushed her cigarette into the paper cup and reached for another without missing a beat. Her fingers trembled slightly as she lit it. Withdrawal was a bitch with claws. "Same nine mil put them both down. BlueBullets," she said flatly.

Lori sat straighter.

"You heard me," Marti continued, smoke trailing from her lips as she talked. "Kane's signature ammo—the fancy shit he used back when we played cop-and-crook at Falls City PD." She sucked hard on her filter and kept going. "Hitchcock had history with Kane. Long one. He knew LaLoLa too—might've even been fucking her, if whispers are true. When LaLoLa vanished off the map, Hitch starts poking around."

She paused long enough for Lori to make eye contact.

"Too close to whatever Kane's hiding," Marti said coldly. "Gone."

Lori stood then sat again, unsettled by ghosts neither of them had invited into the room.

"Kane's insurance scams are background noise," Marti continued, swinging her legs off the desk and almost catching Lori in the knee on purpose. She didn't apologize; if anything, she grinned as Lori glared at her thigh brushing past hers.

"This is about protection rackets for bad Shadow," Marti went on as she paced now, cigarette hanging between two fingers like a weapon no one dared confiscate. "Kane's cutting deals with whoever is cooking those poison batches—probably skimming profit while offering cover when things go sideways."

Lori leaned back in her chair like someone physically pulling away from an unpleasant truth.

"So let me get this straight: Kane runs fraudulent claims to pay his bills and dirty Shadow to build his empire?" she asked.

Marti turned with a wicked smile curling across her face.

"That's what I'm saying." The words dripped satisfaction like venom from fangs.

"Kane's not just dirty—he's diversified."

She perched again on Lori's desk corner, their knees close now.

"And Rufus?" Lori asked quietly.

Stillness crackled between them before Marti answered.

"He's still editing security footage for Kane," she said slowly, like each word cost something hard-earned. "Video magic so no one sees who really pulled triggers."

"But Rufus called him 'old friend,'" Lori insisted softly.

Marti inhaled deep and blew smoke across Lori's monitor screen just because she could.

"Yeah," she said finally, voice sharp enough to slice glass but laced with something sour underneath. "Rufus Montgomery served at Falls City PD back in the same dark-ass days I did."

A pause stretched long enough for thoughts to get dangerous.

"And that fucking video..." Marti muttered as something bitter flashed behind her eyes.

Whatever they were unraveling—it had teeth now.

Big ones.

"So Kane killed Hitchcock?"

Marti didn't answer right away. She dragged deep from her cigarette, staring through the rain-muddled window like the answers were hiding in the gray blur beyond.

"Same gun that took out LaLoLa," she finally said, her voice a low rasp. "BlueBullets. Kane's favorite calling card back when he was still pretending to play cop in Falls City."

Ash fluttered into her half-empty coffee cup. She crushed the butt out against the inside rim, already lighting another before her fingers stopped trembling. The lighter snapped like punctuation.

"This isn't just about two bodies nobody cares about," she said. "It's an empire. A greasy, blood-soaked empire built on fraud and flavored poison."

She flicked ash toward the floor without looking because where the fuck was it going to go?

"Kane's got Rufus rewriting digital trails like a god-damn cyber-ghost, Juanita laundering the claims like clockwork, and Ari Stirling pulling strings from the clean side of town. Insurance fraud on one end, dirty Shadow on the other."

Lori sat perfectly still in her chair, eyes sharp. "LaLoLa was pushing into his territory?"

"She was raising hell," Marti said flatly, pacing now, cigarette loose between her fingers, smoke trailing behind her like a rumor. "Claimed his latest batches were killing off her regulars. Called it out. Loud."

"And then disappeared."

Marti turned fast toward Lori. "And he's tied to it with the bullets."

Her boots clicked loud against the floor as she walked back and dropped onto Lori's desk without permission or apology. Their knees nudged. Marti didn't move.

"Hitchcock started poking around after LaLoLa vanished," she said quietly now, watching Lori with something unreadable behind her eyes. "Got himself shot with the same BlueBullets just days later."

Lori's breath hitched—whether from what Marti said or how close she suddenly was was anyone's guess—and then came silence.

Chapter 26

Marti leaned forward just enough for her knee to slip between Lori's thighs, not breaking eye contact.

"What did Rufus say again?" Marti asked, voice silky and slow now. Dangerous. "That his old friend owed him big?"

"You think that friend is Kane?"

"Don't think." Her smile curved but never made it to warmth. "I know it's Kane. Rufus worked tech at Falls City PD five years ago. Same time Kane was there." Her lips twitched again—but now it was bitter and sharp-edged with memory. "Same time I was there."

The words hung between them like knives.

"The same time that fucking video surfaced," Marti continued as she lifted her cigarette to her lips again and exhaled into the space between them, curling smoke around every truth she'd never wanted to say aloud. "The one that wrecked my badge and flushed my career down a toilet full of lies."

"You think Rufus doctored it," Lori whispered.

"No." Marti shook her head once, emphatic, eyes dark as bruises. "I think Kane told him to do it."

Her hand moved lazily across her throat in a slicing motion.

"If it was just one favor... he'd be gone by now," she said softly. Too softly.

"No need to keep paying him off unless there's more."

Lori went still in that way people do when they understand something awful but can't yet say it aloud.

"Rufus has life insurance," she murmured.

"Fuck yeah he does," Marti snapped back without hesitation, running a hand through her hair before dragging again on her cigarette hard enough to burn through half of it in one go. "And since Rufus sucks at everything except making ones and zeros dance like puppets? That insurance is a video."

Her eyes glittered like cold steel under fluorescent lights.

"Of a murder," Lori said slowly.

"Mhm." Marti nodded once, sharp and final as judgment day.

"Not just any murder," Lori added, voice tightening with tension and fear and maybe something else too raw to name yet. "Something... revolting enough to burn everything down."

"Something public." Marti's voice dropped low again—a growl wrapped in silk.

"Something that wouldn't send him to prison," Lori whispered.

"No." Marti grinned without humor at all this time as she rolled ash off the edge of Lori's desk with one delicate finger. "It would make prison look like vacation."

They sat there in heavy silence as rain hit glass like applause from ghosts who'd seen every sin firsthand.

"Whatever Rufus has... it makes Kane kneel," Marti whispered finally.

Lori stayed where she was, arms folded but not defensive: just holding herself together while Marti lapped across the floor like a tiger with a vendetta. "Even if we had footage," Lori said, "we'd be lucky to get anyone in uniform to touch it. He's a hero and you're a—."

"Vindictive bitch," Marti added.

"And if Kane gets wind of this?" she added, softer now, dangerous in its calm. "If he doesn't put a bullet in your spine, he'll paint you as the embittered ex-partner who went off her meds."

Marti stopped moving. Just... stopped. One boot still cocked mid-step, frozen between fury and revelation as she stared out the window like it might open up and show her a world that made sense.

"Oh, he'll try," she said. The words came cold and crisp, like someone chiseling resolve out of spite instead of granite.

She turned slow, eyes gone glacier-sharp.

"That's why we hit him where he doesn't see it coming."

Lori arched an eyebrow with surgical precision: the kind of move that usually came right before calling bullshit or undoing buttons with her teeth.

"And where's that?" she asked.

Marti leaned in close enough for their legs to brush beneath the desk, casual as gravity, electric as regret. She didn't step back. Neither did Lori.

"Someplace outside his payroll," Marti said, like the words themselves were contraband. "Someone willing to shove a match into the powder keg he's been dancing on."

She paused. Kicked her desk hard enough to send an empty coffee mug skidding off the edge. "Fuck me," she growled. "Who the hell would actually do that?"

"Sounds like one hell of a gamble," Lori said, but even her doubt came dressed in velvet now: less objection, more invitation.

Like foreplay in warpaint.

Like they were already halfway into a plan neither could name but both wanted deep enough to taste.

Marti smiled, not sweetly and not safe, and met Lori's eyes with something feral humming beneath the surface.

And maybe it wasn't telepathy, maybe it was just inevitable: dangerous women thinking dangerous thoughts at exactly the same time.

Either way?

They were already in it now.

"First thing's first," Marti said, tossing a stack of crumpled notes onto the desk as if they might bite her. "We need to find this video I just fucking imagined out of nowhere. Then we can sort out which assholes in the precinct haven't sold their souls. Huff or Venezia, maybe."

But even as the words left her mouth, Marti felt the familiar weight settling back on her chest, the one that had nothing to do with Kane or Rufus or insurance fraud. The one shaped like a seventeen-year-old girl.

Lori must have seen it in her face, because her fingers stopped drumming and her voice went soft. "Marti, I know Kane's your white whale or whatever, but what about Serra? It's been days. No word, no leads. You don't sleep, you barely eat, and nobody seems to give a shit that a girl vanished into thin fucking air."

She took a drag and let it out, watching it curl toward the ceiling as if it might spell answers if she stared hard enough. "Got a tip from one of the girls who works Eighth and Madison. Northeast corner of the Financial District. Said she saw someone who looked like Serra hitting up an ATM that night."

Lori blinked. "What made her think it was Serra?"

"Serra dropped a unicorn necklace." Marti stubbed out her cigarette with force. "Naomi—"

"Naomi?"

"Picked it up. Recognized it in the photo. I checked with Francesca. It's Serra's."

"So if it was really her…"

"We find that ATM footage," Marti said, rolling her shoulders back as if she needed to stretch off all the anger Kane hadn't earned yet. "We figure out if Serra took out cash, or someone else used her card."

"Jesus, all this crap about videos. Did Francesca ever say anything about credit charges or ATM withdrawals?" Lori leaned forward, her body caught between concern and adrenaline.

"Nope. Not beyond the movie ticket." Marti grabbed her phone off the desk with the grace of a woman ready to slam it through drywall. "Let's find out if that's because she forgot… or because she didn't want us to know."

She punched in Francesca Stanfield's number and didn't bother with small talk when the woman picked up.

"Francesca? Need a straight answer: did Serra have access to your bank account?"

There was hesitation on the other end; Marti could hear her squirming.

"She didn't have her own," Francesca said. "She used mine sometimes."

Marti clenched her jaw tight. "Check your transaction history for the night Serra disappeared. Any withdrawals past midnight?"

A pause. Nails clicking on an acrylic screen.

"Yes," Francesca said. "There was a withdrawal at 1:36 a.m."

"You're just mentioning this now?" Marti snapped, all patience gone.

"I, I didn't think it mattered," Francesca whispered.

"It matters." Marti's voice came cold as winter steel. "Send me a screenshot of your statement."

She ended the call before Francesca could apologize again. Before she could tear that bitch a new one.

Turning to Lori, she pushed back from the desk and stood like something coiled too long in place.

"That ATM fits our timeline," Marti said. "Now we confirm if it was Serra using that card, or someone else playing dress-up with unicorns and missing girls."

Lori nodded, eyes sharp now instead of scared.

"So fuck Kane for now. Let's get our hands on that footage," she said.

And just for a moment, underneath fear and fury, there was something else between them: shadows dancing across skin not yet touched, things not yet said humming in their silence.

They were chasing ghosts now.

But ghosts always left fingerprints if you knew where to look.

Marti swung around Lori's chair like she was on a playground, which, technically, she wasn't, but whatever, and leaned over her shoulder. The transaction screenshot Francesca had sent was pulled up on screen. One blurry figure. A timestamp. $50 withdrawn at 1:36 a.m. from machine number 12364.

That was it. That was all they had.

Before Marti could open her mouth, Lori was already hacking away, fingers dancing across keys like she was disarming a bomb instead of digging through databases. Marti stayed close, watching her work, inhaling the scent of citrus shampoo and whatever perfume Lori always wore that made Marti want to do extremely unprofessional yet absolutely expert things.

"Falls City First National!" Lori shouted suddenly, stabbing a finger at the monitor.

Marti flinched, then rolled her eyes and took a step back. "Jesus, tone down the enthusiasm before I have a heart attack."

Reluctantly clutching onto the thread of excitement, Marti paced once before snapping into focus. "Alright: get me a list of everyone who works security or janitorial at that bank branch. If we want that footage, we're gonna have to get creative."

Lori's face scrunched up as if she'd smelled something foul, or maybe as if she already knew what Marti was about to suggest.

"There's no easy way," she muttered, pinching the bridge of her nose.

"Sure there is," Marti said. "Bribery. Deception. Mild seduction."

Lori groaned. "Please don't say you're thinking of dragging your sex worker friend into this again."

"She's very talented," Marti replied. "Guards can't man cameras if they're getting their cocks sucked in the breakroom."

"Jesus Christ." But Lori didn't say no right away.

Marti shrugged, unapologetic. "We set off an alarm somewhere else in the building; keep them moving while we ghost in and out."

"That's not 'creative.' That's felony stupid." Lori looked up at her with those sharp brown eyes that could cut glass, or undress you slowly depending on the angle. "If anything goes wrong we end up arrested or worse."

Marti exhaled and dropped onto the edge of Lori's desk, letting her boots scuff against cabinet drawers beneath it. She tilted her head toward the screen again.

"Fine," she said. "We pose as maintenance contractors doing camera system inspections. Real official-like." She lifted two fingers in mock salute.

Lori blinked at her once, then smiled as if she'd just remembered how damn smart Marti could be when she wasn't being reckless and half in love with chaos.

"That could actually work," Lori said. "If we spoof IDs and schedule it right, slip in during an overlap shift, no one would even question it."

"Exactly my kind of operation," Marti smirked. "Find out who at National handles maintenance, and then find out their boss. We harass the boss."

Lori spun to her keyboard and pulled up another window. "Falls City National Bank contracts their tech work to GDH Security," she muttered as she typed.

Marti leaned close to her ear (it wasn't necessary; it just felt good) and said, "Print us some badges then, boss lady."

Lori grabbed her phone without pause and snapped a pic of herself first, smiling dead-on as if it was for a Fuck-Her profile pic instead of government fraud, then turned the camera toward Marti.

"Smile," she said.

"Bite me," Marti replied, but held still as the flash went off.

"Now go busy yourself," Lori said all mom-like. "I think both the Turnet and Pigeon files need some work."

Once Lori started uploading everything into the magic hell program she used for forgery these days, Marti toddlered back into her office: a room full of caffeine stains and chaos.

She dropped into her chair and pulled out Hazel Turnet's file from under a pile of gum wrappers and old receipts that might've qualified as evidence if anyone wanted to look too closely.

Hazel Turnet: rich bitch flavor-of-the-month for Sezam unless proven otherwise.

Marti flipped through her notes, the ones she'd scrawled out after too many energy drinks and not enough sleep. Criminal record? Clean. Warrants? Nada. Recent employment? Nothing shady there either. She'd even run genealogical background in case Sezam had fallen for his long-lost cousin or something equally fucked. She came up dry on incest too, thank God.

Her gaze landed on one last unchecked line: Family employment.

She sighed as if someone was forcing her to eat kale chips at gunpoint and opened her laptop again.

The Turnet family had some kind of thrift store empire in Falls City: secondhand shops with over-designed logos that screamed influencer board gone wrong. She clicked through site after site with zero interest until...

Wait.

Her finger stopped above the mousepad.

Something flickered across the screen, something small but off enough to tickle that sixth sense she only got when danger or bullshit was involved.

Marti sat up. Her focus sharpened like a razor blade pressed beneath skin.

Well well well, Hazel... what exactly are you hiding in plain sight?

"Lori!" Marti yelled, not bothering to look away from the screen. "I have a think: and fuck me, it's weird."

Lori appeared in the doorway like a summoned ghost. Her sleeves were rolled, ponytail half-falling out. "You serious? What is it?"

"How do you feel about uniforms?" Marti asked, fighting back a smirk.

"What kind of question is... what did you find?"

Marti clicked twice and blew a strand of hair out of her face. "Later. I want to see your pretty little ID magic first. Priorities."

Behind her, the printer wheezed and clicked as if dying for a smoke break. Lori grabbed the ejected cards with one hand, flipped them over with ease.

"GDH Security," she said. "Fresh off the lie press."

Marti plucked them from her and held them up to the light. "Goddamn, these look real."

"They are real," Lori said with a flash of teeth. "Just... not legally."

"This might actually fucking work," Marti muttered, eyes narrowing as if daring the universe to fuck it up.

Lori leaned against the wall, arms crossed but glowing too bright for someone trying to play it cool.

"You gonna tell me what you found or keep edging me all day?" she asked.

Marti grinned. "Oh honey. We're just getting started."

Chapter 27

The office looked less like a workplace and more like a crime scene with snacks: half-eaten donut on top of blueprints, cigarette ash dusting corners of an old keyboard, two mugs that had surrendered any hope of being washed.

Marti kicked her boots up on the desk, sipped what barely qualified as cheap whiskey. The light outside dipped into amber territory. Shadows crawled like lazy fingers across the floor.

Across from her, Lori had gone full nerd mode: reading glasses low on her nose, brows furrowed, mouse clutched as if it held state secrets.

"You done giving yourself an aneurysm yet?" Marti asked.

Lori didn't look up. "Almost. This bank camera maintenance system has some serious vintage charm from 10 years ago." Five lifetimes in technology years.

"I ask again," Marti said, dragging smoke from her cigarette. "You have everything we need or should I start writing my own will?"

"Yes." Lori hit enter with force. "I can guide us through their system blindfolded at this point. God bless my overpriced engineering degree."

Marti stood and wandered toward her with that mix of grace and threat she carried when Shadow was starting to burn off.

"You think I hired you for your degree?" she asked, tossing Lori's hoodie at her without warning.

Lori caught it midair but narrowed her eyes. "Didn't you?"

Marti smirked and perched on the edge of Lori's desk as if she owned every inch of it, including Lori herself. "What was your first assignment?"

"The Henderson file," Lori replied. She blinked uncertainly. "Wait... no... oh my god: the toaster?!"

"Ding ding." Marti tapped ash into a nearby mug with an air of triumph. "That toaster wouldn't toast unless you sacrificed a goat under a full moon."

"And you thought my Electrical Engineering degree made me qualified to fix your demonic kitchen appliance?"

"Well," Marti drawled, "you fixed it."

"I cleaned it! The lever was stuck because there were crumbs jammed in the bottom." Lori threw up her hands like a frustrated magician revealing their trick.

"So theoretically," Marti said, eyes gleaming with mischief, "I could've just hired someone who owns Lysol and a brain stem."

"I swear to god" Lori started. Marti broke into laughter and lifted both hands in surrender before things escalated into paperwork or murder.

"Kidding!" she said between chuckles. "Kidding. You're brilliant; you can write code drunk on two hits of Shadow while explaining thermal conductivity to an idiot with a gun in his mouth."

"What? Oh, never mind." Lori crossed her arms but couldn't suppress the flush climbing up her neck: maybe that was pure rage. Hard to tell sometimes.

"You're also hot when you lecture me about electronics," Marti added as smoke curled between them like punctuation.

"Don't push your luck," Lori said. Her lips twitched just enough to give herself away.

"Oh baby," Marti murmured as she leaned closer, voice low as sin. "I build luck from scratch."

Lori chucked her pen at Marti. "You're such a fucking jerk. You actually had me going."

Marti caught it midair like she'd been waiting for the moment all her life, grinning slow and smug. "Okay. Found a dump that sells used maintenance coveralls. Let's go dress like rejects from a disgraced union."

Turnet's Clothes House crouched on the corner as if it a bored cat just waiting for a mouse to wander by. Peeling green paint flaked off the bricks like dry skin, and the neon sign overhead spat out light in irregular pulses: TUR-NET'S CL SE H USE. It gave off the charming energy of electrical failure and regrettable life choices.

The door squealed open on rusted hinges, spilling them into a basement that smelled like divorce settlements: stale perfume battling mothballs for territorial dominance. Lori gagged behind her hand.

"Cozy," Marti said, eyeing a pile of sequined bras next to what looked like a trench coat with dried blood on the sleeve. "Let's find our sexy-asbestos janitor outfits."

They waded into the maze of racks. Each turn revealed forgotten relics of fashion disasters: shoulder pads that could take flight, denim acid-washed past redemption, one sad sequin glove hanging from a plastic hanger like a war memorial.

"God, these clothes are older than your commitment issues," Lori muttered, sifting through a rack of polyester jumpsuits.

"I heard that," Marti sang from across the aisle, emerging with two coveralls in shades of 'corpse blue' and 'plague gray.' Stains optional, rips included free of charge. She tossed one at Lori.

Lori caught it against her chest, staring at it as if it might start moving on its own. "This is supposed to fool security?"

Marti shrugged one shoulder, already stepping into hers. "Confidence and camouflage, babe. Plus no one looks directly at maintenance unless they're mid-murder."

"We aren't janitors," Lori said, eyeing the filth pressing against their chest.

"Trust."

Lori hesitated before pulling hers on over her clothes with a sigh loud enough to register on seismographs. The fabric gave off a scent somewhere between bleach and broken dreams.

"You smell like an exploded chemistry lab," Marti said.

"And you smell like regret." Lori adjusted the sleeves with disgust.

They moved toward the register, Marti tossing cash down while shooting the cashier a look daring him to question their fashion sense. He chose silence.

Dusk swallowed what little sun remained as they stepped outside again, coveralls hanging off them as if they'd just survived an industrial accident with style.

Lori twisted the front zipper between her fingers as they walked toward the car. "Are you absolutely sure this'll work?"

"Nope," Marti said as she slid into the driver seat and lit up another cigarette. "But we've come too far to chicken-shit out now."

The car coughed to life and rolled down cracked asphalt toward downtown's financial district: crime scene imminent.

"We're doing this for good reasons," Marti added around her cigarette, smoke curling from her lips like punctuation marks in their shared bad idea. "Good-ish reasons."

"Good-adjacent," Lori offered.

"Exactly." Marti reached out, brushed Lori's thigh deliberately, not comfortingly, and revved the engine just enough to make them both feel alive again.

The bank loomed up ahead: square-jawed architecture drowning in self-importance. Tinted windows glared down at them as if they were judgmental lenses behind which money bred in captivity. One block away, Marti killed the engine.

They stepped out into thickening shadows and city silence broken only by distant sirens and Lori's nervous breathing. The buzzer sat beside bulletproof glass like an afterthought or a dare.

Marti pressed it with the confidence of someone who'd never considered consequences once in her life. A soft click answered back.

Inside was chilled air and suspicion; three suits behind desks half-watched them through narrowed eyes as if waiting for them to break character.

Marti approached reception without breaking stride or making eye contact with anyone but the Plexiglass Jesus nailed behind the front desk.

"Tim Mantle," she said, straight-spined and sharp in stained coveralls that somehow still made her look dangerous instead of deranged. "Head of security."

The receptionist blinked twice before nodding and disappearing through a plain steel door behind her station without comment. Just enough time for Lori to lean close to Marti's ear and whisper:

"If we survive this, I'm making you buy me dinner that doesn't smell like formaldehyde."

"Deep breaths," Marti murmured, low enough that only Lori could hear. "And unclench your fists unless you're planning to punch him. Tempting, I know."

Lori nodded once, fingers twitching as if they were itching for a fight or a keyboard, maybe both.

The door clicked open with an ominous hiss, and out came Tim Mantle: six feet of capitalist-grade suspicion wrapped in a discount blazer. His jarhead eyes did a slow rake over them, taking in Marti's grease-slicked coveralls and Lori's too-polished smile, as if he was trying to decide which one would fuck up first.

"Can I help you?" he asked, voice cool as dry ice.

"Hi, Tim." Marti offered her hand because that's what you did before metaphorically kicking someone in the nuts. "We're with GDH Security. Cops sent us; some bullshit about faulty ATM footage not lining up with the timestamps on their reports." She held up her ID with one hand and motioned for Lori to do the same. Twin flashes of laminated plastic and fake authority.

Tim didn't take her hand. He crossed his arms as if he'd rehearsed it in front of a mirror labeled I Am Important. "First I'm hearing of it."

"Paperwork probably got lost between bureaucratic ass cheeks," Marti said, smile tight enough to cut glass. "But hey, that's what we're here for. Just need access to the system managing the ATM camera. We're not touching the machine itself."

He hesitated as if he was debating if he had enough muscle mass to toss them both out. He didn't. Eventually he gave them an annoyed grunt that might have passed for consent in certain circles.

"This way," he muttered, spinning on his heel.

Chapter 28

Tim Mantle was not a happy man. Didn't matter. He led them through sterile corridors that smelled like toner and failed ambitions until they hit the security room: two chairs, five monitors, and just enough space for passive aggression to flourish.

Lori slid into place, a professional dissecting her prey, and started tapping at keys with precision. Tim loomed behind her like a bad thought she couldn't shake.

Marti knew when it was time to run interference.

She wandered toward the corkboard on the back wall and tilted her head at a network topology map clinging there as if it had something to hide.

"What's this?" she asked, channeling every dumb intern who ever asked how email worked.

Tim glanced at her before his eyes snapped back to Lori's hands. "It outlines our internal server architecture," he said. "Visual aid for tech staff."

"Huh." Marti tapped one finger against her bottom lip and let the pause stretch long enough to get awkward. "Seems risky to leave something like this out where any asshole can see it, no offense. Protocol says unsecured schematics are an automatic red flag."

Tim's jaw twitched. For one second she thought he might growl.

Instead, with a theatrical huff that would've earned him applause in community theater, he yanked the map down and shredded it into confetti-sized regrets before tossing it into the trash can as if it had personally offended him.

"Happy now?" he barked.

Marti offered him a sunny smile that screamed fuck you very much. "Ecstatic. Less paperwork for me."

She glanced sideways. Lori was still working, still calm under pressure in a way Marti found sexy when combined with focused silence and those capable fingers flying across keys as if they were born there.

"Let's wrap this up quickly," Tim snapped, glaring daggers nobody cared about.

"Almost done," Lori said without looking away from the monitor, voice steady as sheet steel while her reflection flickered across security feeds looping behind her.

Marti stepped closer to Tim so she could smell his rising irritation, or maybe that was just cheap aftershave trying too hard.

"So," she said, turning toward another panel of switches and blinking lights designed to look impressive on TV dramas, "what kind of backup system you guys running for footage? Offsite redundancy? Real-time mirroring? Or do we have another potential issue? Don't give me that look. It's my fucking job to help you keep your job. And your money."

Tim exhaled hard through clenched teeth and fixed his glare on Marti as if she'd personally insulted his mother's meatloaf recipe. "We use standard offsite storage proto-col," he snapped. "What are you implying? That we don't know how to do our fucking jobs?"

Marti blinked at him, eyes wide and full of fabricated innocence, and leaned close enough that their shoulders nearly touched.

"We're just doing our jobs."

Tim scowled so hard his eyebrows nearly fused. "Right."

Lori clapped her hands once, loud enough to make Tim twitch. "Got it!" she declared, slamming the laptop closed and spinning her chair toward them as if she were a game show host revealing a prize behind Door Number Two. "System's clean. All set."

"Lovely," Marti purred, already halfway to the exit. She tossed a lazy wave over her shoulder at Tim. "Thanks for your stellar cooperation."

He muttered something deeply ungrateful as the door swung shut behind them.

Outside, the sky was still that dead gray that made Marti crave a hit of something stronger than nicotine just to feel alive. They walked to their shitty little car parked half a block away: no-questions-asked plates, rusting bumper, zero fucks given.

"I can't believe he bought it," Lori murmured, pulling her hair into a knot as they walked.

"He bought it because I'm charming and terrifying," Marti said, lighting up a cigarette as if she were in a noir film with nothing left to lose. "And because sometimes you roll the dice with a straight face and pray no one notices your hands are shaking."

They got into the car. Lori laughed softly as she slammed her door shut, but it didn't reach her eyes.

* * *

Back at the office, they peeled out of their disgusting maintenance coveralls with theatrical flair, like strippers reluctantly moonlighting as private investigators. Marti caught hers before it hit the floor and held it up between two fingers.

"These things are kinda hot," she mused. "Might keep 'em for sexy times." Her smirk edged into wicked territory as she disappeared into her cluttered office.

"Stars and stripes forever," Lori called after her, flopping into her desk chair with exhaustion.

She cracked her knuckles and got to work pulling up the bank surveillance files. The computer fans whirred like tired bees trying not to die. Five minutes later she jabbed at the screen.

"Found something." Her voice had shifted; it was edged now with adrenaline instead of sass.

Marti reappeared beside her, a boring old cigarette between her lips. They stared at grainy black-and-white footage timestamped from an ATM at 1:36AM. Serra appeared, hair pulled back tight, jeans cuffed high, and stepped up to the machine. Inserted card. Waited.

Then she turned suddenly to her right.

"What was that?" Lori whispered.

Before anyone could answer, he entered frame: a man moving fast with coiled violence tucked into every line of him. He grabbed Serra by the arm like he owned her bones and smashed his fist against her face so hard she folded without sound.

Marti's cigarette trembled between two fingers before falling onto Lori's mousepad.

"Fuck me," Marti hissed. "Run it again."

Lori did, hands steady now even if her heart wasn't. They watched every frame like they were trying to summon god from pixels.

Marti leaned in close, her breath fogging the edge of the screen. "Stop. Right there." She stabbed a finger forward.

She paused as if she'd been punched in reverse when his face came into focus for half a second on the tape: pale skin under an old ball cap, features twisted sharp like broken porcelain glued back wrong.

The man looked directly at the camera as he dragged Serra offscreen like she weighed nothing more than regret.

Predatory didn't cover it.

"That face…" Marti muttered through gritted teeth. Her jaw flexed hard enough you could hear tendons protest.

"Rufus fucking Montgomery." Her voice was reverent in that way people whisper names that come wrapped in blood-soaked headlines and personal history too taboo to say during daylight hours.

Marti didn't feel her fist crack the screen until shards of cheap monitor glass rained down like confetti. Rufus's face split in two across the spiderweb fracture. Her knuckles were bleeding and the monitor hissed as if it was offended.

She shook out her hand, pain blooming behind her wrist, and splattered blood across Lori's button-down: the good white one she only wore when pretending professionalism.

"Fuck." Marti stared at the smear like it had betrayed her. "Sorry about your shirt."

Lori blinked down at the red spot just below her collar. "It's fine," she said, voice tight, like everything inside her was trying not to scream. "You need to stop punching electronics."

Marti ignored that part. She paced, boots thudding against the tile in a rhythm that made Lori wince with every step. She was coiled tight, rage simmering below her skin, ready to boil through at the wrong word or wrong look.

"I mean it," Marti said, voice low. "Rufus Montgomery; IT guy for Falls City PD turned full-blown garbage fire of a human being. We know about the insurance fraud. Now kidnapping? Maybe murder? Fuck knows what else." She leaned forward on Lori's desk as if gravity had a vendetta against her. "We have to find this asshole."

Lori didn't argue. She moved to the supply cabinet and pulled out gauze and tape that expired back when zip phones were cool. "Sit," she ordered.

Marti sat.

"This is going to sting," Lori said as she peeled open the bandage. She worked slow, gentle, almost intimate if you ignored the blood and context.

Marti watched her fingers work: methodical, clean. Lori wrapped her hand in silence like it was a ritual, some kind of unspoken thing between people who knew each other past casual flirtation and into battlefield mechanics.

Then her computer dinged.

"It found an address," Lori said. She didn't look up from bandaging duty until the final knot was tied.

Marti yanked back her hand before it could feel too much like affection. "Send it to my phone."

"You're not going alone," Lori said.

Marti had already stood up.

"Marti."

"Lori."

"Marti."

"That's cute," Marti muttered, halfway through the door. "Like I listen."

* * *

Falls City never bothered cleaning up after itself; every gutter carried secrets and cigarette butts no one dared trace back to origin stories. Marti parked a block from Rufus's listed address because habits die harder than men, and sometimes just as bloody.

The fire escape groaned under her weight: third floor, busted window latch, peeling paint that stuck to her palms when she pried it open like an old wound.

Inside: chaos without character.

No closets. No dresser. Just a filthy mattress on bare floorboards surrounded by empty snack bags.

No computer, no holo-tab, no displays, keyboards. Nothing but unorganized tech guts he'd harvested from dead desktops across departments

And Serra?

Nowhere.

Not even a ghost of her. No hairbrush left behind or half-drunk sippy cup of coffee going stale with hope.

Marti scanned again just to be sure but found nothing except mounting bile in her throat.

"Fuck me," she muttered, teeth clenched around all the things she couldn't do yet but wanted to, like peel Rufus's skin off with words alone.

She slid back out the way she'd come; down three stories of rusted regret. She hit pavement fast enough to make herself dizzy.

Driving back to the office was a blur: neon signs flickered past as plans rewrote themselves, none of them useful enough to cut through failure or fury.

Back in motion but nowhere close to okay, Marti gripped the steering wheel tight and whispered into the hum of tires on wet asphalt. "I'm coming for you, motherfucker."

And this time, there wouldn't be a screen between them.

Chapter 29

Marti made it to the office in record time. Past three red lights, two pedestrians missed and a junkie in a fucking bike lane screaming at the world.

She stalked into the office and was immediately met by Lori. "Jesus, Marti. Don't kick the door like that. If you break it you have to buy it."

"Nothing at Rufus's place. What the fuck do we do?" Marti snarled as she stalked to the window. Maybe Bertha was around to curse at.

Lori's fingers moved in rapid strokes. "On it." Click-click-click. "Stirring the hornet nest." Tap-tap-tap. "'Rufus Montgomery assaulted Serra Stanfield.' And...boom. Anonymous tip sent."

Marti leaned against the cracked window frame, arms folded, jaw clenched tight it hurt.

"That won't be enough," she said. "They'll bury it unless we shove it down their throats with documentation and a crowbar."

Marti turned from the window, her bandaged hand throbbing in time with her pulse. "We're missing something. Rufus didn't just wake up one day and decide to kidnap Serra. There's a pattern."

"His insurance file was clean. Well, except for the fraud." Lori pulled up the document again, scrolling through pages of corporate nothing. "I mean, nothing about Serra."

"Exactly." Marti stalked closer, leaning over Lori's shoulder. The smell of her shampoo cut through the office's usual cocktail of burned coffee and desperation. "So where's the rest? Where's the shit that made him snap? It isn't at his home."

Lori's fingers stilled on the keyboard. "You think there's more at FCPD."

"I know there is." Marti straightened, pacing again. "IT guys don't just leave. They get fired. And when cops fire someone, there's always a paper trail. Complaints, incident reports, all the shit they bury in digital filing cabinets."

"Even if that's true, we can't just waltz in and—"

"He might still have access. What if there's something there?" The words came out sharp, urgent. "Think about it. Lazy fucks at FCPD probably never revoked his credentials. He built half their system."

Lori swiveled to face her fully. "Marti, that's insane. Even if I could get close enough to ghost in, we're talking about hacking a police department. Federal crime territory. Prison-orange-jumpsuit territory."

"Serra's been missing for more than three weeks." Marti's voice dropped low, dangerous. "He's had her for three fucking weeks. What if she's—"

"Don't." Lori stood, closing the distance between them. "Don't finish that sentence."

They stood there, too close, breathing each other's air. Marti could see the calculation happening behind Lori's eyes. Risk versus reward, prison versus finding Serra.

"I can do it," Lori said finally, quietly. "If I can get within range of their network, with a legitimate login to piggyback on... I can slip in through the back door. Find what we need."

"You sure?"

"Nope."

"If they catch you—"

"They won't." Lori moved back to her desk, already pulling up new windows, fingers flying. "But we'll need a way in. A reason to be there that doesn't involve you trying to punch another cop."

Marti's laugh was bitter. "Fresh out of good behavior points."

"Then we get creative." Lori glanced up, something fierce in her expression that made Marti's chest tight. "Serra's counting on us. On you. So we find a way in, we get what we need, and we find that son of a bitch's hiding place."

"You're cute when you get all riled up like that," Marti laughed as she lit up a cigarette.

"I get cuter," Lori corrected her. Lori sighed and rubbed at her temple as if she could massage sense into the world through will. "How do we get in? C'mon Marti, you're the ex cop."

"Ex for a reason. They don't just let you waltz in. We have to have a plan." Marti took a deep drag and flicked her ashes on the floor.

"Okay... what if we wore coveralls and pretended to be janitors again? Like at the bank?" Lori offered.

Marti scoffed so hard she choked on it.

"Oh yeah, that'll go great," she said. "I'm on every wall in there under 'Do Not Admit.' Right next to that poster of a kitten clinging to a branch."

"To be fair, you're scarier than that kitten," Lori grinned, glancing at her with eyes that lingered.

Marti ignored the heat creeping up behind her ears.

"You couldn't just hack in from here?" Marti asked without hope while watching Lori smack the side of their monitor like an old TV.

"Not without this piece-of-shit screen turning into an actual fireplace."

Marti walked over and yanked the plug from hers. "Use mine."

Lori blinked at her but didn't argue; just swapped them fast and got back to work like it had never been broken.

Marti stared at nothing while thoughts spun through her head like razors in a blender.

"What if Rufus is greasing palms to hide the video?" she offered after a moment, too quiet for anger, too loud for peace. "Or they never recovered the ATM footage from that night? Maybe he's blackmailing someone high up: Chief Franklin? Christ." She slammed her fist against her thigh.

"All possible," Lori murmured without looking up. "But theories don't get us evidence."

"Nope," Marti said. Her mouth twisted into something sharp and close to smiling, as if she'd just remembered who she used to be before everything went sideways.

Lori turned toward her then. There was something there in that look: curiosity laced with something darker than attraction but twice as electric.

Marti grinned.

"Let's break some fucking rules."

Lori's eyebrow ticked up. "That's hot. Go on."

Marti grabbed a pen off the counter, spun it once between her fingers as if testing gravity, then pointed it at Lori like a weapon. "Step one: you get whatever sketchy software lets you hijack a police computer with nothing but a user ID and good timing. I'll handle the circus act. Fuck 'em up good."

Lori let out a short laugh, already thumbing through her phone. "Jesus, Marti. You ever just ask nicely?"

"Where's the fun in that?"

The screen lit up as Lori downloaded the necessary tools. "You know this is wildly illegal, right?"

Marti snagged her own phone from the table and dialed quickly. Her voice dropped into business mode: low, lethal, no room for questions. "It's Marti. Twenty minutes." She hung up before whoever-it-was could say a word.

She turned on her heel. "Come on. We're crashing the police station."

Lori blinked. "We really are, huh?"

Marti was already halfway to the door, her energy spiking as if she'd mainlined caffeine and chaos. "Dead fucking serious."

Lori hesitated. Only for a heartbeat. Then followed.

"In and out," Marti said as they hustled down the stairs. "While I'm talking pretty to HR, you're gonna log into one of their terminals using Damian Kane's credentials: 'dkane28.' Password is the season plus the year: 'fall55.' Because that idiot never met a security warning he couldn't ignore."

"You want me to pretend to be Detective Detention-Fantasy?" Lori asked, climbing into the passenger seat.

"That's the one." Marti slammed the car into gear. "Buckle up; we're about to charm our way past armed men and questionable ethics."

The engine roared awake as if it was pissed off to be disturbed. Marti tore out of the parking lot like someone dared her not to cause an accident, swerving around cars and burning through a red light while pedestrians scattered in her wake.

They pulled into the police department's lot with tires screaming like backup singers at a rock concert.

Marti jumped out first. "Let's go make some mistakes."

They crossed the lot shoulder-to-shoulder, their pace brisk enough to raise eyebrows but not alarms. Yet.

A bored security guard making origami cranes at the front desk barely looked up until Marti stepped into his eyeline with that predator smile she wore like lipstick.

"I'm Martina Starova," she said, flashing a badge she no longer had any right to carry. "I need Keira Persky in Human Resources."

The man put down his crane and picked up his desk phone without comment but kept either suspicion or interest locked on them while he talked.

After thirty seconds of murmured bullshit, he hung up and gave them a nod that said "you're someone else's problem now."

"She'll see you," he grunted.

"Of course she will," Marti muttered, stalking down fluorescent-lit hallways like she owned them. Which she once did.

Lori kept pace behind her, trying not to sweat through her shirt.

"Keira!" Marti called ahead as they turned into HR. The woman waiting in the doorway had arms crossed over a generous chest and dark eyes that lit up as if she'd spotted dessert on legs.

"Martina fucking Starova," she said with more glee than anyone should show in HR. She extended her hand to Lori without looking away from Marti's face.

"Keira Persky," she introduced herself as they shook hands.

"Lor—"

"You haven't changed at all," Marti said with that same near-smile from earlier; the one that promised trouble or sex or both.

"It's been almost a year," Keira replied, stepping aside and ushering them in without bothering with small talk niceties.

Marti guided Lori toward a chair outside the office door with one hand on her lower back, a press of contact so subtle it could've been accidental if Lori weren't aware of every place Marti touched her lately.

"Twenty, no thirty minutes. You wait here," Marti instructed, something wicked curling under every word. "Play Candy Crush or hack government servers: whichever gets you off faster."

And with that, Marti disappeared inside with Keira and closed the door behind her with an audible click of intent.

Lori's laptop booted without fanfare, the glow on her face too faint to reflect in the frosted glass of Keira's office door. The hallway was gray, fluorescent-lit, and reeked of municipal furniture polish. From the bench outside the office, she looked like any other bored plus-one: a partner waiting out bureaucratic theater. Marti had gone in three minutes ago with that brittle smile she used when preparing to do something too fucking pleasant.

Lori exhaled slowly and got to work.

She connected to the precinct's guest Wi-Fi first, not because it was useful, but to keep up appearances. The real network floated just beneath the surface, unsecured in the way only government IT could be: confident, underfunded, and asleep at the wheel.

She sniffed packets for two minutes, filtering the noise down to a local IP range. From the stream of regular heartbeat pings and a predictable traffic pattern, she isolated the active session: the unlocked terminal in the back office. Keira's desk. Her MAC address was sloppy, hardcoded, and conveniently tagged with her name.

Lori spoofed her laptop to mimic the terminal's address family, then mapped a route into the subnet. One port remained open: 445. Glass OS file sharing. She almost smiled.

Username: dkane28

Password: fall55

Just like Marti said. He had the imagination of wet dry-wall.

The login landed her on his mapped home directory without a stutter. His folder names were all lowercase, clumped and obvious: documents, casework, backup1, pron, yesterday.

She tunneled into each, pulling everything including the porn. There was no way to know where any of the important data was, if there was any at all. In the last folder, a single video file blinked at her: camview_09-28.mp4. Forty-two megabytes. Big enough to jump out. Big enough to matter. She snagged it, along with a handful of other recent files, all timestamped within the last 72 hours.

Nineteen minutes in. No alerts. No signs of counter-measures. She sat back, eyes drifting toward the office door.

Inside, Marti was mid-distraction, her voice sharp, cutting through the dull acoustics like a serrated edge. A bang. Something metal. Keira said something unintelligible, then a muffled "Ow." Another bang.

Lori glanced up. No one in the hallway. No one looking at her.

She closed her laptop, letting it sit idle on her lap as if she were watching a movie instead of committing a felony.

Eleven minutes left.

The real danger wasn't the hack, it was the boredom that came after. Sitting still, feigning calm, waiting for Marti to finish her hands-on fieldwork with a civilian asset. while her own heart kept the rhythm of a countdown timer.

Outside, someone laughed down the hall. A printer choked and restarted. Overhead, the lights buzzed with bureaucratic indifference.

Eight minutes.

Inside the office, silence. Then footsteps. A chair scraped. A sigh. Marti's. Unmistakable.

Lori shifted her weight, set her laptop into its case, and crossed her legs like she'd just finished checking her email.

She didn't know what was in the files, but she knew one thing:

Whatever it was, it would hurt someone.

And it had better not be Marti.

Chapter 30

Falls City Police headquarters disappeared behind them like an old bruise, faded but still tender if you pressed too hard.

The car ride back to the office was just fifteen minutes, since Lori didn't take Marti's shortcut through pedestrian walkways and went all the way around, but not short enough for Lori.

Marti reeked of everything Lori had missed: sweat and soap layered over fresh sex. The windows were shut tight and so was Lori's jaw as she stared ahead, pretending she hadn't heard every slap of skin through the thin walls earlier. Pretending she didn't want to murder or fuck someone. Maybe both.

Marti didn't glance over once. She drove like she always did, reckless and speeding, and Lori hated how good she looked doing it.

When they got inside, Marti headed straight for the bathroom without a word. The door slammed shut behind her.

Lori stood alone in the dimness before dropping into her chair hard enough to make it creak in protest. The computer blinked on with a soft hum while her eyes settled on the busted monitor still lying cracked on the floor from yesterday's explosion of violence. Maybe frustration or both; with Marti it usually came as a buy-one-get-one deal anyway.

"Fucking idiot," Lori muttered under her breath as she connected her phone to the port.

A loading bar crawled across the screen as stolen files started transferring from police HQ to their drive: digital sins laid bare in grayscale pixels.

Click. Open. Read. Close. Rinse. Repeat.

Behind her, water cut off.

Marti emerged wrapped in steam, not literally this time but close enough. Her hair was damp at the edges where water met skin still flushed from earlier exertion. She smelled better now, cleaner, but somehow that made it worse.

Lori's heartbeat kicked up as Marti dropped into the seat beside hers and pulled out her phone like orgasmic silence hadn't just filled their hallway twenty minutes ago.

No messages from Francesca Stanfield.

Big surprise there.

"Find anything?" Marti asked without looking up.

Lori clicked open one of the scanned PDFs, throat dry like she'd swallowed gravel. "Yeah," she said. "You're gonna love this."

She turned the screen toward Marti so they could both stare at it together: an official Informant Agreement with Rufus Montgomery's signature scrawled at the bottom as if he'd just signed off on selling his soul for a pack of smokes and loose change.

Kane's handwriting was all over it, sloppy but clear: "Do not arrest Rufus."

Dated two days after Serra went missing.

"Son of a fucking bitch," Marti snapped, gripping the desk so hard her nails carved little half-moons into the cheap wood veneer.

"Any clue what he's holding over Kane?"

Marti's jaw worked as if she was chewing glass. "Rufus has something. Has to. Worth shielding him, and worth that extra twenty crisp he wants shoved up his ass."

Lori nodded, her gaze flicking back to the monitor. "Then we figure out exactly what that something is."

"It's gotta be about the Gomes mess." Marti's voice dropped an octave, thick with conviction and nicotine burn. It had to be.

Lori clicked through a folder labeled YESTERDAY in all caps: never a good sign. She hovered over a new video file, dated less than 24 hours ago.

She hesitated.

Hit 'play.'

"Shit," she breathed. "Look at this."

Marti leaned in, and there he was.

Kane.

Dragging Serra like a bag of laundry headed for the incinerator.

"That motherfucker," Marti hissed, her body tightening like a spring coiled too long. Her cigarette trembled between two fingers before she shoved it between her lips and took a drag deep enough to make her lungs protest.

The flickering screen cast an ugly green light across her face as if it were warpaint from another world. "Play it again," she muttered, voice gone gravel-raw.

The footage stuttered and rolled: Kane, pixelated but unmistakable, hauling Serra by the arm into some unknown room before grabbing her throat in hands that looked too calm, too deliberate for panic. He controlled the scene as if he'd done it before, as if he'd practiced on something smaller than a girl.

Marti didn't blink.

"Pause," she barked, stabbing a finger toward the screen. "Right fucking there."

Lori froze the frame mid-movement. There, by Kane's shoulder, a flicker. Just for a second.

"There." Lori zoomed in and pointed at the glitch: half a shadow vanishing in an instant without any reason in physics or logic to excuse it. "Sloppy digital splice. Rufus cut this footage."

Marti reached for her cigarette but realized it had burned down to filter. She flicked it into the ashtray with violence. "Get the VideoTruth program loaded up," she said through clenched teeth. "If Rufus faked this, we blow his filthy deal wide open."

The office phone blared its shriek into the thick air. Both women flinched.

Caller ID lit up: FRANCESCA STANFIELD.

Marti answered with one finger punch to speakerphone.

"Where is my daughter?" Francesca spat out. Not asked; demanded with all the poise of a woman unraveling by threadbare strands of composure.

"We're working on it," Marti said, pushing every word through teeth gritted tight enough to crack enamel. She looked over at Lori, who gave one of those small nods that meant nothing and everything at once.

Francesca's breath hitched through static-laced silence. "Please... please find her..." Her voice cracked open soft and wet as bruised fruit. "I can't lose my baby."

Marti felt it then: that sharp ache behind her ribs as if emotion tried to claw its way out through bone. She reached for another cigarette with hands that wouldn't stop shaking.

"You just lit one," Lori murmured beside her, gentle this time, not judgmental, as if maybe Marti burning herself down completely would finally stop her hurting inside.

Smoke curled around Marti's words as she spoke into the speaker again: "We're close, Francesca." Her tone tried to hold firm but came out more frayed than fierce. "Closer than we've ever been."

"Not good enough!" Francesca shouted back, half pain and half fury.

Click.

Silence wrapped around them again like smoke tendrils from Marti's second cigarette: not comforting, just present and choking as fact.

They both stared at the screen still frozen on Kane's smug face mid-assault.

The shadows on the wall didn't dance. They loomed now, coiled and waiting to strike if either woman dared look away first.

* * *

When the silence had grown thick enough to suffocate them, the eyes all but bled in desperation, the door of their office burst open. Francesca entered angrily, her perfect appearance contrasting with her furious expression. She was not alone. A menacing figure loomed just behind her, an icy presence that made the air feel heavy with dread.

"What the fuck?" Marti hissed, the cigarette held tight between clenched teeth as she stood up.

"Meet Kevin Gardner," Francesca spat, her voice trembling with anger and fear. "He's taking over."

"I know who the fuck he is. What is this?" Marti asked, squinting as she studied Gardner's imposing form. He was a man she knew all too well—a local drug lord and her ex-client. Their last encounter had ended with Marti taking a bullet, a constant reminder of the dangerous game she played.

"Check your account," Gardner growled, his wide-set brown eyes locked onto Marti's like a predator sizing up its prey.

Lori hesitated, then grabbed her phone, opening her bank app. She gasped when she saw that a large payment had been transferred into the account.

"Alright, Gardner," Marti said, trying to suppress the tremor in her voice. "Why are you here?"

"Because I want Serra found," he snarled, his chiseled jaw clenching in rage. "And you're going to do it."

"Francesca, what is this?" Marti glanced at the frantic mother, searching for answers that might help her make sense of the situation.

"Serra is my granddaughter," Gardner revealed, a darkness clouding his words. The room seemed to shrink under the weight of this revelation.

"Fuck," Marti replied, forcing herself to meet Gardner's furious gaze. "I'll find her."

"Good," he growled, stepping forward until he was mere inches away from Marti. She felt the heat of his anger, a fire that threatened to consume them both. "Because if you don't, I'll kill you."

Marti swallowed hard, steeling herself against the onslaught of his verbal abuse. She knew better than to show any vulnerability.

"Twenty-four hours," Gardner snarled, slapping her across the face in anger. "Find my granddaughter or I will tear you apart with my bare hands." Marti believed him.

As he slammed the office door on his way out, the glass shattered. Marti stood motionless, the stinging slap lingering on her skin like a brand. Francesca followed him, her worried eyes flicking back to Marti one last time before disappearing into the night.

"Damn it," Marti muttered, rubbing her swollen cheek. Her fingers twitched again, craving the numbing embrace of Shadow. But she knew she couldn't afford to succumb to her addiction now.

"Twenty-four hours," she whispered to herself, the words echoing through the room like a death knell. The shattered remains of the office door reminded her of the urgency of their task.

Marti shook her head, determined not to let fear paralyze her. She turned to Lori, her eyes alight with resolve. "Let's make a plan to trap that bastard," Marti said, allowing herself a small smile. It was time for them to turn the tables on Rufus Montgomery.

As they sat down to plot their strategy, Marti took a hit. She channeled the drug into determination, steeling herself against the fear that threatened to choke her.

"Do we follow him?"

"No."

"Do we confront him?"

"No."

"Do we contact the authorities?"

"No."

"Do we try to gather more evidence first?"

"No."

"What about setting a trap?"

"Yes."

"How?"

Marti's only answer was a shrug.

"Rufus is a goddamn wizard with video editing," Lori said, brow creased, fingers already dancing over the keyboard. "What if we bait him with a fake job?"

Marti tilted her head, cigarette smoldering between two fingers, watching the ceiling as if it might offer divine confirmation. "Yeah. Yeah, that works. We put up a request for something dirty; something that reeks of 'help me hide this body' vibes, and wait to see if he bites."

"If he does?" Lori's grin was halfway there.

"Then we've got him." Marti stubbed the cigarette out on the edge of the ashtray, grinding it in like it had wronged her. "We catch him mid-crime. Proof he could have doctored that Kane footage. And maybe," she glanced at Lori, pulse quickening, "maybe pressure him into telling us where Serra is."

Yeah. Pressure. That's a good word for it.

They exchanged a look that said what neither wanted to say aloud: Serra could be dead. Already carved up and dumped somewhere no one would ever find her. But hope was as stubborn a bitch as Marti, and neither of them moved to kill it yet.

Forty-three minutes later, Lori slammed her palm onto the desk like she'd just won a game show.

"Got his greasy little profile right here."

Marti leaned in, squinting at the screen. "The fuck is this mess?"

"Night Nexus," Lori said. "It's kind of like jobber site meets the dark web, but with better spelling and less dick pics."

"A jobber site?" Marti asked.

"Exactly. People offer... services. No questions asked, no judgment passed." She clicked around with flair, then opened another tab. "Here's yours."

Marti stared at the profile for two seconds before her jaw tightened like a bear trap.

"'Professional Problem Solver,'" she read aloud. "'Specializing in situations conventional methods can't touch.' Oh fuck off. 'Former intelligence background with selective moral flexibility?'"

Lori reclined in satisfaction, biting her lip to suppress a cackle.

"I will murder you and write my own alibi," Marti muttered, still scrolling.

"Keep going," Lori said.

Marti did. "'Combines tactical precision with creative improvisation...' Jesus Christ. 'Not squeamish about necessary unpleasantness.' Oh look: 'Rates negotiable depending on ethical compromise required.' And here's my favorite: 'Will not harm innocents, engage in human trafficking... or file late tax returns.'"

Lori lost it, laughing so hard she wheezed.

"The tax thing really sells your brand," she managed between gasps.

"I sound like an unhinged dominatrix who freelances in black ops," Marti growled, but even as she said it, she felt the corners of her mouth betraying her resolve.

"Oh please," Lori said through tears. "You don't remember Mint City? That curator you seduced while stealing back the prototype? Or Fenner Morgan? You got him to confess by pretending to be his dead wife."

"That was Halloween-themed strategic misdirection," Marti mumbled.

"That was ghost roleplay and I have the receipts."

Marti opened her mouth to argue but couldn't think of anything that didn't prove Lori's point harder than silence did.

"See?" Lori tapped on the screen again. "Selective moral flexibility."

"If I didn't love you just a little bit," Marti muttered, "I'd be gagging you with Ethernet cable."

Lori rolled her chair closer until their knees touched under the desk and gave Marti a slow smile; one that made promises even her voice hadn't caught up to yet.

"Let's set our trap," she said.

Using the alias Liliana Alvarez (chosen because it sounded like someone who sent bloodstained corsages to prom dates), Lori crafted their bait: a message requesting Rufus's services for an 'urgent edit' involving blurred faces and audio distortion on sensitive material.

One click later and it was done.

Digital hook set.

Blood in the water.

And if Rufus so much as sniffed it, they'd be waiting with jaws wide open.

Chapter 31

Minutes later, Rufus bit.

He messaged back with a speed that made Marti's lip curl, words dripping with greasy excitement. Eager to "help Liliana" blur some faces and clean up the sound on what he guessed was a damning little video. Maybe blackmail. Maybe porn. Maybe both. Rufus didn't ask questions; he just wanted in.

They volleyed messages, each one dialing his anticipation higher, until he begged for an in-person meeting. Marti agreed, tossed out the Crimson Crown as their rendezvous point, and told him she'd be there in an hour.

"Hooked," she said, bumping Lori's shoulder as if it was game day. "Now we gut him."

Lori didn't smile. Her brow furrowed enough to leave tracks. "He's going to recognize you."

Marti froze. "Fuck." She scrubbed a hand through her hair. "You're right."

"He knows your face," Lori pressed. "We need someone else to play Liliana."

Marti opened her mouth, but Lori beat her to it.

"I'll do it."

Marti blinked. "You?"

"I've seen how this guy writes. He thinks every woman wants to fuck him, so all I need is a tight dress and dumb eyes." Her voice was flat, but her jaw was set like concrete. "You can run interference from the shadows."

Marti frowned. She didn't like it, didn't like Lori anywhere near that leech, but the logic stuck. Clean and cold.

"If anything goes sideways," she said, leveling her with that cop look: the one that made perps shit themselves, "you walk."

"I will," Lori said.

Marti didn't like it when people agreed too fast, but fuck if that confidence wasn't hot.

* * *

The Crimson Crown looked as if it had been dragged out of a noir film and hosed down with beer sweat and broken dreams: the kind of place where good intentions went to die behind the bar or under someone's zipper.

Perfect, as always.

Marti adjusted her holster and checked the time again.

Twenty minutes.

Her nerves chewed on bone, but she ground them down with caffeine and focus.

Lori sat in the idling car two blocks away, red lipstick perfect, neckline lower than usual (her idea), and eyes locked on the rear-view mirror as if she was watching herself transform into something dangerous.

"Remember," Marti said through the burner phone wedged between her shoulder and ear as she slipped around the back of the bar. "Keep him talking; don't give him shit unless I say so."

"I've got this," came Lori's reply, smooth as silk soaked in gasoline.

"And I got you."

Marti hung up before Lori could comment on that little slip up.

The alley stank of old piss and week-dead cigarettes. Marti tucked herself into a shadow beside a dumpster oozing something wet enough to shine under streetlight and tried not to think about what it might be digesting.

She pulled her coat tighter, collar turned up against both wind and recognition.

She had eyes on the back door. Rufus wouldn't see her till he bled for it.

Then:

"Need a light?" rasped a voice behind her.

Fuck me with a chainsaw.

She turned just as a guy peeled himself from the darkness: a twitchy bastard who looked like withdrawal personified, sunken cheeks, darting eyes, knife already out as if he thought he was the boss of this conversation.

"Wallet," he hissed, blade catching firelight from a busted bulb overhead. "Now."

Marti didn't answer. She let instinct take the wheel, hand sliding low to grip metal smooth against leather.

Gun drawn in half a breath. Finger tightening.

Bang.

One shot caught his arm; he screamed and stumbled forward anyway, steel flashing once more before biting into her stomach like a snake. Pain bloomed, hot and sharp, and then he was gone, knife clattering behind him as his blood trail painted an exit across cracked concrete.

Marti sank to one knee by instinct more than choice, hand pressing hard over her own wound while her other still gripped the gun.

"Fucking amateur," she muttered through clenched teeth.

Somewhere inside the bar, Rufus probably waited for Liliana Alvarez with his pants half-zipped.

And outside?

Marti bled into shadows not even rats bothered with; queens don't scream when pawns scratch them on their way down.

She still had time before Lori stepped into danger dressed like temptation itself.

Time enough… maybe… to stand back up.

"Shit," Marti hissed, blood warm against her side as she stumbled into the alley's half-light. Her pulse hammered like a war drum inside her skull. Plan was already fucked six ways from Sunday. She snatched the knife from where it had skittered during the scuffle and lobbed it into a sewer grate with a satisfying clang. No knife, no problem.

Gunfire on this block didn't even earn a proper glance. A few heads turned. Nobody cared.

She winced and straightened, ignoring the sting of the asshole's little love tap under her ribs: the kind of shallow stab that annoyed more than killed. Not enough to drop her, but enough to make every breath feel like gravel.

Besides, it hit mostly fake flesh. Mostly.

The Crimson Crown loomed as if bad decisions were wrapped in neon and sour regret. Marti pushed through the door and was greeted by the holy trinity of rot: stale beer, cigarette smoke, and fryer grease that had fossilized. She scanned the booths. No Rufus, half-zipped or otherwise.

Fuck.

She slid into a booth near the back, out of sight and close to an exit, and texted Lori.

"Inside. Back right."

Across shitty pleather cushions and sticky floors, Lori entered with her legs for days and enough sway to guarantee trouble. She drifted toward the bar by the slot machines as if she belonged there, which she didn't, and looked around, zeroing in on Marti swaddled in shadows.

"Everything okay?"

Marti considered how many ways she could say no without sounding like she was about to puke blood or cry.

"Fine. Keep eyes up."

Pain pulsed behind her eyes as she kept scanning. This shithole always coughed up ghosts when she least wanted them. Tonight it coughed up Damian fucking Kane.

He was parked at the far end of the bar, swirling vodka and seltzer as if it might tell him his future. His eyes met hers across fractured glass and low light.

Marti didn't blink.

Kane did; just once. Then he bolted for the door before his drink hit the counter.

Coward.

The sucker-punch landed hard in her gut anyway. Betrayal tastes metallic when it's fresh; burns going down like cheap whiskey and broken trust.

"Son of a bitch," she muttered, fingers tapping out another message with nails that still had someone else's blood under them.

"Set up."

Lori's reply was instant.

"Specify?"

Her stomach twisted as she typed his name.

"Kane. He saw me. He knows what we're doing."

She watched Lori fight not to flinch, scanning every face around her now as if they all had knives behind their backs. Marti shook her head once, low and slow: not yet. Not until they had Rufus in a zip tie or a body bag.

Twenty minutes dragged by like molasses over broken glass before Lori ditched her drink station and walked toward Marti as if nothing tasted better than danger that wore leather boots and apathy like armor. They passed each other subtle nods; a shared language made from too many nights pressed together behind dumpsters or file cabinets or worse things they'd never name aloud. Then Marti stood from the booth with all the grace of someone trying not to bleed on their jeans.

Outside, night wrapped around them thick as breath on glass. The car sat tucked halfway into an alley that smelled like piss and promises no one kept. They slipped inside fast, too fast. Marti fired up the engine while Lori checked over their shoulders for men pretending to be shadows.

Marti's grip on the wheel was ironclad as they peeled off into streets drunk on fog and secrets no one left behind willingly. Lori broke first.

"What the fuck was Kane doing there?"

Marti kept her gaze forward, jaw clenched so tight it hurt to speak.

"I think we were set up," she said, voice flat as asphalt. "The fight, the no-show."

Now that adrenaline was fading, Marti knew she looked rougher than usual because Lori wouldn't stop staring at her side as if skin shouldn't be leaking crimson through black hoodies in polite company.

"You're hurt," Lori said, gentle but firm, like everything else about her lately: soft voice wrapped around steel spine. "What happened back there? Are you okay?"

Marti scoffed and waved it off with a flick of two fingers as if dismissing death itself was just part of Tuesday night foreplay.

"It's nothing."

"Asshole."

"I got stabbed before I even stepped inside." Her voice dropped into something close to manic glee. "But I shot him in the arm."

Lori's lips parted in disbelief, then snapped shut before spilling whatever curse or confession tried to crawl out first.

"You are such a jerk sometimes," she whispered, half pissed-off, half something else entirely that curled between them in electric silence thick enough to chew on.

Marti grinned sideways through blood-stained teeth.

"Sometimes?"

Chapter 32

Lori was half-out the fucking window again. One knee propped on the sill, the other leg dangling uselessly while her arm stretched toward the rusted fire escape. The stray cat huddled there as if it had a vendetta against basic affection. Her grip on the frame was death-grip tight: knuckles bleached white, shoulder trembling from the strain.

"Goddamn it," she hissed, fingertips brushing fur and catching nothing but air as the little bastard hissed and bolted.

Marti watched from the couch, coffee cooling by her knee, cigarette forgotten between two fingers. Lori's hips shifted with every movement, dress clinging in all the right places. Her ass tilted up as if temptation was an accident.

Marti took a drag just to give her hand something polite to do. "I think Rufus planned that robbery."

Lori didn't look back. "First it was Kane. Now Rufus? That's what we're doing now? Conspiracy talk while I risk a spinal injury for a fucking cat?"

Marti rolled her eyes toward the ceiling, smoke curling out of her mouth. "Feels like he set us up."

Lori grunted. "Or maybe he just ghosted us. Chicken-shit move either way."

"Wouldn't be out of character." Marti leaned back, sighing into the leather with bitterness you couldn't fake. "He's always struck me as soft in the spine and hard in excuses."

With one last curse under her breath, Lori gave up and scrambled back inside, hair damp from leaning too far into drizzle. Marti smirked as she took another drag.

"I get it," she drawled. "Wanting pussy that doesn't want you back."

Lori turned just enough to flash her a dirty smile; half challenge, half heat. She crossed the room with purpose.

She kneeled beside Marti, fingers brushing under her shirt without asking for permission first. Not that they ever played by those rules. The pads of her fingers skimmed along puckered skin and neat little staples peppered across Marti's ribs.

"You've stopped bleeding," Lori murmured, voice low and even. Her touch stayed gentle but not tentative; it knew exactly where it could go and how long it could linger before becoming something else. "Lucky you've still got someone around to patch your dumb ass up."

Marti winced as she sat straighter. Her breath caught at how intimate pain could feel in the right hands. Lori's were never wrong.

"It's a fucking setup," Marti growled, teeth gritted as if she was trying to chew through steel. "Kane at Crimson Crown? What, did the universe just roll snake eyes on my life again?"

Lori paused mid-bandage, fingers smeared with dried blood and antiseptic. "Could be coincidence."

Marti let out a snort so loud it turned into an ugly cough. "Coincidence?" She yanked her torso away from Lori's careful hands, scowling as if she wanted to punch the idea in the face. "Sure. And I'm just a knitting enthusiast with excellent taste in bullets." She swept one hand down her body: torn jacket, Shadow-stained shirt, blood stiffening in thin lines across her ribs. "People don't stalk you into death traps for shits and giggles."

Lori pressed a fresh bandage over the deepest gash, fingers steady even if her voice wasn't. "Still. It's not like he came after you."

"No," Marti said, words thick with suspicion. "He left."

She stared at the wall behind Lori's head, at splotched wallpaper peeling at the corners as if it was too exhausted to hang on, and didn't say anything for a long time.

"Because he wanted to be seen," she muttered, "without having to get his hands dirty."

Lori sealed the bandage with surgical tape, then leaned back on her heels. Her brows lifted. "You think he's working with Rufus?"

Marti didn't answer right away. She tilted her head back and closed her eyes, counting thoughts instead of seconds.

"No," she said, voice sharpening like a blade finding its groove. "You remember what Rufus said when I met him as Bertha? Him saying about that twenty crisp payment?"

"Yeah, but..." Lori stopped as something clicked behind her eyes. Her mouth moved before she finished thinking it through. "Oh shit. You think Kane was there to pay him off?"

"Has to be." Marti shifted forward with a wince, testing the limits of her shoulder and ignoring every nerve that screamed no thanks. "Kane didn't look surprised to see me; he looked guilty as fuck." Her grin twisted itself into something meaner. "He wasn't there for me. He was meeting his blackmailer."

Lori blinked. "Wait, so Rufus kidnaps Serra, Kane finds out… and Ruffie-boy plays cleanup by making that fake video?"

"And gets Kane to sign the Informant Agreement," Marti added, nodding to herself now. "That way nobody arrests him for actual crimes while he's busy laundering this mess."

Lori crossed her arms under her chest, the motion framed in sharp lines of muscle under damp cotton, and leaned against the desk, eyes narrowed.

"And Kane is doing this because…?"

"Because Rufus faked the Gomes escape video. Made it look like me instead of Kane. He's got Kane by the short hairs," Marti said as she swatted away Lori's attempt at ministrations.

"And now Rufus wants twenty crisp to keep quiet," she said. Her voice had that lazy drawl she used when she'd figured something out before Marti did and wanted credit for it anyway. "Probably thinks flashing cash will impress me. Liliana." She looked Marti up and down as if she might be priced too low on the open market. "Kane expected Rufus at the bar to give him the money… and then you show up instead."

There was a beat of silence.

"You're worth twenty thousand dollars," Marti said. Marti's eyes dragged along Lori's frame, still kneeling there, still radiating heat from earlier touches, and smirked without humor.

"Is that all? Fuck you," Lori snapped, jaw tight enough to splinter teeth as she slammed the first aid kit shut.

Marti didn't flinch.

Didn't apologize either: not now, not ever.

She stood up, blood singing in her shoulder like gunmetal lullabies, then met Lori's glare head-on.

"You're worth everything he has," Marti said.

And for one breathless second neither of them looked away.

The silence clamped down between them like a bear trap, teeth sunk deep, until Lori's phone buzzed. One sharp little chirp that cut through the heat and the tension and everything else neither of them wanted to name.

Marti pinched the bridge of her nose, fingers smudged with blood and ash. "Fuck's sake," she muttered, voice hollowed out but still carrying that serrated edge. "We need to figure out what happened to Serra before these fuckers stuff her story six feet under, slap a concrete floor on top, and call it closure." She flicked her gaze toward the glowing screen. "Who's texting?"

Lori didn't answer right away. Her anger unraveled: rope slipping loose from around her shoulders, replaced by something softer, almost confused.

"It's my sister," she said finally. "Aiden jumped off the roof again. Broke his arm this time. They're at the hospital."

"Aiden?" Marti arched a brow. "You got secret kids I should know about?"

Lori huffed out something between a sigh and a laugh. "Nephew. Just a kid, thinks he's indestructible. Last week he made wings out of pizza boxes."

Marti blinked. "Ambitious."

"Fucking exhausting," Lori said, thumbs moving across her phone as she typed something back, probably reassurance wrapped in emojis and ILY.

"You need to go handle that?" Marti asked, already expecting yes, already prepping for alone again.

But Lori just locked her phone and tossed it onto the table as if it had never mattered. "He'll be high on painkillers and milking this for ice cream before I hit the parking lot. I'll swing by in the morning; it's our thing, me bringing breakfast."

"So you're staying." Not a question.

"Until we figure this out," Lori said, voice low now, full of something weightier than obligation.

She moved as if gravity didn't apply to her, graceful as sin, as she dropped beside Marti on the battered sofa, one leg crossing over the other. Those legs should've come with warning labels.

Marti noticed anyway.

Noticed everything.

And said nothing at all.

* * *

Every thread stank of Rufus or Kane, usually both, and neither one had ever been worth shit in daylight, let alone in the dark. Every time Lori tried to steer Marti to other possible explanations, Marti jerked the wheel right back.

Rain hammered the windows like it wanted a goddamn seat at the table. Thunder rolled overhead as if judgment day was running late.

"We trying Rufus again?" Marti asked after another dead end detonated between them.

"Sure," Lori said, already dropping into her chair with that dangerous ease she wore like perfume. She pulled up their fake Liliana profile before Marti could change her mind. Her fingers hit keys in a flurry of deceit; typing faster than most people could come up with a decent justification for murder.

She didn't look away from the screen. Just typed: Why didn't you show at Crimson?

Boom. Sent.

As if answers showed up faster when you shoved the question down someone's throat and smiled while doing it.

Far off but not far enough, thunder cracked again. Distant gunfire dressed as weather.

The reply came back quick.

"I got there, but there was blood everywhere. I couldn't go in. I was scared."

"Your blood scared him off," Lori snorted. "Coward," she typed, then sent it before Marti could weigh in on whether provoking assholes was strategic or just her kink.

Another message popped up: "You're a bitch, Liliana. You'll pay for insulting me."

"He's pissed," Marti muttered, not hiding her smile as Lori nuked the fake account with one final click. Bye-bye, Liliana.

And then Marti's phone started shrieking on the table as if something alive that hated being ignored.

She glanced down. Froze. "What the fuck? Keira never calls me."

She answered anyway, because regardless of what she said out loud, Keira called to somewhere deep in Marti most nights; even if that call involved fewer clothes and more bruises.

"Keira?"

"Marti, please. I need your help."

Marti sat bolt upright.

Keira didn't plead. Didn't sob. Didn't do anything except drip sex and heat and walk away smelling like expensive sin. But there she was now, cracking apart over the line as if something terrible had found her soft parts.

"Alright," Marti said. "Breathe and tell me what's going on."

"I don't know who else to call." Her voice hiccupped through static and tears. "Can you meet me? Kransten Park."

Kransten Park? Now? No one asked anyone to meet at Kransten unless they were selling drugs, buying pain, or planning to die soaked and anonymous under a streetlight.

Still.

"I'll be there soon." She hung up before Keira could offer more details that would make saying no impossible.

When she turned around, Lori was looking at her as if she'd grown a second head: or worse, caught feelings.

"You sure that's smart?" Lori asked, suspicion curling tight around each word like barbed wire gift-wrapped in concern. "Could be a setup."

"She's not like that," Marti said.

"Right," Lori drawled. "Because this has nothing to do with your pussy making decisions again."

Marti grabbed her gun from the desk drawer without commenting on that particular truth bomb. She checked the chamber by muscle memory and stuffed it into her jacket like an old habit she'd never unlearned.

"It doesn't matter," she muttered as she headed toward the door, "I'm going."

She snagged a Fentafill like she was taking candy from a dish, and let it go down dry.

The rain greeted her outside like an old lover with anger issues; fists pounding every surface without apology or rhythm. Her boots hit puddles hard enough to send water flying behind her as she moved through streets drowning under stormwater.

The glow from streetlights smeared across wet asphalt as if someone tried to paint shadows with firelight and grief and failed at both.

Kransten Park loomed ahead like a mouth waiting to close around something breakable.

Marti kept walking anyway.

Chapter 33

Keira stood beneath a skeletal tree as if she hadn't decided whether to bolt or beg. Hair plastered to her face, jacket sticking to her too-thin frame. She looked like a ghost trying to pass for human. Marti slowed, eyes sweeping the edges of the park: no watchers, no vans, no sudden movement from the dark. Just thunder chewing at the sky overhead and Keira vibrating like live wire.

"Jesus," Marti muttered. "You look like shit."

Keira startled at her voice, then let out a breath that shook harder than the lightning above them. "You came."

Marti pulled her coat tighter around herself and stepped closer, boots squelching in mud that smelled of sewage and blood memories. "Of course I did."

"They're going to kill me," Keira said, skipping past greetings as if they were luxuries she couldn't afford. "Kane called me in after you left my office. Said he saw everything on his little hallway cam. He knows you were there."

Marti swore under her breath, sharp and guttural, and glanced toward the streetlamp swallowing their shadows whole.

"Look, you can go to HR, tell them it—"

"Not the sex. He thinks I told you something," Keira rushed on. "I didn't, but it doesn't matter! He threatened me. Said his guys would come by my place tonight to… do things." Her voice broke on that last word as if it couldn't bear the weight of what she meant.

Marti's stomach twisted.

"How does he think you leaked anything?" Marti said, blinking against memory.

"He's paranoid." Keira's hands fluttered toward her face and dropped again. "Something big's coming down and he's unhinged. He kept asking about files; records I don't even have clearance for."

A bolt of lightning split the sky open behind her, illuminating tear tracks and fear tattooed across her expression. Marti felt her fingers curl into fists and forced herself to stop.

She reached out, wrapping an arm around Keira's waist and pulling her close. Standing that close made it easier to breathe somehow. Keira didn't resist. She melted into Marti's chest with a soft gasp, skin cold through layers of fabric.

"Fuck him," Marti murmured into damp hair. "You're staying with me tonight."

She dug into her pocket and shoved the keys into Keira's trembling hand.

"My place," she said, soft but firm enough to cut glass. "Don't open the door for anyone who doesn't know all three safe words."

Keira blinked up at her through raindrops.

"You have three safe words?"

"Just a joke. Don't open the door to anyone but me."

That earned half a nod before Keira stepped away, clutching the keys as if they might be holy. "1344 Raven-crook?"

"1344 Ravencrook."

Marti watched her disappear into the night before turning toward the office with murder pooling behind her ribs.

*　*　*

The door slammed so hard behind her it shook dust from the ceiling tiles.

"Kane threatened Keira." She threw it out like a grenade as Lori turned from the monitor.

Lori's brow cinched tight enough to wrinkle time itself. "Why the hell would he target Keira? She didn't give us jack."

"No shit," Marti snapped, pacing hard enough to bruise tile through boot heels. "And he knows that, but he's spiraling so fast he doesn't care anymore."

"Because you fucked her?"

"He thinks she gave me files. She doesn't even have clearance," Marti said, dragging fingers through wet hair. "But Kane. Maybe he knows we found something but doesn't know how. Blames Keira. Maybe Rufus asked for the money, and then I show up near whatever little peep show he has going there. Get caught on camera talking to HR. It lines up just right to make him sweat bullets."

"He thinks you've found something and you're going to HR to...?"

"Get my job back. Tank his career." Marti pulled out a Fentafill with shaking hands, threw it into her mouth and swallowed dry.

"Rufus backs Kane by framing me over Gomes," she said, voice gone low and mean. "Then Rufus fucks up and attacks Serra, and he needs Kane's help. Kane puts him on the no-arrest list. But Rufus gets greedy and fired and desperate and wants money. And I see Kane at Crimson Crown, ready to pay him off."

"And he doesn't know you don't have proof of the payoff. Or the Gomes video." Lori's eyes flared wide.

"No proof yet."

"And now our poor admin gets death threats for screwing with you." Lori leaned back against the desk but kept looking at Marti as if messing with her could get you killed. Which clearly it could.

Marti stared at nothing.

"Serra's dead," she said. "And Kane knows it."

Lori stiffened as if she'd been slapped with ice water.

"You don't know that."

"I do." Marti lifted one brow but didn't soften anything else about herself. "They found out who she really was: Gardner's granddaughter. No way she walked away from that alive once Rufus found out and told Kane."

"You're just being cynical again."

"Realistic," Marti corrected with zero apology in her tone. "Hope doesn't rescue corpses."

Lori opened her mouth, closed it again, and looked suddenly interested in staring down at her feet instead of meeting Marti's gaze.

Neither of them spoke for several seconds while thunder rolled outside as if sky-borne judgment had decided to join their crisis planning session.

"And we have not much time left to find her," Lori muttered without looking up.

Marti sighed long and jagged enough to strip rust from metal and crossed the room until their hips brushed together at the edge of the desk.

"Without Serra or her body, we're dead in the water," Lori said, still committed to her deep and meaningful examination of her boots. "She's not at Rufus's place; I checked. She has to be somewhere else he knows, somewhere familiar."

Marti snorted. "Kane's?" The word left a bitter taste, and she shook it off. "No. Kane wouldn't babysit a corpse. He'd toss her in the grinder and frame Rufus for the noise."

Lori chewed on her bottom lip as if she was one wrong word from breaking skin. "Maybe Rufus just dumped her. Remote stretch of nowhere. Somewhere even the rats don't bother with."

"Fuck it," Marti muttered as she lit a cigarette with steady hands. "Go home. Enjoy your last night on earth."

"Marti!"

"I'm kidding."

"You're not."

Marti waved a smoke-trailing hand as if she could swat the guilt away. "Fine. Go. Sleep the sleep of someone who doesn't have blood on her boots yet. We've still got time, unless we don't, but who gives a shit anyway?"

Lori didn't move.

Marti watched her over the rim of her coffee mug, hoping that Lori might say fuck it and drag them both back to her place where they could pretend-forget together.

Instead, Lori grabbed her coat with the air of someone who hadn't given up but wanted to.

"I'll grab some food," she said as she opened the door. "And coffee strong enough to burn a hole in hell's floor." Then, over her shoulder: "Don't get high while I'm gone; promise me that much. We need both of our brains for this. Back soon."

Marti just nodded into her ashtray.

She didn't even get past the first page of notes she had no desire to read when the door opened again.

Lori stuck her head in, cheeks pink with embarrassment or cold or something that made Marti want to drag her in by the collar.

"Got all the way to my car before realizing I forgot my phone," she said, rummaging through her desk. She held up the phone in triumph and added with a crooked grin: "It's like walking out without pants."

Marti didn't smile.

Didn't blink.

She stared past Lori like something had lit up on the wall behind her.

"Wait." Her voice dropped an octave and picked up speed. "Wait wait wait... why the fuck was Serra's phone found in that alley behind: what was it, the Clown? Crowd? Not at the ATM where we know she was grabbed?"

Lori froze mid-step, sheepishness gone.

"I checked," she said, stepping further into the room now that Marti had gone full bloodhound mode. "There is no bar called 'The Crowd.' The kid got it wrong. We don't know where—"

"Teenagers are garbage at getting names right," Marti snapped. She stubbed out the cigarette hard enough to crack ceramic (thank God it was metal) and stood up fast enough to make Lori step back. "What did you find? Any near-matches?"

Coat forgotten, Lori crossed back to the desk and pulled out a wrinkled page from inside her jacket pocket.

"Of course. There's a list," she said, reading quickly now as if adrenaline made memory easier: "The Rusted

Crow, Crow & Compass, The Midnight Crowd, Wandering Crow Tavern, Crown & Crow Tavern, The Crimson Crowd, The Black Crow Public—"

"FUCK!"

"What?"

"The Crimson Crown," Marti snapped as if saying it louder might conjure Serra whole and unhurt beside them. "That dive where Rufus drowns his regrets and pick up bad ideas. That's where he was supposed to meet us but ghosted instead."

Her eyes were wide now, the dangerous kind of wide that meant things were clicking fast and ugly inside Marti's head.

"Oh my God," she whispered. "Serra might actually have been there."

Lori swore under her breath as if trying not to make it real by speaking too loud.

"Not 'crown' or 'clown,'" she murmured, eyes narrowing into focus again. "Crown."

She looked at Marti.

"It makes sense..."

Marti nodded, already reaching for another cigarette and checking if she had enough gas in the tank for war.

"...Rufus would feel safe there." Lori swallowed. "Maybe... god... maybe Serra was in a dumpster out back."

"She's gone," Marti said, lighting her cigarette with the kind of finality that came with funerals or quitting a job you never liked. "But if she set foot inside that place, if even her shoe scuffed the fucking floor, we need to know. Something. Anything we can hurl at Gardner before he shoves us into a grave and calls it closure."

She blew smoke toward the cracked ceiling.

"Alright." Her voice sharpened. "We hit the Crimson Crown early: like ass-crack-of-dawn early. No bartenders, no busboys, just shadows and locked doors. We go in quiet, rip the place apart, and pray to whatever sadistic god's listening that she left something behind."

Lori arched an eyebrow. "So... breaking and entering is officially on our to-do list now?"

Marti didn't flinch. "Always has been."

Silence.

That look between them was a signature on the decision. Fuck legal. Fuck smart. They'd already rolled too far down this hill.

Marti leaned back against the couch, eyes on the ceiling, trying to lay out the bar as best as she remembered. Exits, security cams, kitchen door, washrooms.

"We go quiet," she said again, more to herself than Lori. "In and out."

Outside, the city snarled past tired neon and twitching brake lights. Inside, everything stilled like a held breath before a bad decision.

Plans made.

Someone was going to bleed.

Chapter 34

4:02 AM.

The city didn't give a damn if you were trying to be quiet. It slopped rain and motor oil down the alley like it was swabbing out its guts, and Marti stepped right into it, hoodie low over her eyes, boots hissing on wet pavement. Neon flickered in puddles like someone's bad memory. The air reeked of carbon monoxide and cheap decisions.

The Crimson Crown crouched ahead: dirty brick stacked like teeth behind rusted signage that might've once been red. Now it just looked tired, like everything else in this part of town.

Marti's gun rode her hip, metal against skin through torn denim. No safety net, but hell, it was something solid when the rest of the world felt like water. She glanced at

Lori beside her, both of them pressed tight to the wall as if they'd practiced this, as if they knew how easily second acts turned into funerals.

Then came the back door, smug beneath its little padlock, practically begging to be shot.

"Fuck me," Marti muttered, running one finger along the rusted hasp as if she might seduce it into opening.

She looked around for something helpful: a pipe, a crowbar, divine intervention. The alley offered her a broken bottle and a condom wrapper playing dead by the drain. Great.

She sighed, frustration pooling where patience used to be. The lock was still locked. Her fuse wasn't.

She pulled the gun and fired; one clean shot.

The sound cracked off bricks as if God had slammed a filing cabinet shut on someone's hand.

Lori ducked behind her hood. "Jesus fuck! Subtle much?"

Marti holstered the gun with a grin sharp enough to cut concrete. "Cops don't patrol here unless someone calls in rich."

The lock hung open in two jagged halves as if it regretted its choices.

They slipped inside, door dragging on warped hinges, into bleach-stained dark that smelled like rot trying to pass for sterilized.

"Downstairs," Marti said as she headed toward a dark stairwell.

The basement breathed around them. Pipes above clattered out Morse code confessions against a ceiling low enough to make tall people apologetic. Every step slick with grime. The floor felt alive under their soles, not in a sexy way, but in a way that suggested it might shift and swallow you whole.

Everything inside looked abandoned by someone who gave up halfway through cleaning and decided arson was easier: collapsed cardboard boxes, yellowing mop buckets full of swamp water, chairs stabbed together with duct tape and spite, shelves hoarding expired tomato soup next to gallon jugs of industrial cleaner with labels peeled off like secrets no one wanted to admit existed.

Marti's boot clipped a beer bottle stuffed full of piss instead of beer. Classy touch.

The furnace wheezed from the corner as if it had asthma and no will to live.

And holy shit did it stink down there, like death wearing mildew as perfume and whispering sweet nothings about black mold into your ear canal. The air curled into Marti's lungs all wrong, thick and greedy, as if it had plans for her insides she didn't agree to.

Her chest clenched tighter than Lori's jeans. Fuck! Fuck that thought right now. Claustrophobia crawled out from wherever she'd buried it years ago and started rubbing its hands together with glee.

"Come on," she growled under her breath, shoving aside a piece of soggy cardboard that disintegrated in her hands like zombie skin on contact. "Goddamn it... where was she?"

Her fingers shook as they moved through stacked shadows and forgotten filth, digging for clothes, shoes, anything that Serra might have left behind.

Hope was always messiest when you actually went looking for it.

"Nothing," Lori snapped, a stack of plastic containers crashing to the ground as she whipped her arm out. "Fucking useless."

Marti didn't flinch. Her eyes scanned the basement like it owed her something personal. "Keep looking."

The shadows didn't just sit in the corners; they poured through the air, thick and wet like oil. Somewhere between the rats and mildew, Marti's heart pounded like it was trying to punch its way out. Every box upended, every shelf stripped added weight to the dread curling in her gut.

"We've checked everything," Lori hissed, brushing cobwebs from her arms with a shiver that wasn't from the cold. "Where the hell is it? There must be something."

Marti bit back a scream. Not at Lori: at herself, at fate, at Serra for being gone where Marti couldn't follow. "Upstairs," she said, voice tight as piano wire. "Maybe."

The stairs groaned under their boots. The air shifted as they climbed; mold and rot giving way to stale beer and the echo of regrets soaked into velvet carpeting. Tables stood like abandoned altars, empty glasses catching what little emergency light flickered overhead.

"Scan everything," Marti murmured, her voice sharp enough to cut glass. "If she left anything behind..."

Lori nodded and peeled off toward the bar while Marti stalked left, eyes slicing through shadows until they landed on a hulking silver door tucked behind an overturned high-top table.

Then, it hit her.

That smell, just under the surface. Like copper and rot. She'd smelled it before. Twice. Once in a tenement crawlspace in '49. And once behind a butcher shop where a dealer had tried to ice a body like pork. This? This was the same damn scent.

"There." Her finger jabbed toward the walk-in freezer as if it had personally offended her.

The door was padlocked: a thin industrial bolt that screamed 'stop thief' in chrome. Designed to keep out light-fingered employees, not adrenaline fueled private investigators with a fuck of a lot to lose. Marti didn't blink before her gaze found a rusted industrial mop leaning nearby.

She snatched it and jammed the handle into the hasp with fury.

Metal screeched against metal. Lori came running. The lock popped with a reluctant snap.

Then came the stench. Obvious. More sure.

"Oh fuck me sideways," Lori gagged, stumbling back and throwing her sleeve over her face as if it might do a damn thing.

Marti's lip curled as rancid air hit her straight in the throat: something between dead meat and chemical failure. She turned away but didn't step back.

"You know what it is," she said. Voice coated in steel shavings. "Hold the door open."

Lori hesitated for a heartbeat.

"I'm not fucking around," Marti growled, not hiding how close panic sat behind her teeth. "It locks from inside."

"Right," Lori said, planting herself against the frame as if she could physically keep time from closing it on them both.

Marti's hands were shaking. They revealed what she refused to admit. Claustrophobia screamed in her ears, and she ducked inside.

The freezer sucked away warmth with greedy fingers. Her skin went tight. Ice crusted on old food boxes and plastic containers scattered across shelves at odd angles, as if someone had started rearranging for storage and given up halfway through prep.

Her boots crunched over frost slicks as she moved toward the deeper dark at the back wall. The flashlight on her phone threw silhouettes across metal surfaces, making monsters out of mop buckets and ketchup-stained cartons.

"You see anything?" Lori called out from somewhere outside normalcy.

"Not yet." Marti grit the words through clenched teeth as breath steamed in quick bursts, fast enough to fog up thought if she let it.

Claustrophobia skittered up her spine like a cold neon sign flickering back on after years of disuse: TRAPPED BITCH GET OUT NOW.

She kept moving anyway.

Then there, in the far corner under bags of half-thawed fries and god-knows-what else: blue tarp, wrinkled as if someone had tried to forget it existed but didn't have enough conviction to throw it away.

Marti stared at it for half a second before biting down on whatever part of herself wanted to stall this moment forever, and yanked it back with both hands.

Serra looked up at her with frozen eyes that hadn't closed properly. Her body contorted mid-prayer or protest under layers of ice-burned skin and makeup now smeared like bruises across bone-pale cheeks.

Marti didn't scream. An electric jolt screamed through her. Her spine sang like someone had dropped live wire down the back of her jacket. Her lungs seized. The walls of the freezer closed in like a vice made of dead girls' ghosts and ice. She staggered, gasping, one palm flat against the cold belly of the nearest shelf as her chest crushed in on itself.

Fuck.

Her vision splintered: white, red, shadows. Still Serra stared past her with those open, frozen eyes as if she was waiting for Marti to explain why it took so long.

Marti swallowed bile. "Lori," she managed, teeth grinding together as if that would hold the sentence down. "I found her."

There was a beat. Then Lori's voice cracked through the static: "Serra?"

"Yeah," Marti rasped. "She's here. All of her."

Lori didn't answer right away. No sobs or panicked breathing over the comms, just a hollow silence that hit harder than any scream.

"Pictures," Lori said, voice dry and tight as if she'd wrung out all the water just to speak. "Take pictures."

Marti wiped sweat, or tears, off her face with the back of her hand. Pulled out her phone with fingers that didn't want to work and started taking shots. Click. Click. Hands first: thin gold ring around her pinky, sparkly nail polish, chipped. Then clothing: jeans, t-shirt for a band she'd probably never heard of, no shoes. Face, body, done.

Enough to convince Francesca it was real.

Enough to make Gardner not kill them. Maybe.

She eased the tarp back over Serra's body with hands that felt more like claws now, gripping too hard and shaking too much, and backed out fast before she started talking to corpses again.

Lori lowered her own phone (she'd been filming) and the freezer door slammed with an echo that chased her halfway across the room.

Marti pulled out her Shadow inhaler and dragged deep until chemical calm clawed its way into her bloodstream.

"Cool," she muttered, even though everything inside her screamed otherwise. "Just fucking peachy."

Marti caught Lori's arm before she could bolt past.

"You okay?" There was no way that wasn't rhetorical, but Marti asked anyway.

"Yeah. You?"

Marti let out a laugh sharp enough to cut skin. "Oh, I'm fabulous. Found a frozen girl in a meat locker and now I get to call Daddy Warcrimes about it." She tugged Lori toward the alley exit by sheer rage alone. "Come on."

The rain outside hit like broken glass: cold and mean and full of sirens in waiting.

Chapter 35

The fluorescent lights buzzed overhead like hangry wasps. Marti's fingers left smudges on the glossy photograph as she studied Rufus Montgomery's face. A constellation of acne scars and barely-contained malice looked back. Her stomach turned.

Five years ago, she'd have known exactly what to do. Now? She wasn't sure of anything anymore.

Serra Stanfield's case file lay spread across her desk like entrails at an autopsy. Seventeen years old. Honor roll student. Missing for more than three weeks before they found her in the freezer. Marti's gaze flicked to the wall clock, each tick feeling like an accusation. Her hands trembled slightly as she reached for her empty coffee cup. Withdrawal. Or guilt. The lines had blurred months ago.

Falls City's neon glow filtered through the venetian blinds, painting prison-bar shadows across the desk. The office always felt smaller at night, when the world outside compressed into these four walls and the weight of decisions hung in the stale air. A brown coffee ring stained Serra's school photo, bisecting the girl's smile, the kind of unintentional metaphor that made Marti's chest ache.

She shoved back from the desk. Her chair's wheels caught on the worn carpet as she stood. Three steps to the wall. Four steps back. Her Doc Martens scuffed against the floor with each turn. The leather jacket she wore—too heavy for the stuffy office—stayed on. Armor against the night. Against choices she didn't want to make.

Marti's phone dinged.

Embarrassing. She hadn't even heard it ring.

She snatched it. Keira. She dialed into her voicemail and listened.

"Marti it's me. I'm out of here. Heading to California. Away from all this shit. Chief Franklin was not happy when I talked to him. I think...I don't know what I think. I'm gone. I'll drop you a line once I am settled. Yeah. Bye."

Marti erased the message. One good fuck gone, and Kane and Rufus were to blame,

"This is bullshit." Her voice cracked across the room. "Rufus has a face like a hammer; how the hell have the cops not ID'd him yet? He should be halfway to GenPop by now."

The door hinges protested as Lori slipped in, fresh coffee in one hand and case notes in the other. The dim light caught her short blonde hair, creating a halo effect that seemed obscenely out of place in their grim reality.

"You say something to me?"

Marti shook her head.

"You've been staring at that photo for an hour," Lori said, setting the coffee down carefully away from the documents that mapped Serra's final days.

"Thanks." Marti didn't reach for the cup. Instead, her fingers found Rufus's photo again, thumb tracing the edge. "Look at him. Every damn stereotype of a predator wrapped in one package. The kind of guy who makes your skin crawl before he even opens his mouth."

Lori perched on the edge of the desk. Her green eyes, sharp, and assessing, studied Marti's face, seeing past the facade. "That's not what's bothering you though, is it?"

Marti's laugh caught in her throat, emerging as something hollow and broken. She tossed the photo onto the desk.

"Five years ago, I'd have called this in immediately." She ran a hand through her tangled hair. "Now I'm sitting here wondering if I should just…" Her voice dropped to a whisper. "We know where this is going to go."

"And?"

The coffee sat untouched as the prison-bar shadows lengthened across the desk, across Serra's divided smile, across the face of the man who'd taken her life.

"The system that betrayed you," Lori added softly, her silhouette framed against the grimy apartment window.

Marti's fingers found their way through her short black hair, leaving it standing in jagged spikes. The gesture, automatic as breathing when she was stressed, didn't help clear her thoughts. "Yeah. But that's not an excuse, is it?" The whiskey in her desk beckoned. She poured a finger into her coffee. "I do this every fucking time. I want to save these murderous pieces of shit just so they can go to prison for a year or two before getting off on some technicality bought by whoever the fuck. Where's the fucking line?"

Lori turned from the window, her face half-shadow, half-harsh light. "There isn't one. That's the point." She moved closer, each word precise as a knife cut. "Despite everything you believe about yourself, you're a good person who believes in law and order and justice."

The truth in those words knocked the air from Marti's lungs. She dropped onto the couch, springs groaning beneath her like they shared her pain. "Christ. You need to write a book of inspirational quotes."

"My therapist. I swear to God she has a book of inspirational quotes that she just launches into sometimes." A hint of a smile softened Lori's face as she settled beside Marti, their shoulders touching. The faint scent of her perfume cut through the perpetual smell of old takeout and cheaper whiskey. "While you're busy being self-destructive and dramatic, I go to therapy."

The warmth of Lori's shoulder against hers made Marti want to say fuck everything, and fuck Lori. Hard and often. Outside, sirens wailed the city's constant soundtrack. "You know what you have to do," Lori continued. "You've known what you were going to do since you found that evidence. You're just afraid of being disappointed again."

Marti's head fell back. The water stains on her ceiling formed continents on a map to nowhere. She traced their outlines with tired eyes. "And again." Her voice came out rougher than intended.

Behind her closed eyelids, she saw Kane's face. That easy smile across their shared desk, the casual way he'd slid the evidence bag into his drawer. Just this once, Marti. For the greater good. The memory tasted like ash.

"You're not Kane." Lori's voice cut through the memory. She'd always had that knack, reading Marti's mind when it wandered to dark places. "That's why you always try. It... Falls City isn't about bringing justice to the world. It's about making sure you don't drown in the corruption." Her hand found Marti's, squeezed once. "It's who you are, the person who does the right thing, even when you know it won't work."

Marti opened her eyes, turning to face her friend. The certainty in Lori's expression made something tighten in her chest. "Even if it means helping the department that threw me under the bus?"

"Especially then." Lori stood, the couch springs shifting with her absence. She smoothed her skirt with tender hands, the gesture at odds with the chaos of Marti's mind. "Because that's exactly what separates you from them. Justice ahead of revenge, even when revenge would be easier." She paused. "Even when revenge would feel better."

The phone felt heavier than it should as Marti picked it up from the cluttered desk. Her thumb hovered over the screen, then scrolled through contacts. Names of people who no longer took her calls flashed by until she stopped on one. "Detective Caspian Huff," she said, the name bitter and hopeful all at once. "He's honest, for sure. If anyone will handle this right, it's him."

The guy had half a dozen commendations on the wall and a frayed sticky note taped to his monitor that just said: Tell the truth. No matter what.

Lori's hand found her shoulder, squeezed once. "You're doing the right thing."

Marti nodded, but didn't hit the call button yet. She just stared at Huff's name, wondering if doing the right thing would feel better this time around. Somehow, she doubted it.

She hit call before she could reconsider, then pressed the cold phone to her ear. Each electronic pulse of the ring tone stretched into eternity, matching the thud of her heart against her ribs. Her gaze drifted to the photos spread across her desk: evidence that would either save a life or raffirm her cynicism.

"Martina Starova." Huff's voice finally broke through, carrying the weary rasp of too many hours on shift. "This is unexpected."

"Yeah, well." Marti's fingers twitched toward her cigarette pack, then curled into a fist. Not now. "Don't get used to it."

She swallowed, watching a car's headlights sweep across her apartment ceiling. "I've got something you need to see. About Serra Stanfield. Missing teenager."

A pause. Papers shuffled in the background. When Huff spoke again, his voice had cooled. "Missing? That's not my case."

"It should be." Marti leaned forward, her chair creaking beneath her. "Because it's not missing persons anymore. It's homicide."

His sharp intake of breath carried through the line. She could picture him sitting straighter, reaching for a pen.

"I've got evidence against Rufus Montgomery," she continued, running her finger along the edge of the nearest photograph. "Solid evidence."

"That weird guy who used to work in IT? Go on." The professional edge had returned to his voice, the tone she remembered from stakeouts and case breakthroughs, before everything went to hell.

Chapter 36

Marti stood, unable to remain still with the tension coursing through her. She paced to the window, watching raindrops trace jagged paths down the glass.

"I have security footage Serra taking out money at an ATM, being attacked right there. Montgomery's face is visible," she added, turning back to her desk. "Those distinctive acne scars catch the security light. The night the girl disappeared."

More rustling papers. A drawer opening and closing. "You're absolutely certain about the identification?"

"I'm just getting started." Marti pressed her forehead against the cool glass. "I've got photos from the Crimson Crown showing a body being stored in their freezer. It's Serra. And I've got proof that an employee at an insurance company where Rufus worked, fraudulently redirected a claim payment to Crimson Crown. Twenty crisp about the same day Serra went missing. A fee to store her body."

The line went quiet. She could hear Huff breathing, processing. "You sure?"

"Wouldn't be calling if I wasn't." Marti picked up one of the photos, studying the grainy image for the hundredth time. The face that had haunted her for weeks stared back, caught in a moment of calculated violence.

"How exactly did this evidence come into your possession?"

Marti's lips twisted. She caught her reflection in the window. A ghost of her former self, haunted by cases both solved and unsolved.

"I did the job the fucking cops wouldn't. Mom went to Falls City PD and they did jack shit. Found the payout working an insurance fraud case. All legit."

Huff's heavy sigh filled the silence between them. "I suppose we deserved that. It's getting bad." A pause. "But if I'm going to do this right, I need something I can take to a judge to get a search warrant. Don't want this thrown out with cries improper collection."

"The bank security video is something you can get yourself, but you need to move fast. You don't want it deleted." Marti tapped the grainy surveillance images spread across her desk. "I can send you probable cause for a warrant for the Crimson Crown, then you use the body to get the banking video to show it was Rufus."

"Listen to you," Huff said, the phone line crackling slightly. "Being all procedural and shit." Something in his voice softened. "This is solid work, Marti."

Marti's fingers froze mid-tap. Her throat tightened. She hadn't realized how much she'd been waiting to hear those words – from him, from anyone who remembered the detective she used to be.

"I'll take it to the Judge Patterson," Huff continued, papers shuffling in the background. "She's usually good about after-hours warrants when the cause is solid. Shouldn't take more than twenty minutes. You want to watch the search from across the street? Just—"

"Keep my distance? Yeah, I'd fucking love it."

"I was going to say 'be subtle,' but…"

Marti snorted. "Not exactly in my skill set."

"Some things never change." The gruffness in Huff's voice couldn't hide the warmth underneath. "Send me the photos and video. I'll see you at the Crimson Crown."

The line clicked dead. Marti set her phone down and exhaled slowly, unclenching muscles she hadn't realized were tight. The tension that had coiled around her spine for days loosened just enough to notice.

Lori appeared in the doorway, leaning against the frame with arms crossed. Her eyes darted from Marti's face to the scattered surveillance photos.

"It's done," Marti said. "Huff's taking it to Patterson as soon as you send him all the shit. Skip the insurance stuff, that's not relevant to Serra's death."

"How does it feel?" Lori asked, stepping into the room.

Marti ran her fingers along the edge of her desk, tracing a groove worn by years of the same nervous habit. "Like…" She paused, searching for the right words. "Like finding your favorite gun in a drawer you forgot you had."

"That's either poetic or disturbing." Lori's mouth quirked up at one corner.

"Little of both." Marti stood, leather jacket creaking as she shrugged it on. "I'm going to watch the search. Send him that stuff?"

Lori nodded. "On it, boss."

"Good girl." Marti grabbed her keys, metal jangling against her palm. "What would I do without you?"

"Drown in paperwork and drugs, not necessarily in that order." Lori's smile faded. "Watch yourself out there."

Marti nodded. The door clicked shut behind her.

Twenty-five minutes later, the Crimson Crown's neon sign cut through Falls City's perpetual acid mist, red light pulsing across wet pavement. The 'C' in Crown flickered erratically, sending spasms of crimson across the brick fa-cade. Marti hunched lower in her seat, the car's defroster fighting a losing battle against her breath on the windows.

She'd chosen this spot with care – the shadow between streetlights, positioned behind a delivery van with a clear sight line to the club's entrance. Close enough to see every-thing, far enough to vanish if needed.

Rain pattered against the windshield in uneven bursts while Marti's fingers matched the rhythm on the steering wheel. First it was forty minutes. Now, an hour and a half. Ninety goddamn minutes waiting, watching the Crown's dark windows like they might suddenly confess their se-crets. The street had emptied except for a couple of beater cars and the occasional drunk weaving between puddles. Inside that bar, Serra lay dead. Waiting to be rescued. Re-turned.

A pair of headlights cut through the mist, their beams distorted by the rain. Marti straightened as Huff's car eased to the curb in front of the bar. She recognized it. But where the fuck were uniform? And Forensics?

He didn't exit immediately. Just sat there, a shad-ow behind rain-streaked glass, staring up at the Crown's neon-dead facade. His head swiveled slowly, scanning the street until he locked onto her car.

Huff stepped out into the rain without bothering to pull up his collar. Not a good sign. He bypassed the bar entirely, his gait heavy as he approached her car, water darkening his shoulders. Marti's gut twisted. She knew that walk. That slight hunch. The way his gaze fixed on the ground instead of looking ahead.

The passenger door creaked open. Cold air rushed in alongside the smell of wet wool and disappointment. Huff lowered himself into the seat with careful precision, like a man with invisible bruises. Water dripped from his hair onto the collar of his rumpled suit. He closed the door and stared through the windshield at the bar.

"Judge wouldn't sign," he said finally, voice scraping like shoes on gravel. His fingers worked at a loose thread on his coat sleeve. "Patterson is a night judge. An idiot. I'll try tomorrow, first thing. Benson is scheduled to be working."

The steering wheel creaked under Marti's grip. "Tomorrow is a lifetime," she said, each syllable brittle. Her thumbnail dug into the worn plastic.

"I'll stay here tonight and watch the place. Nothing in or out." Huff's jaw tightened, a muscle jumping beneath stubbled skin. His eyes remained fixed on the Crown. "I can't get in right now. Then tomorrow I can—"

"You know you can't." A laugh clawed its way up Marti's throat. "Christ, Huff. We both know without the warrant, it's too risky. You are in the wrong department. They'll call it overreach. Hold you and the department accountable, throw out any evidence found. Without the warrant, you've got nothing."

"Starova, I…This is a solid case. I can work with Missing Persons. We'll get her. There is no evidence they are going to move the body. I can work with MisPo and get eyes on the bar," Huff said as he jabbed is finger into the dash.

"I know you'll try." She twisted in her seat, knee bumping against the gearshift. "Huff, you're one of the last good guys. I know you'll do it right."

Huff's silence filled the car like smoke. He rubbed his thumb across his knuckles, eyes dropping to his lap.

"I have to try it the right way," Huff said, voice barely audible over the rain. "You know that."

"I do, man. I wanted Serra returned home to her mother." Her voice cracked, and she swallowed hard. "A kid who never made it home from the movies. What I wanted was to believe that doing things the right way still meant something in this city."

Huff's hand moved toward hers, then retreated. "It does, Starova. I just need a little time. Really nail the bastards. All of them. Not just Rufus, but whoever the fuck is letting him store a little girl's fucking body in a freezer."

Rain drummed harder on the roof. Both of them had faith in the man. Both knew faith counted for nothing in Falls City.

Huff exited with the careful precision of a man stepping around landmines. Marti tracked him in the rearview as he walked back to his car, each step deliberate, shoulders hunched against some invisible weight. His taillights flared red, then dwindled down the rain-slick street.

The Crimson Crown's neon sign sputtered overhead, washing her face in pulses of bloody light. On-off. Guilty-innocent. Justice-corruption.

Her phone sat heavy in her palm. She wanted to trust Huff. She did trust Huff. She just didn't trust the system he worked for.

She had to let Gardner know where his granddaughter was. No way was that little girl going to spend one more night in a goddamn freezer.

Chapter 37

Marti didn't hesitate. Pulled up Gardner's number on speed dial because she couldn't afford second thoughts right now.

He answered first ring. His voice bled anger through every word: "Starova."

"Kevin," she started. "I…I f—," Marti said, the words like ash in her mouth.

"Shut the fuck up."

It caught Marti off guard. What the fuck was his problem?

The silence stretched, charged with something terrible. Then:

"You unbelievable fuck. You stupid fucking fuck!" He didn't even take a breath. "My warehouse. Seventh and

Cross. Right the fuck now!" His demand for attendance was nothing she could deny him.

But he hung up before she could figure out what the fuck was going on.

Had Patterson told Gardner about the warrant request? Or Huff? What the fuck was going on?

Marti stared at her phone, Gardner's fury still ringing in her ears. Whatever had set him off, she was walking into a shitstorm without knowing why. She needed backup. Not the kind that carried guns, but the kind that carried facts.

She scrolled to Lori's number.

"Marti? It's almost midnight—"

"I need you to meet me. Now." Marti pulled away from the curb, leaving the Crimson Crown's neon glow in her rearview mirror. "Gardner just called. He's pissed about something, wants me at his warehouse immediately."

"What happened? Did the police—"

"Huff can't do anything tonight. Tomorrow. I don't know what the fuck is going on. But whatever's going down, I need all our evidence on Rufus. Everything, the insurance files, the video analysis, the timeline, the photos. All of it."

A pause. Then Lori's voice, suddenly alert: "You think he knows about Serra?"

"I think I'm about to find out. Can you get to the office and grab everything? I'll pick you up in fifteen."

"Already moving."

Marti ended the call and pressed harder on the accelerator. Whatever game Gardner was playing, she wasn't walking in defenseless.

In fifteen minutes, Marti pulled up to the curb where Lori was standing in the rain. Lori hesitated for a moment while Marti leaned over and opened the car door with twitchy fingers and nerves fried on Shadow fumes.

"We should call detective Huff," Lori said.

Marti snorted so hard it hurt. "And tell them what? A drug lord called me to his warehouse because he doesn't need your bullshit jurisdictional policy? Huff needs time to establish his reason for the warrant, that's all."

"But—"

"He'll kill us both if I don't show," Marti snapped.

That shut Lori up long enough for Lori to do up her seatbelt. Then:

"If I have to die, I'm glad it will be with you," Lori said, hand tight around Marti's wrist.

"Nope." Marti didn't yell, just peeled Lori off as if someone defusing a bomb strapped with emotional guilt instead of wires and C4. "Not dying."

Marti peeled around a corner, honked for no reason, and swore. "If shit goes sideways…"

"Then I run," Lori promised, breath warm near Marti's cheek now, heartbeat visible just beneath thin skin at her throat. Her eyes were wide but steady this time, electrified by fear and fury both.

Marti looked at those eyes for three full seconds longer than she should've. Then nodded once.

"Good," she growled low in her throat as heat curled under sternum-level panic like kindling daring someone to light it. "You stay behind me, you do exactly what I say."

The engine growled and everything shifted.

The city was a wet snarl of steel and glass, rain coming down like someone upstairs was pissed off for real. Neon signs bled color over the asphalt, smeared and twitching like a dying pulse. Marti's wipers fought a losing battle against the storm as their car nudged deeper into the city's industrial rot.

Lori sat stiff beside her, chewing on her bottom lip like she was starving. Her fingers gripped her phone so tight Marti thought it might snap. The screen glowed faint in the dark, playing hellish reruns: Rufus dragging Serra into a shadowed alley. Serra's body cooling somewhere behind them, all wide eyes and no breath.

"You okay?" Marti asked, which was bullshit, because of course she wasn't.

"I've seen worse," Lori lied. Her voice cracked on "worse."

Marti didn't push. She cracked her window instead and lit a cigarette with shaking hands she pretended were steady. Smoke curled around her mouth like a secret she didn't want to keep anymore. "We need to be civil enough not to get our asses capped," she muttered. "Gardner's got a temper and a trigger finger."

"I can be civil," Lori said, and it sounded like both a promise and a prayer.

A hard right onto an unmarked road swallowed them whole. Whatever passed for streetlights here flickered more than they glowed; dying sodium bulbs bleeding piss-yellow halos across weed-choked pavement. Warehouse hulks loomed like sleeping giants that never woke up sober.

"Jesus," Lori breathed, squinting through the windshield at the industrial graveyard ahead.

"Don't invoke Jesus," Marti said around her cigarette. "He stopped showing up to these neighborhoods a long time ago."

The car bounced over potholes deep enough to swallow lesser vehicles whole. Something crunched under them: glass or bones or maybe just yesterday's bad decisions. Lori made a noise in her throat, not fear exactly, but something adjacent.

Marti gave her a sideways glance. "Y'know there are better ways to chase an orgasm than following me into Gardner's den."

Lori shot her a look that might've been scandalized if it weren't also aroused. "You offering alternatives?"

"Later," Marti said. "Assuming we're still breathing."

The warehouse appeared out of the gloom as if summoned: tall, mean-looking, and flanked by six glossy black cars lined up like undertakers at a mob funeral.

"Looks like everyone showed up for the fucking intervention," Marti murmured.

Lori's breathing turned ragged; shallow little hits barely enough to keep oxygen flowing to that bright brain of hers. Her hands trembled now, not from cold, and her shoulders were square despite it. Brave girl.

Marti's chest twisted in ways cigarettes couldn't solve. She killed the engine. Silence pressed in except for rain hammering on metal overhead.

She took one last drag, then flicked the butt out into the storm where it sizzled against concrete like punctuation at the end of a bad sentence.

"You ready?" she asked, even though she already knew.

Lori swallowed once, hard, and nodded without speaking.

Marti opened her door with that same calm she wore when facing down junkies with knives or cops with lies caught between their teeth. Every instinct screamed turn back, but she'd never been good at listening to herself when self-preservation was involved.

They stepped out into the rain together; wet hair plastering itself across foreheads and cheeks as if the universe was trying to hide their faces for them.

Lori hesitated for half a breath before stepping closer than necessary, shoulder brushing Marti's arm like armor shaped from skin and want.

Marti didn't flinch away.

Her palm slipped low against Lori's back, hot through soaked fabric, as they approached the looming doors ahead.

"Stay close," she said softly but sharp enough to cut glass. "Keep your mouth shut unless you're bleeding or it's something I need to hear."

"What if I see something?"

Marti gave her a sideways smile that didn't reach her eyes but damn near melted Lori anyway.

"If you witness nothing," she said, "you've got nothing to confess."

The warehouse gaped open like a broken jaw, swallowing them whole the second they stepped inside. Smelled like wet concrete and the kind of fear that had fangs: old blood, piss, maybe regret. Fluorescent lights flickered overhead, buzzing like pissed-off hornets. Broken windows blinked against the dark; some boarded up, some just jagged holes pretending to be eyes. A graveyard of chairs huddled in one corner as if they'd witnessed too much and didn't want to talk about it.

Marti could hear the low grown of someone already at Gardner's mercy.

Chapter 38

"Playtime's over, asshole," Gardner said, voice slick as oil and twice as flammable. He stood dead center, brown eyes burning holes through her as if he could tunnel into whatever secrets she might be hiding behind her bone structure.

Henchmen flanked him: jittery meatheads trying to look casual about the violence vibrating under their skin.

Marti stopped three feet from him. Enough space for movement if it came to that. Not enough to run.

Gardner's lip curled. "Thought you could keep me in the fucking dark about my granddaughter?"

"Kevin, I—"

"Save it." His hand sliced the air. The sound alone shut her up better than a muzzle.

"I saw the damn footage," he growled. "I know Kane's behind this."

"Kane? Kane didn't—" Marti started again, but his fist was already flying.

No warning, no buildup. Just fury and knuckles straight into her gut so hard she folded like wet cardboard around it.

Her lungs forgot how to breathe for a second. She doubled over with an ugly gasp as two goons grabbed her arms and yanked her upright again. Another goon had grabbed Lori by the arm. Marti could see her wince.

"Let Lori go," she rasped, tasting bile and Shadow withdrawal at the back of her throat. "She won't say anything."

Gardner glanced sideways at Lori. He gave a bored little nod as if letting her live was barely worth the calories. One of his men unhooked his hand from Lori's arm.

Lori stumbled forward on high-alert legs but stayed quiet, smart girl, and pressed close enough that Marti felt every tremble leaking off her body like static discharge.

"Stick close," Marti told her, voice shredded raw. "Eyes down unless you're ready to scream or stab."

Lori nodded once and stared hard at the cracked concrete as if it held all life's answers, just needing someone desperate enough to look for them.

Cue dramatic entrance: more henchmen dragging something limp and bloody between them like garbage they weren't paid enough to carry carefully.

It was Kane.

Even through split lips and swollen eye sockets, Marti recognized him. She smiled a little because the bastard deserved worse.

"Kane," Gardner hissed as if saying his name gave him indigestion. "You thought you could fuck with my family?"

Kane's head dangled from his neck as if it wasn't fully attached anymore. He blinked up through blood-crusted lashes and tried for words.

"I didn't—"

Another fist shut him up before he got past the contraction.

Marti twisted against the hands holding her still. "Gardner," she snapped through clenched teeth. "Listen to me. Kane didn't take Serra."

"You hate Kane." Gardner's brow scrunched up as if he actually couldn't compute logic with that much testosterone in his bloodstream. "Why are you protecting that little shit?"

"I'm not protecting him." Her chest burned every time she tried to breathe around it all; pain and panic and old guilt clawing their way up against each other in her throat. "I'm telling you he didn't do it. I have—"

The back of a hand shut her up. Gardner stepped closer until she could smell dried sweat under designer cologne: expensive rage in a bottle. "Explain the goddamn video then!"

"A video? I don't—," Marti said, voice cracking despite herself.

"Exactly!" Gardner thundered. "You didn't send me the fucking video of my Serra being kidnapped by this piece of shit! I need him to tell me where she is."

"I try tell," Kane mumbled through blood.

Marti hesitated just long enough for silence to punch its own kind of hole in the room before finishing the sentence that gutted her every time:

"We found Serra. Us. Lori and I. Got pictures. Got video. Got the real video. Even called the cops."

Gardner froze mid-breath. A woman, Francesca, wailed in the background.

"She's dead," Marti said. No drama now, just truth sharpened down into a fist into her ribs.

"You don't need to hit m—"

The back of Gardner's hand silenced her, murder painted across his face: a Rorschach test of grief gone feral.

He drove his fist into Marti's jaw without hesitation or ceremony.

Pain ripped sideways through her skull as something cracked; a tooth? Her dignity? She hit the floor along with half a mouthful of blood.

Marti laughed once, a small thing choked between pain and pride, and mumbled through swollen lips: "Always the face."

Lori flinched at the spray of red across concrete near her boots but still didn't look up.

Good girl.

Stay down. Stay quiet.

Marti spat another glob of blood onto the floor because she'd rather lose teeth than give Gardner anything real to chew on, and because maybe if Lori saw how bad things could get, she'd finally stop looking at Marti as if she was still worth saving.

"Let me fucking show you," Marti said, her voice shredded raw and barely audible through bruised lips. "We have proof. Real goddamn proof."

Gardner scowled as if he'd just sniffed a lie, then flicked his fingers. A silent order. His men unclenched their fists from her arms and stepped back.

Marti winced as she rubbed her jaw, teeth buzzing like metal under pressure. She reached into her jacket slow enough to make a point but fast enough to piss someone off and pulled out her phone, gun glinting right behind it.

She smirked at Gardner. "Your boys frisk like prom dates."

"Fucking get on with it," Gardner snapped, voice slicing the air like a blade. He didn't flinch at Marti's presence or whatever haunted fire she dragged along behind her.

Marti didn't flinch either. She thumbed open her phone with hands crusted in blood and fingerprints, the screen smeared like it had been through hell—and maybe it had.

"Photos of Serra," she said. Then, quietly, to Francesca: "Don't look."

Her voice cracked softer than before—like an apology wrapped in razors. Like she wished she could take the world back five minutes before it broke.

"Remember her smile, not this." She turned toward Gardner, eyes hollow but steady. "Have one of your goons take a look. You'll get digital copies later. Lori's got every-thing catalogued."

One of Gardner's muscleheads stepped up like he'd rather walk into traffic. He took one glance—and recoiled like someone had shoved roadkill under his nose. His face collapsed around itself.

Gardner clocked him. So did Francesca, fists curling into nothing with nowhere to go.

The man didn't speak, which somehow said too fucking much.

Then Gardner moved, snapping his head toward Kane like an animal scenting blood. "You did this!" he bellowed, storming toward the detective tied to his chair like broken furniture waiting for trash day.

"No!" Marti lunged between them without thinking, ribs screaming and the sharp tang of blood coating her tongue again. "It wasn't Kane!"

Gardner's gun came up like a question nobody wanted answered.

"Then who?" His voice cracked, fury twisted around grief until neither could stand on their own.

Marti froze for half a second—not because she didn't know, but because saying it out loud meant letting go of revenge she'd been nursing like an old wound.

"Rufus Montgomery," she spat. Every syllable dripped venom and bile and old rage left out in the sun too long. "Some walking stain who thought playing gangster made his dick bigger."

Her whole body was trembling now—not fear. Fuck fear. Rage this old came fossilized.

"He's the one who sent the video," Gardner said as he snapped his fingers and some thugs peeled away into the dark while new ones appeared from nowhere like roaches with better suits.

"Can I see?" Marti asked.

Gardner spun on her like a bomb going off. "No you can't fucking see! This isn't entertainment, Serra wasn't a fucking sideshow!"

Marti didn't blink at the scream. "We've got Rufus on footage dragging Serra from an ATM," she said calmly—too calmly for how fucked everything was.

Gardner's eyes narrowed, sharp as broken glass under bare feet. "I've got footage too," he growled, fishing out his phone like he meant to bludgeon someone with it. "And mine shows Kane taking her."

"It's fake," Marti shot back before he could blink wrong. "We pulled ours directly from the bank servers. Lori worked her magic. We've got metadata. Proof colder than your dealer's heart."

She stepped forward slowly, careful not to spook him. Or herself.

"Kane's not your guy," she whispered, an edge of pleading cracking under her words. "Not for this."

Gardner didn't move, but his hand tightened on the trigger like it was all that tethered him to reality.

The silence hit hard and wide.

Then he pulled it anyway.

Chapter 39

Blood spilled out from under Kane like ink across cement. Venous red against gray floors that didn't give a fuck about pain or guilt or justice. Crimson bloomed from his thigh in slow motion as if gravity couldn't keep up with how many ways he'd bled for this already.

He hissed hard through gritted teeth. The only sound other than a gurgle he was capable of making right now.

Marti didn't even flinch at the gunshot. She just spoke over it with dead calm: "The Crimson Crown."

Everything stopped moving inside that moment.

"That's where Serra is," she said flatly. "Back freezer."

Gardner swayed—not much—but enough that anyone watching would know it hit home.

Behind him Francesca let out something fragile enough to break glass—a gasp tangled with disbelief and grief that hadn't found its shape yet.

"I called a detective I trust," Marti went on, keeping her eyes fixed on Kane like they were tethered by threads no one else could see. "He couldn't get a warrant today—bullshit about insufficient proof or internal politics—but maybe tomorrow." She exhaled through clenched teeth. "Crimson Crown's on Spark Street near East 9th. Good guy, but he's watching the place. Keeping a vigil." She hoped adding that would keep Huff alive.

That cracked something open.

"We'll get her!" one of Gardner's guys barked before bolting toward the shadows with three more in tow—boots pounding echoes into concrete as they vanished toward vengeance or ruin or both.

"I didn't give my footage to the cops," Marti added without apology. "They can haul their asses over if they want it legit." Her gaze cut sharply toward Lori now. "Eyes down."

She dove into Lori's jacket pocket without warning—familiar as owning it—and yanked out her holo-tab like she'd just pulled a knife from under her thigh holster.

"Here." She slammed it into Gardner's hands hard enough to make it count. Bright screen flickered awake without shame or softness.

ATM footage rolled grainy and raw across the display: Serra stepping up to use the machine—and then Rufus Montgomery ghosting into frame like some slasher-flick fucker under bad lighting and worse intentions. A hand over Serra's mouth so fast it made you choke—and then gone again into shadow as her legs kicked wildly above ground level.

"That," Marti bit out between clenched molars, "is what happened."

Gardner stared blankly at the screen before dragging his own phone out again and stabbing at it until another video played—the same setting but now Kane under the hood instead of Rufus.

"Which goddamn version is real?" he demanded through gritted teeth that wanted to crack bone instead of words.

Marti swallowed air that made no promises and held out his phone beside hers with trembling fingers that wouldn't stay still even if someone paid them off to behave.

"Look here," she murmured fast and sharp. "See how fat the attacker's hands are? Compare them to Kane's—they don't match." Her voice cracked sideways before catching itself again. "Let Lori run your clip through our software—"

"Fuck your software!" Gardner barked. "Why set Kane up?"

"I don't know!" She screamed back without meaning to—then caught herself halfway through breathless panic and reeled everything back down into something rougher than calmness should be allowed to feel. "Kane is Rufus's handler—a registered informant protector per official channels." Her throat went dry again as she glanced at Kane bleeding beside them all over someone else's mess.

"We've got papers filed just days after Serra disappeared," Marti said miserably, staring at a man whose body might not last long enough for truth to do any good at all.

"I think Rufus figured out I was onto him, that I'd found pieces, and panicked," Marti said quietly now, eyes shrinking inward around memory and dread both lighting up behind them at once. "So he framed Kane thinking I'd fall for it."

"When we searched Rufus's place?" Lori asked suddenly from nowhere.

Everyone turned because everyone had forgotten she existed for a moment there in all that rage and bloodlust and noise.

Marti froze mid-thought and swore loudly enough to peel paint off walls.

"Oh fuckfuckfuck... yeah." Her brows furrowed deep enough to drown in as realization sank claws beneath skin already paper-thin from damage done earlier tonight, or longer ago than that depending on which trauma you measured time by these days.

"He had rigged alarms—I must've triggered something when I searched his apartment looking for Serra," Marti rasped out past bloody lips starting to stick together now from dehydration and too many lies unspoken until tonight exploded them loose everywhere all at once.

"He hoped I'd bite down hard enough not to ask questions." Her laugh came jagged and humorless.

"He helped frame me five years ago too," she added bitterly then didn't stop once she'd started bleeding truth aloud again.

"Altered video showed me where Kane really was when another little girl died," she whispered hoarse now despite herself.

"Kane knew the truth would end his career so he let Rufus tank me instead. They're still working together, Insurance scams using doctored surveillance feeds."

She paused only long enough to feel bile stir behind her tongue.

"One of their payoffs went straight to Crimson Crown."

She swallowed hard. "Maybe... maybe Rufus rented storage there—for Serra."

Everything inside her twisted violently sideways but kept standing somehow because someone had to say these things aloud even if they tasted worse than death going down.

Gardner stiffened visibly.

Something changed behind his eyes—not rage anymore. Recognition.

Calculations finding their answers written in blood. Then...

Gun met skull with an ugly crunch that echoed forever.

Kane collapsed instantly. Dead weight hitting cement. Gardner followed with a vicious kick to his ribs even though Kane wasn't moving anymore.

"Tell me," he growled, rounding on Marti as if she'd lit the match that burned down his life. "How long has that fuck known my granddaughter was dead?"

Marti tried not to recoil but something inside broke anyway.

"The day after, I think," she whispered, voice raw and fraying around the edges. Her legs buckled beneath her weight and she grabbed Lori without thinking, pure reflex, to keep from folding into herself entirely.

There was a pile of chairs off near the wall as if someone expected people might need places to collapse eventually. Marti yanked two free and shoved one behind Lori before falling into hers as if she'd spiral straight through reality itself if she didn't sit now.

Lori sat beside her silently shaking, knuckles white on her thighs and chest rising too fast for comfort.

Marti leaned toward Gardner slightly, not close enough for threat but close enough for truth.

"We'll stay put," she said quietly. "Out of your way. Trust me, Kevin. I found Henry for you, didn't I? I let the fucker shoot me and never said anything to anyone about it. You owe me."

It wasn't cowardice.

It was survival masquerading as surrender; and Gardner knew it.

"Fine," Gardner grunted. No conviction, just fatigue dressed as authority. "But you try anything, anything, and I will put you down."

Marti didn't argue. She didn't even look at him. Her fingers were digging for her lighter like it was a lifeline and not a poor excuse for self-control. "Can I smoke?"

He nodded.

The flame caught, the tip glowed, and Marti inhaled like salvation came in filter-form. She tilted the cigarette away from Lori so the smoke wouldn't hit her directly; it felt absurd, considering the blood on the floor and the stink of betrayal in the air.

She blew a soft stream toward her boots instead. "It's gonna be okay," she murmured, voice low enough to pretend none of this was happening. "Just stay close."

Lori leaned in, barely touching but warm beside her as if a tremor waited to bloom into an earthquake. "Alright," she whispered, and it broke Marti a little more.

Marti was on her second cigarette when the warehouse door slammed open.

Rufus stumbled inside as if guilt had animated his limbs, flanked by two men who looked like they'd failed out of goon school but passed with flying colors in intimidation. His eyes locked on Kane first: slumped over and half-conscious. Then they scraped across to Marti as if he'd seen a ghost that hated him back.

The shit finally figured it out, Marti thought.

"They're setting me up!" he yelped, voice cracking under its own weight. "They're setting me up!"

"No one gives a fuck," Gardner snapped before squeezing off a shot that whizzed past Rufus's ear close enough to singe regret into his skin.

Rufus shut up.

If his pants had been dry before, they weren't now. The smell hit all at once: piss and panic mixing into something sharper than blood.

One of the hired gorillas dragged over a chair. The screeching legs against concrete cut through bone. He shoved Rufus into it before knotting a rope around his waist. Limbs free but locked in place, as if Gardner wanted him capable of squirming when things got bad.

Marti stood, cigarette dangling from her lips as she approached the two assholes who'd made sure her life went up in smoke.

"I want five minutes," she said without turning back. Her voice didn't raise.

Gardner nodded once before correcting himself. "Two," he growled.

Fair enough.

Chapter 40

Marti flicked ash onto the floor and stalked forward until she stood toe-to-toe with memory and failure incarnate. Kane looked bad and it made her feel good: blood dried under his nostrils, eyelids fluttering as if they were trying to decide whether waking up was worth it.

And Rufus, fucking Rufus, just frozen beneath a layer of flop sweat, as if he still had the motherfucker, hope.

"What the fuck did you do to me?" Marti asked Kane first because if there was anything left inside him worth reaching for, she needed to know before she killed it off.

He blinked at her as if she'd spoken another language.

So she turned on Rufus instead, the real snake here, and let her fury do the talking.

"I saw it," she said. "The Gomes video? I saw the god-damn original file."

Rufus swallowed but said nothing.

"I wasn't even fucking there." Her voice spiked with disbelief more than rage. "Kane let Gomes escape, not me! You edited me into it. You altered the fucking footage to make it look like I screwed up!"

She flicked the cigarette at his feet; it sizzled on the piss-soaked concrete. She stepped closer until there wasn't enough space between them for lies anymore.

"You goddamn fucker," she hissed through clenched teeth, face inches from his. "You set me up... You piece of shit... Why? Was that your price for getting ahead? Throwing me under a bus while Kane jerked himself off behind closed doors?"

Kane stirred then, a groan more than words, but it drew Marti's attention anyway. She spun toward him, fury still red-hot in her throat.

"You ruined me! You took everything!" Her fists clenched until her nails bit into flesh; that pain helped her stand upright longer than she should've been able to.

Kane flinched, not from her voice but as if some part of reality had clicked back into place inside his busted skull. His lips moved uselessly; whatever apology or denial he tried got lost somewhere on its way out and came instead as a vague gurgle that could've just been blood choking back clarity.

Marti let out a shaky breath that wasn't quite surrender and wasn't quite relief either. She turned again toward Rufus because someone had to answer for this shitshow and she was tired of screaming into silence.

Her voice cracked, betrayal slicing through steel like acid through silk. "Why would you help him destroy me? What did you get out of this? A raise? A blowjob? Some handshake promise no one intends to keep?"

Rufus didn't speak, not really, but something curled at the edges of his pocked face: not fear or shame or even regret... just satisfaction laced with malice between yellowing teeth.

It looked an awful lot like victory.

"Five grand," Rufus sneered, spitting the words at her like they tasted foul. "That's all Kane gave me to fake the Gomes video. Five crisp to fuck your career right into the dirt. Plus my sweet gig at SecureGuard. Steady income for every video I cleaned up for him. Insurance claims, evidence tampering, whatever he needed. Without worrying about other snooping IT geeks watching over my shoulder. Been making bank off his cases for years." His eyes glittered with malice. "And it was worth every goddamn cent to watch you fall apart."

Marti stared at him, her mind racing through possibilities, trying to understand what she'd done to earn this level of hatred. "Why?" The word came out raw. "Why me specifically?"

Rufus's grin widened, showing too many teeth. "You don't even remember, do you? Figures. Just another day at the office for Detective Starova." He leaned forward, savoring the moment. "Jeb Montgomery. Ring any bells?"

The name sounded vague, like a childhood tune someone was humming off key. She did remember, barely. A domestic violence call that escalated. The girlfriend dead, the boyfriend covered in her blood, claiming it was an accident. Open and shut case.

"You didn't even try to understand," Rufus went on. "Didn't care that she was cheating on him, threatening to drain him dry. You just cuffed him and walked away like he was some rabid dog."

Marti's gaze went flat, voice colder than steel. "I arrested a fucking animal, Rufus. He beat a woman to death with his hands. That wasn't heartbreak. That was murder."

"You don't know what really happened!" Rufus barked, voice cracking. "You never looked deeper—"

"I didn't have to."

Marti leaned in, voice low but brutal. "She had twenty-three broken bones. Her jaw was shattered. He hit her until her face stopped being a face. I saw what he did. I stood over her body while he sat in the next room with her blood under his nails, crying about how she made him do it."

"But, but..." His voice dropped to a whisper, more dangerous than his shouting. "My parents never recovered. Dad started drinking again after fifteen years sober. Mom... Christ, she wouldn't even say Jeb's name after the trial. We went from Sunday dinners and birthday parties to nothing. Complete fucking silence. All because you arrested Jeb."

"You're lucky I didn't shoot the fucker," Marti said, staring into the face of a man who didn't see the truth.

Rufus's eyes glittered with unshed tears of rage. "Three years later, he hanged himself in his cell. Couldn't live in a fucking cage. So when Kane offered me five grand to fuck with some video evidence, and it turned out to be your case..." Rufus shrugged, but his hands were shaking. "It felt like Christmas morning. Finally, a chance to make you feel what my family felt. You deserved it."

The words detonated inside her skull like a grenade going off. Everything she'd believed about herself, every sleepless night she'd spent blaming herself for the Gomes escape, every drink she'd used to drown the guilt, every drug. All of it based on this twisted fuck's revenge fantasy for a case she'd barely remembered.

"You piece of shit!" The scream tore from her throat, raw and primal. She lunged forward, her fist connecting with his jaw so hard the impact shot up her arm like lightning. His head snapped back, blood spattering from his split lip.

"Five years!" She hit him again, this time in the gut, and he doubled over as much as the restraints would allow. "Five fucking years I blamed myself! I thought I failed that girl, thought I wasn't good enough, wasn't fast enough—"

Another punch, catching him in the ribs. He wheezed, gasping for air.

"You destroyed me for a case I worked right! A case where your psycho brother killed an innocent woman!" Her voice cracked with fury and anguish. "You want to know what I remember now? I remember her face. Twenty-two years old. He beat her skull in because she wanted to leave him. And you, you sick fuck, you made me think I was the monster."

She grabbed him by the hair, yanking his head up to meet her eyes. "How many bottles did I empty thinking it was my fault? How many nights did I lie awake wondering what I could have done different? You didn't just fake evidence, you made me hate myself."

Her voice dropped to a whisper more terrifying than her screams. "I should kill you right now."

From the sidelines, Lori moved, but too slow. "Marti, no."

Gardner stepped in as if he'd been waiting his whole life for this moment. He grabbed Rufus by the wrist and yanked his arm back with a twist so brutal it sounded like wet branches snapping in half. Something tore. The radius bone didn't just break: it tore through skin, white and slick and glistening red.

Rufus screamed, high-pitched and pathetic, and not even Marti's fury could make her ignore the grotesque beauty of it.

Gardner grinned, one hand still clamped on Rufus's mangled arm. "Heard you liked watching people suffer," he said. "Thought I'd return the opportunity."

Marti stalked forward, her boots loud against tile smeared with blood and sweat. Rufus tried to curl in on himself, sobbing through clenched teeth.

She crouched beside him, close enough to smell the panic peeling off him like old paint.

"This still funny to you?" she asked, gun resting against her thigh like a sleeping animal ready to wake up mean.

Gardner twisted again.

The chair creaked under Rufus's weight as he bucked and screamed.

"Stop!" Lori's voice cut across the room, but there was no authority left in it; just raw fear straining at the edges. "Marti, please!"

Rufus wasn't talking anymore. Just whimpering between snot-choked breaths, eyes rolling as if maybe this wasn't real and would vanish if he blinked hard enough.

Marti raised the gun.

She didn't think about it; her body moved as if vengeance had become muscle memory after all these years of rot and silence and pretending justice still existed somewhere beyond a badge or bullet.

"Please." Lori again, closer now, trembling hand reaching toward something neither of them could name.

Marti froze with her finger curled around the trigger like a lover's neck.

Rufus deserved it. Kane too. Dying would be mercy next to what was coming from Gardner, but Marti wasn't looking for mercy anymore.

Her vision shimmered at the edges; rage overloaded her system like static crashing through glass. And underneath it: Lori's voice like wind slipping beneath a locked door. Just breath and hope wrapped in one last plea.

She closed her eyes.

Fuck. Fucking consequences.

The safety clicked back into place louder than thunder in that silent room.

Marti shoved the gun into its holster and stepped back as if it burned her skin to walk away from him breathing.

"Jesus Christ," Lori breathed out, swallowing relief like it might choke her.

Marti dropped into the nearest chair without grace, legs going loose beneath her as if deciding not to kill someone had drained every volt of current from her bones.

She wasn't crying, but something sharp twisted behind her ribs anyway.

"You didn't do it," Lori whispered, less awe than disbelief laced around gratitude she didn't know how to say aloud yet.

And Marti just stared ahead, silent and shaking, as everything she hadn't done threatened to break her harder than anything she ever had.

"Are we good now?" Marti asked, voice sandpaper-rough, like she'd gargling glass and guilt.

Gardner didn't look up, just gave a curt nod, eyes somewhere past her shoulder. "Thanks for finding my granddaughter. You can go."

Marti turned, but something glinted near her boot: white against the blood-dark concrete. She crouched, fingers closing around it.

Her tooth.

She held it up between thumb and forefinger, squinting like it might still be useful. "Dental work goes on your bill," she muttered.

Gardner barely blinked. "Fair enough."

"Expect padding."

He sighed as if he'd made peace with the woman. "Wouldn't have it any other way."

They left him there. Marti and Lori stepped into the chaos-stained rain, survivors of some war no one would write songs about. The warehouse moaned behind them; screams slithered through cracked windows like ghosts that hadn't realized they were dead yet.

Outside, the car sat where they'd left it, untouched. A shitty little miracle covered in grime and secondhand regret. Marti slid into the driver's seat, lit a cigarette with shaking hands, and cracked the window: just enough to keep from suffocating.

She didn't start the engine yet.

Silence stretched between them, thick as dried blood. Neither said anything for a long time.

Then Lori spoke first, voice low as if she was worried talking too loud might shatter something inside them both. "You okay?"

Marti let out a sound that wasn't quite a laugh and wasn't quite human. "Define 'okay.' You?"

Lori turned toward her, eyes rimmed red but not crying anymore, not visibly anyway. "I don't know if I'll ever be okay again," she said, each word shaped like walking barefoot over broken glass. "But... we're alive. That has to mean something."

Marti took a long drag and stared at the dashboard as if it were about to answer for God. "Sure," she said. "Alive means something."

Another beat passed before she flicked the key forward and let the engine rumble awake beneath them.

City lights smeared across the windshield as they drove: acid-colored halos bleeding through fog and filth. Sirens wailed somewhere distant, threading between buildings like wolves on heat trails. The kind of music this city never stopped playing: despair in minor keys with backup vocals from the damned.

Marti followed the road from instinct more than intention, street after street folding behind them like pages in a book she didn't want to read anymore.

Then Lori asked it, the question hanging since they stepped out of that hellhole.

"Where do we go from here?"

Marti didn't answer right away. Her gaze drifted to a woman passed out on a bench beneath a billboard advertising hope in pastel colors: some rehab center run by people who'd never felt real withdrawal claw through their veins at 3AM.

"Forward," Marti said.

It tasted like rust in her mouth.

That one word. Fuck. It almost undid her more than any bullet could've hit home.

A moment passed before Lori reached over: just fingertips on Marti's thigh, light but enough to make Marti tense like prey caught under someone's boot.

Marti glanced over at her and saw not just bruises or trauma or ash but someone still breathing in all the ways that counted. Someone who knew what she'd done in that warehouse, and what she hadn't, and stayed anyway.

She wanted to kiss her then, hard and selfish, lips bruised from more than violence. She didn't move. Didn't let herself tip over that edge yet.

Instead, she gave a half-smile that felt more real than anything had in weeks and tapped ash out the window onto streets that deserved worse than cigarettes and lies tossed their way.

"Yeah," Marti said. "Fucking forward."

* * *

The motel room smelled like mildew and broken promises. Forty dollars cash, no questions asked, the kind of place where screams got ignored and blood washed out easy if you knew which detergent to use.

Marti sat on the edge of the bed, hands shaking as she tried to light a cigarette. Third match finally caught. The flame danced, throwing shadows that looked too much like Kane's face in those final moments. Not when he died, but when he realized he would.

"Let me see," Lori said, kneeling in front of her.

"It's nothing."

"Bullshit." Lori's fingers were gentle as they lifted Marti's shirt, revealing bruises already blooming purple-black across her ribs. Marti smiled. "Jesus, Marti. Where's your tooth?"

"Front left pocket." Something about the way Lori's breath hitched made it feel like a perfectly safe place for a tooth.

Lori disappeared into the bathroom and Marti sent Huff a message. Okay? Simple. Had to find out if he was still alive.

Lori came back with a threadbare towel soaked in luke-warm water. She cleaned the blood from Marti's split lip, her knuckles, the scratch marks on her throat. Each touch deliberate, careful, like she was handling something that might shatter.

"They're dead," Lori said finally. Not a question.

"Yeah."

"Good."

The word hung between them, heavy as a confession. Lori's hand stilled against Marti's cheek.

"Rufus killed Serra," Marti said. "Kane protected him. There was no way we could have stopped Gardner." She took a long drag, exhaled smoke that tasted like copper and regret. "Even if we could have had the arrested, state would've given them both the needle anyway, if they'd lived long enough to see trial."

"Gardner—"

"Did what he does." Marti's laugh was hollow, scraping. "Funny thing about that man. Sometimes he wears a three-thousand-dollar suit to pretend he's better than all the other killers. But he still knows exactly where to put the bullets."

Marti's phone buzzed. Yes. He was okay.

Lori stood, moved to the window. Outside, neon bled through rain-slicked glass, painting her profile in shades of pink and blue. Beautiful and dangerous, like everything else in this godforsaken city.

"We can't tell anyone," she said.

"Especially not the cops." Marti stubbed out her cigarette in an ashtray already overflowing with someone else's sins. "Besides, we didn't see anything. Just heard loud noises. Gun shots. Maybe fireworks. End of story."

Lori turned back, something unreadable in her eyes. "You think we're safe now?"

Marti wanted to lie. Wanted to promise her something better than this cheap room and the taste of violence still coating their tongues. Instead, she held out her hand.

"Come here."

Lori crossed the room, let Marti pull her down onto the bed. They lay there fully clothed, Lori's head on Marti's chest, listening to each other breathe. Outside, sirens wailed their eternal song. Inside, two women who'd seen too much held each other like drowning things, waiting for dawn or death, whichever came first.

Chapter 41

Rain slammed down like it had a vendetta. Bigger than just a weather pattern, as if the city itself was grieving, angry, and too goddamn tired to pretend otherwise. Umbrellas were a joke. Black fabric strained and snapped in the wind, doing about as much good as tissue paper in a flood.

Marti stood just shy of the burial canopy, soaked to the thighs despite the umbrella she barely bothered holding anymore. Lori leaned into her, pressing closer every time someone shifted behind them. The rest of Falls City's who's-who lined up in neat rows like obedient mourners: the mayor with her fake solemnity, Police Chief Franklin giving all the right pained expressions for the cameras that weren't even there. And of course Francesca Stanfield and her father, and Kevin Gardner. They were the only ones who looked like they might actually tear out their hearts and toss them into the grave along with Serra.

But yeah. Everyone pretended not to notice the cluster of drug lords watching from under their matching black coats, sunglasses on even though it was darker than a crypt under tree cover.

"Think they're here to repent?" Lori asked, her lips moving against the wet air more than Marti's ear. A corner-of-the-mouth smirk played behind the words, even if her eyes were pure steel.

Marti stared at the casket getting lowered into mud thick enough to swallow secrets whole. She let out a slow breath she didn't bother hiding.

"They're not here for peace," she said, voice flat as rainwater pooling around her boots. "They're here because they're scared. Serra should've been off-limits; rivals or not, nobody touches children. So now they're wondering whose kid is next."

Lori hummed, barely audible under the drumming rain. "Still feels theatrical."

"Everything's theatrical in this city," Marti replied. "Even grief comes with stage directions."

The words came out automatic, but something twisted in her gut as she said them. Stage directions. Like the ones Kane had written for her five years ago, casting her as the fuckup who let Gomes escape. She'd played that role so well she'd forgotten it was fiction. The Gomes case. Christ, she could still see that little girl's face sometimes when she closed her eyes. Heart gone. How the fuck does even that happen? For five years, Marti had carried the weight of thinking she'd failed Sabrina Kogoya. Her parents. Herself.

Except she hadn't. The truth sat in her chest like broken glass: sharp, painful, impossible to ignore. Kane had Rufus edit him out and her into that video like she was nothing more than pixels to be rearranged. Five grand to Rufus, and her whole life became a lie she'd been living without knowing it.

A woman sobbed behind them, raw and ugly, the kind that grabs you by the throat whether you want it or not. Francesca was folded in on herself as if her spine had given up trying to hold her together. Her father held her upright with both hands on either arm, but it wasn't doing much good. She wasn't going to make it through this clean.

Maybe not at all.

Marti turned away before she could feel anything dangerous. Empathy was a slippery slope, and she'd already slid down further than she meant to when Gardner called to invite her to the funeral.

The crowd began to fall apart soon after; umbrellas turning away like black petals shirking from light, leaving behind soggy footprints and silence that felt louder than any sermon.

Gardner approached as if his bones had forgotten how to walk without breaking somewhere inside him. His jaw was tight enough to crack teeth. And his eyes; his eyes made Marti want another cigarette and six more feet of distance between them.

Before he could speak, Lori stepped back, gave space, which made Marti almost love her again for getting it.

"Thanks," Gardner said, voice hoarse but carved from granite anyway.

Marti nodded once. That was all she could manage without leaking something unprofessional across her face.

"I wanted..." he started. He stopped himself before whatever sentimental shit was about to happen did happen instead of getting buried under it. "It mattered that we found her."

"I wish we'd found her sooner," Marti said. "Alive."

The word 'alive' stuck in her throat. How many people were still alive because she'd thought she was too broken to save them? How many cases had she turned down, how many leads had she let go cold because she believed she was the detective who'd let Gomes escape? A fraud playing at being a PI, always one step away from fucking up again.

"Should have gone to you first, not the cops. Waste of time. Bet you would have found her alive." His mouth twitched like he almost had something else to say, then didn't bother censoring what came out next: "The fire at Crimson Crown... wanted everything in that place erased."

Marti met his stare head-on this time.

"Wiped it clean," he said, even though water still poured off his collarbone and into his coat collar.

Her fingers twitched around the handle of her umbrella as if they wanted a weapon instead.

The fire hadn't just taken the bodies of Rufus and Kane: it had devoured every fucker who'd touched the Serra mess, and anyone dumb enough to help cover it up. One of the biggest fires Falls City had seen in a decade, and all she could feel was that bitter flick of satisfaction. Burned clean, like bleach on blood. And if that made her a monster, monsters didn't lose sleep.

But monsters also didn't spend five years drowning in guilt that wasn't theirs to carry. The rage was still there, simmering under her skin, but now it had a different texture. Not just anger at Kane and Rufus for what they'd done, but at herself for believing it so completely. For letting their lie reshape her into someone smaller, someone broken.

"Listen," Gardner said, his voice soft. As if he didn't want to piss on the moment too hard. "I told my people to respect you. You won't have any problems with us again."

That landed somewhere unexpected inside her, sharp and warm like a shot of whiskey she wasn't ready for. Gratitude? Maybe. Or just the strange clarity of someone keeping their fucking word.

She nodded once. "Thanks," she said, rain trailing down her face like tears she wasn't sentimental enough to shed. "Take care of Francesca."

"Always." His voice was heavy with something unspoken: grief, guilt, whatever cocktail he was choking down. He turned away to where Francesca still sobbed beside the grave as if the sky might drown her out.

Marti walked to the car where Lori pressed close next to her, both soaked through as if they'd been pulled out of a storm drain instead of just standing in one. Her fingers wouldn't cooperate with the keys; they shook enough to make her curse under her breath.

"You okay with it?" Lori asked without looking at her, voice low.

Marti kept fumbling for a second before answering.

"They're dead," she said. "That's fine."

Lori waited, as if she knew there was more coming.

"I thought I'd feel something," Marti added, shoving the key in and turning it until the engine screamed awake. "Closure or peace or some bullshit people write about in books. They destroyed me. But I just feel tired."

She paused, fingers gripping the steering wheel. "Five years, Lori. Five fucking years I thought I was the cop who let a killer walk. Every drink, every line, every shitty decision I made because I figured I was already worthless. All of it built on their lie."

"But now you know the truth," Lori said softly.

"Yeah, now I know." Marti's laugh was bitter as burned coffee. "You know what the fucked up part is? I was good at my job. Really good. The Jeb Montgomery case that Rufus was so twisted about? I worked it clean. By the book. Saved other women from ending up like his girlfriend. But I let Kane and Rufus convince me I was nothing."

She lit a cigarette with shaking hands, took a long drag. "Maybe that's what pisses me off most. Not just what they did, but that I believed it. That I let them rewrite who I was."

"But now you know."

"Now I'm tired."

"'Tired' is better than vengeful," Lori murmured, hand resting on Marti's thigh now instead of her arm; warm even through wet denim, too comforting for someone trying not to fall apart.

Marti looked over at her but didn't speak. She stared at Lori's mouth while it moved, lips parted as if she might say more but hadn't decided yet.

"As long as we're still breathing," Lori said, that soft idealism bubbling up despite everything, "we've got time to heal."

Marti didn't laugh because it wasn't funny. Jesus, sometimes Lori made hope sound like an STD you couldn't shake even if you tried. But maybe that wasn't wrong. Maybe she'd been infected with something worse than hope for the last five years: Kane's version of who she was, Rufus's revenge fantasy playing out in her head every time she looked in the mirror.

"Sure," Marti said. She dropped one hand from the wheel and laced their fingers together as if it was nothing, as if maybe that simple act could keep them grounded when revenge had failed. "You know what? Maybe we do. Maybe I spent so long being the person they made me, I forgot there was someone else underneath."

The rain slicked off the windshield as they pulled away from the cemetery gates.

"Lunch?" Marti asked after a few minutes passed without either of them speaking.

Lori squeezed her hand once before letting go. "Yeah. That burger place downtown? You know: the one where they name everything after serial killers?"

Marti snorted and nodded once.

"Perfect," she muttered.

She wasn't going to start over. It only works that way in the movies. But she was hungry. Fucking hungry. Death and appetite weren't mutually exclusive. That you could swallow horror and keep breathing. That sometimes the only way forward was through the graveyard of who you used to be.

The Gomes case was closed now, really closed. Not by evidence or courts, but by truth burning through five years of scar tissue. She wasn't the cop who'd failed. She was the cop who'd been sabotaged. And maybe that meant she could be something else entirely.

The rain kept falling, washing Falls City clean of nothing.

Continue the Falls City Series

What happens next? Find out in: ***Almost***

January 16, 2026

PI Marti Starova is back in Book 4. She is battling her addictions and a killer who is closer than she ever realized. As the stakes get higher, the rain-soaked streets of Falls City start running red with blood.

◆

The Familiar Dark - Coming March 11, 2026

Ready to keep reading? Pre-order now!

www.ingramcontent.com/pod-product-compliance
Lightning Source LLC
Chambersburg PA
CBHW061044310726
48969CB00004B/1073